The

Amish

Rebel

*A Story of War and Faith
and the men of the
Confederate States Naval Academy*

A Historical Novel

by

Preston Nuttall

*Cover photo: A thirty-two pounder gun mounted in the bow of
a Confederate gunboat. The Photographic History of the Civil
War, Volume Six: The Navies. Francis Trevelyan Miller, Editor
in Chief. Castle Books. New York. 1957.*

The Amish Rebel
Copyright © 2012, by Preston Nuttall.
Cover Copyright © 2012 by Sunbury Press, Inc.
Back cover photo by Lawrence Knorr.

For information about special discounts for bulk purchases, please contact Sunbury Press, Inc. Wholesale Dept. at (717) 254-7274 or orders@sunburypress.com.

To request one of our authors for speaking engagements or book signings, please contact Sunbury Press, Inc. Publicity Dept. at publicity@sunburypress.com.

SECOND SUNBURY PRESS EDITION
Printed in the United States of America
November 2012

Trade Paperback ISBN: 978-1-62006-042-1
Mobipocket format (Kindle) ISBN: 978-1- 62006-043-8
ePub format (Nook) ISBN: 978-1-62006-044-5

Published by:
Sunbury Press
Mechanicsburg, PA
www.sunburypress.com

Mechanicsburg, Pennsylvania   USA

For it is written, He shall give His angels charge over thee. And in their hands they shall bear thee up...
Luke 4: 10-11

Acknowledgments

This book is dedicated to my wife Pat, who also happens to be my best friend, constant companion and editorial sounding board. Her knack for guiding me around literary dead-ends and pointing me in the right direction is uncanny.

Thanks as well to our family and the many friends who have given me constant support and encouragement, in particular Jackie Nash of Augusta County, Virginia who has suggested many intriguing story line ideas, and Jackie Jones of JTEC Consulting, Inc. who has provided valuable technical assistance.

I would be remiss without thanking my publisher, Lawrence Knorr, my editor, Allyson Gard, and the other folks at Sunbury Press for their expert assistance and patience with me throughout this process.

I would also like to extend a special thanks to our Old Order Amish friends in Lancaster, Pennsylvania for the advice and warm friendship they provided during the writing of this book.

Welcome to the world of *The Amish Rebel*. I hope you enjoy it.

Preston Nuttall

Foreword

The Amish have long believed in nonviolence, de-emphasis of individuality, rejection of conveniences not of their own making, and a strict code of social behavior. Their simple, utilitarian way of life, built around these basic beliefs, is often looked at askance for no better reason than it makes them seem different. For three hundred years they have faced social pressures, prejudices and the allure of an increasingly liberal society, yet a determined will and a deep faith have allowed the "plain people" to not just survive but flourish. They are to be admired.

Perhaps the greatest pressure on the Amish emerges during times of war and is brought on by their total rejection of violence. This deep-seated belief is thought to stem from reverence for the violence suffered by Jesus Christ. Though the pressure may cause some young Amish men to volunteer for nonviolent duties, rare indeed are those who forsake their Amish teachings to take up arms.

The fictitious Jacob Buckner was among the latter. Motivated by reasons that tore apart his very soul, Jacob forsook Amish ways and entered the Civil War on the side of his native South. Estranged from his family and community, he found himself in a cauldron of destruction, bloodshed, killing and betrayal as far removed from his simple, self-sufficient Amish life as he could imagine. Whether he succumbed or survived would depend on his inner strength and teachings - the very teachings he had rejected.

The Amish Rebel *is a work of historical fiction. While certain characters, notably Captain William Parker, Secretary Steven Mallory, Commander John Taylor Wood and Midshipmen James Morgan and Palmer Saunders, all of the Confederate States Navy, were actual people, they as well as certain actual events depicted herein are portrayed in a fictionalized manner. All other major characters are fictional and any resemblance to real people living or dead is purely coincidental. The reader's attention is directed to the Epilogue and the List of Suggested Reading for further insight into the story.*

Chapter One

Dry stubble rustled beneath Jacob Buckner's feet as he tramped across the newly cut field, a wooden hay rake across his shoulder. His cotton shirt and straw hat bore the salty stains of a hard morning's work, but a different matter occupied his mind now.

A group of men passed him headed in the opposite direction.

"...and that big fight up Manassas way killed *thousands*." The man's grey chin beard bobbed as he spoke and he walked with a slight stoop. "Everyone's gone crazy, North *and* South." He shifted his scythe to the other shoulder. "If folks would just follow the Bible...say Jacob, dinner's *this* way. Didn't ya'hear the bell?"

"Yes sir, but I'm not hungry just now, Mr. Detweiler."

"Better come along. A skinny boy like you'd best eat every chance he gets. We got another five acres t'cut 'fore dark - and it's not likely to get no cooler."

Jacob hated being skinny, and he hated it even more when someone pointed it out to him. "No thank you, sir. Thought I'd give the animals some extra feed and water." A dry grin creased his face. "Can't have 'em gettin' skinny like me, ya'know."

As the men moved on, Jacob noticed two of them exchanging whispers. They knew what he was up to, he figured. No matter; it was normal for a couple to do their courting as discreetly as possible. Just another meaningless Amish custom, though this particular one suited him just fine. He didn't care for socializing anyhow.

The big barn reeked of straw, horse manure and urine. Jacob walked down the row between the stalls, speaking softly to one horse and then another as they thrust their heads forward for a rub or a handout.

"Hello, Jacob."

The voice came from above. Jacob propped his hay rake against a wall, hung his hat on it and climbed the ladder to the loft. Amy Unger sat on a hay bale next to the loft

1

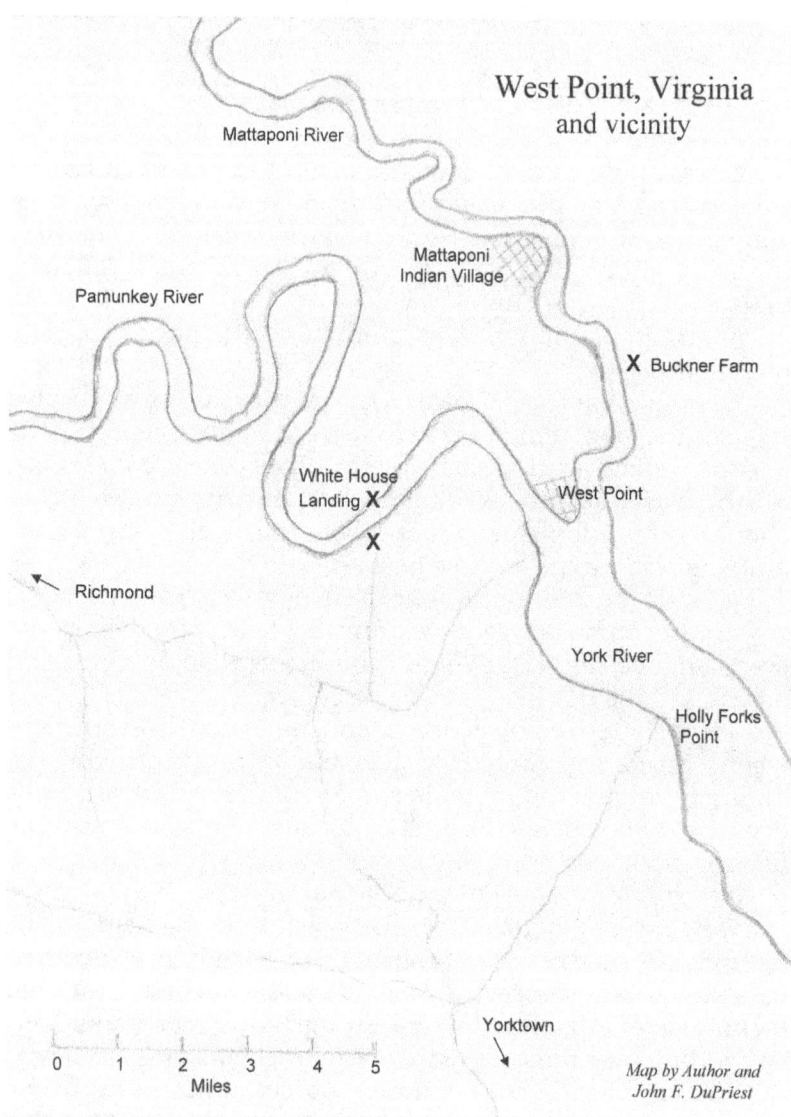

Vicinity of West Point, Virginia, 1861

window. Jacob brushed aside his sandy, sweat-soaked hair and gave her a quick kiss.

"What kept you?" she asked.

"The dinner bell. Thought it'd never ring." He joined her on the hay bale.

A block and tackle for lifting hay to the loft hung outside the open window. In the distance, the marsh-lined Mattaponi River shimmered in the bright sun as it meandered through the Virginia countryside toward West Point. There it would join the Pamunkey to form the broad York River.

But Jacob focused only on Amy. She grew more beautiful each day, he thought, so beautiful that even her plain black dress and white hair cover couldn't hide her beauty. Her figure, her blue eyes, her clear complexion – nothing about her needed man-made help. She would look beautiful even in a burlap sack.

Painfully self-conscious of his tall, scarecrow build and the deep scar on his jaw, Jacob tended to shy away from people, and had a limited circle of friends aside from Amy. He often wondered how she could be attracted to him.

Despite the barn odors, Jacob and Amy came here often to gain privacy. They had been fond of each other for most of their eighteen years, and had grown more serious in the two months since her return from a year in Richmond.

She had been on her *rumspringa*, a custom whereby Amish youth in their upper teens go and live among the 'English', as non-Amish were called, to help them decide whether to accept the Amish lifestyle. Acceptance meant baptism into the church and was considered a lifetime commitment. Amy had chosen that path.

"You been waiting long?" Jacob asked.

"A while. I was eager to see you."

"And me you. I want to talk more about - you know."

"I've been thinkin' about that," Amy said.

Jacob started to speak but hesitated, fearful of appearing confused or stupid. He hated that in people, most of all himself. He sighed and forged ahead.

"Does that mean you...you've changed your mind?" he asked.

"Me? It isn't a matter of *me* changing my mind! I'm committed to the church now, Jacob. It's a matter of *you* changing *your* mind!"

Jacob dropped his gaze. Sure enough, he had said the wrong thing. "I love you, Amy," he said softly. It was the only defense he could muster.

"And I love you," she said. "I want more'n *anything* to marry you, but you know the rules. If I marry you, I'll be excommunicated and I can't raise a family that way, Jacob. You *must* join the church!"

Jacob nodded half-heartedly. "I just can't, at least not yet. No one should join the church unless they're ready and I've got too many questions..."

"I had questions too, but it didn't take long among the English to clear things right up for me. Have you considered doing that?"

"Some, yeah, but if I go I can't, you know, guarantee how I'll feel afterwards."

In truth, Jacob's shy nature caused him to hate the thought of going off and living among people he didn't know, and he wasn't sure it would change anything anyhow.

Amy shook her head. "Nobody can guarantee that, Jacob, but the sooner you find out, the better."

"I know," he said. "I guess I need to make some decisions. Meantime, can we keep seeing each other?"

"Don't know any rule against it," she smiled. "I enjoy our time together."

They talked for a while and Amy left for home. Jacob made good on his word to feed and water the horses, then rejoined the other men as they prepared to resume harvesting hay. It was already early fall and the harvest needed to be finished while the weather remained dry.

Jacob had some serious thinking to do and wasn't in the mood to talk, so he avoided the other men, especially his father, who liked to launch into lectures about this or that Bible passage. Usually he did his thinking on the river bank, but in this case he would have to settle for a corner of the hayfield.

He knew of married couples who were not church members, but generally those were couples that had never joined the church in the first place and even then it was frowned upon. If a church member such as Amy married a nonmember, the results were more serious indeed. Of course, she *could* be using the church as a shelter, Jacob thought. Maybe she didn't *want* to marry him.

No, Amy could never pretend. It was simply that she had already faced the issues he was wrestling with now and had made her decisions. That was as it should be, and he shouldn't try to change her.

But *he* couldn't pretend either. If he couldn't come to the same conclusions as Amy – on his own, without pressure - then they shouldn't marry.

Their fathers were church elders and strict enforcers of church rules, known as the *Ordnung*. He and Amy both knew that if they married without Jacob joining the church, Amy would be excommunicated.

That was just one of many church rules that Jacob felt lacked logic or reason – like those requiring everyone to wear similar clothes and hairstyles, ignore insults and even threats, avoid quoting freely from the Bible, and not using modern tools like the steam engine...

Some he understood, like the importance of family and pooling community resources, but most seemed to do nothing but create a chasm between the Amish and others that led to ridicule and persecution. He himself had been harassed over his odd dress, his soup-bowl haircut, the Amish reputation for meekness.

Jacob didn't want to lose Amy, yet he wondered if he could ever, in clear conscience, join the Amish Church. He and his father had talked often about his feelings and the discussions usually did not end amicably. He saw no alternative but to have another talk, hopefully with different results - but he had his doubts.

* * *

Isaac Buckner was a sixth generation follower of Jacob Amman. He insisted that his family adhere to the Old Order Amish teachings that Amman founded in 1693. Indeed, he had named Jacob after the founder and insisted that his wife Sara, born a Mennonite, conform to the more strict rules of the Old Order.

Isaac sat grim-faced at a table in the study, legs crossed, scraping out the bowl of his corncob pipe using the point of a hand-forged nail. He was looking forward to a good smoke after a hard day in the fields. Smoking was his one worldly pleasure, though he used only tobacco he had raised himself. He shook the pipe's loose contents into a clay ashtray on the table beside him.

Jacob watched from across the table and tried to read his father's thoughts. As usual he couldn't, but he noticed that his mother Sara and younger brother Joshua stayed ominously silent in the kitchen nearby, handling the supper dishes with a feather touch. Tall like his two sons but heavier, Isaac was a physically imposing figure.

"So you're still not ready to commit yourself to our Lord, is that right?" asked Isaac, his chin beard keeping time with his words. "I don't know what else to do, son. We've read the Bible together, I've tried to explain things and answer questions." He scooped his pipe into a pouch of tobacco. "Do you still not believe?"

Always his father's first assumption, thought Jacob, his answer to every issue and every question. "Father, I believe in God and accept the scriptures as His word, but I have questions about, you know, other things."

Isaac frowned and used the head of the nail to tamp down the tobacco in his pipe. They had plowed this ground before. "So as always, the problem isn't faith, but *Amish* faith - our rules, the way we live..."

"I know you've tried to explain, but I...just don't get the reason for certain things," Jacob said. "Why shouldn't we use a steam engine to saw lumber? And what does it matter what kind of suspenders a man wears, or how much ribbon is on a girl's head cover, or who's allowed to grow a beard and who isn't? Our homeland is being invaded, land we've lived on for a hundred years, yet instead of helping defend it like everyone else, we worry about clothes and beards and tools!"

"You're talking about the very *heart* of our faith, Jacob," said Isaac. "All things come from God and all glory goes to God. We bear witness to Him by using only what He gives us – the sun, the soil, the strength of our back. If someone seeks to be different through his dress or his tools, then he's trying to glorify himself, not God." He paused, feeling frustrated. His son was so logical in most ways, yet he couldn't seem to see the logic of this.

6

"We reject violence in every form - obstinacy, anger, cruelty," he continued. "It's rooted in selfishness and shows disrespect for our Lord Jesus Christ, who suffered so much violence on our behalf. And by the way, I know about you and the Unger girl. Amy's a fine young lady and deserves someone who is fully committed to the church."

Jacob had heard all of this before, but still the rationale made little sense. "Oh really?" he snapped. "So it's all right if I join the church just so I can 'qualify' to marry her? Is that a good reason for joining? Or perhaps Amy should marry someone she doesn't love just because he's a church member. Would that be better?"

Isaac pulled his pipe from his lips, blew out the match in his hand and glared at his son. In the kitchen, Sara and sixteen-year-old Joshua held their breath. They had never heard Jacob speak that way to his father.

"I said 'committed to the church'. That would hardly be committing yourself to the church, would it?" said Isaac. "I'll respect your views on anything you wish to discuss, Jacob, but I'll not respect that tone of voice. It reflects arrogance and pride, two things we don't tolerate. Perhaps...it's time you considered rumspringa."

"Perhaps it is," said Jacob.

Both knew it was best not to continue the discussion, at least not now. Isaac lit his pipe and calmly went to smoking. Jacob got up and walked out into the yard. He leaned against a rail fence and gazed toward the river.

He knew he was hurting his parents. They had considered him a potential leader of their community, perhaps an elder to follow behind his father, yet he was questioning everything they stood for.

He simply couldn't accept things that made no sense to him any more than he could accept an illogical answer to a problem. Just as such an answer wouldn't work well in practice, neither would pretending to accept things just to marry Amy. It would ultimately result in harm to everyone – most of all Amy and himself.

He had known all along that he would be lucky to win Amy. At six feet and 150 pounds, he didn't exactly fill out his clothes the way most boys did.

Then there was the deep scar he had borne since childhood. He hated it and had asked for permission to grow a beard, but beards were viewed as 'vain' except on men over forty or married, so he had been turned down.

* * *

Two mornings later found Jacob on the bank of the Mattaponi River a half mile down from his family's farm. The talk with his father had made things worse, and with harvesting out of the way, he wanted time alone to sort things out. It was a beautiful day, and he sat on the bank in the warm sun, a fishing pole in his hands.

He had picked his usual spot. It had a deep hole offshore and a submerged log just upstream from it. The fishing always seemed to be good here.

An hour passed. Jacob watched an osprey circling above the river. The multi-colored bird hovered in midair, gathered in its wings and plunged earthward. It hit the water talons first and emerged clutching a pan-sized fish - a mackerel, from the looks of it. Catching fish surely was easier with a pair of wings, Jacob thought.

There it was again, something playing with his hook, brushing and nudging the bait but not taking it. He jerked his pole for probably the tenth time, but again came up with nothing. No matter. He would as soon be left alone anyhow.

Jacob enjoyed solving problems and usually solved them by sorting things into some kind of logical order, but the situation with Amy was proving difficult - perhaps because it was *his* problem rather than someone else's, he thought. Personal issues were always the hardest.

It seemed simple enough. He wanted to marry Amy, yet he viewed the church's rules as unreasonable, but how could he be certain the rules of others were any better? The answer was equally simple and he was ignoring it, and he knew why. It wasn't the answer he wanted.

Just the thought of going away for a year threw his stomach into knots. To live among strangers, put up with their teasing and have little contact with Amy or his family had no appeal to him, but like it or not, he must face the fact that rumspringa was the only option that offered him at least the *possibility* of an acceptable solution. If other customs and laws *did* prove worse than the Ordnung, then...

Jacob bolted upright and stared downstream. He saw movement a half-mile away where the meandering Mattaponi curved to the right and disappeared behind scrub pines lining the shore. Three wooden columns reached into the blue sky above the pines like three dead tree trunks, except these tree trunks were smooth and varnished and moving silently in his direction. Black smoke trailed off behind them.

A steam-powered sailing ship, and judging from the size and spacing of her three masts, a big one, thought Jacob. Earlier, he had heard cannon fire echoing in the distance. He suspected he was about to encounter the source.

That big catfish that had teased him most of the morning would have to wait. He gathered his fishing gear as he watched the three masts moving behind the pines. He knew he must hurry home, but first he wanted a look at this big visitor.

He gasped as a ten foot high ship's bow emerged around the bend, followed by a sleek hull lined with gun ports. From each port protruded a dark muzzle the size of a fish barrel. He had heard stories of a big Federal gunboat in the area, but had figured the shallow Mattaponi would keep it down on the York, below West Point.

He must remain calm and think. The earlier gunfire probably meant the ship was on a raiding mission - and the Amish farms were less than a mile upriver. How far upstream could such a huge ship go?

The absence of paddlewheels indicated a screw propeller and he had seen enough steamers to know that a screw propeller on a ship this size meant a draft close to ten feet. The Mattaponi wasn't much deeper than that along here. This ship couldn't possibly go much further, but she was around the bend and still coming, the methodic chug of her steam engines clearly audible now.

Jacob picked up his fishing pole and pail of worms and started upriver, but hadn't gone ten feet when he heard the bellow of orders and the splash of an anchor. The ship was heaving to. From a stand of marsh grass, he watched the crew scurrying about the deck. His blood ran cold when he saw them lower a longboat.

He dropped his fishing gear and sprinted for home.

* * *

USS Pawnee - a gunboat of the Arapahoe type. Courtesy, Naval Historical Center

Jacob burst into the barnyard and met his younger brother Joshua, at sixteen already as tall as Jacob and still growing.

"Jacob, what's the hurry? Did'ja catch that big catfish?"

"A Yankee raiding party! Where's Father?"

"What? In the barn I think. I'll get him!"

Joshua disappeared on the run and soon reappeared with Isaac.

"Father, a ship downriver! A longboat coming!" exclaimed Jacob, still catching his breath. "About a dozen Yankee sailors! We must warn the others!"

"No need to *warn* anyone, Jacob," said Isaac. "We must gather the neighbors and *greet* our visitors. Joshua, go and ring the bell."

"But Father, it's a raiding party!" said Joshua. "Shouldn't we...I mean, won't they take our food and... and...?"

"We have plenty, Joshua, and we must share," said Isaac. "These men are our guests and we should welcome them."

"They're *invaders*, Father! They're here to make *war*!" exclaimed Jacob. "If we don't hide our food and valuables...!"

"Jacob, you know that isn't our way!" said Sara Buckner, emerging from the house. "Hide things indeed! We must *offer* them food, not hide it. The scriptures tell us to *care* for travelers in our land. I'll go and draw cool water."

Jacob's face flushed. Would it be so terrible to protect what their hard work had produced, he thought, from men who had no need for it and no right to it, men who were trespassing and prepared to *take* what they wanted? Did his parents think these invaders would respect property when they were here to *conquer?*

A half-dozen neighboring men quickly arrived in response to the ringing bell, but Jacob knew they would only welcome, not defend. He turned away and gazed toward the river, a hundred yards down the slope. The longboat was about to touch shore next to the path leading to their yard.

The sailors, wearing dark blue uniforms with white trim, had banked oars and taken up carbines. In the bow stood a big, grizzled veteran with a small white insignia emblazoned on each sleeve. He had a pistol in his hand, and as the longboat beached, he jumped ashore and waved the pistol for his men to follow. The twelve sailors formed six ranks of two and started up the path.

Mr. Buckner extended his hand as they entered the yard. "I'm Isaac Buckner. This is my family and these men are our neighbors. Welcome to our farm."

The leader ignored him and gazed around. He stood six feet and weighed perhaps two hundred pounds. His face, as leathery as an old shoe from years of wind and salt air, bore several days' growth of grey stubble. On the cuff of each sleeve was a single white star.

"I'm Masters Mate Alonzo Peck of the *USS Arapahoe*," he said, his voice as rough as a cob and cold enough to freeze water. "You must declare your weapons *now*. If we find one later, you'll be considered hostile and put in chains."

The Amish men exchanged surprised glances. Jacob felt his blood heating up. He didn't like the looks of this. Next to him, Joshua glared at the visitors.

"Mr. Peck, there are no weapons in our entire community except a few knives we use to slaughter our hogs and cattle," said Isaac. "We're Amish and don't practice violence of any kind."

"Do tell," said Peck. "And what happens to all that beef and pork? I'll wager most of it goes to the rebel army! Well, from now on the rebs don't get so much as a *mouthful*, ya'understand? Anyone who aids them or interferes with us will be shot! Now all of you stand aside! All right, boys, the first two ranks search the barn and that shed yonder, the next two the house, and the rest guard these men. Move out!"

"Sir, you don't have to search. We'll show you everything we have," said Isaac, his voice calm and even. "We're peaceful people."

"Shut up!" Peck growled.

Moments later two sailors came out of the shed - actually the smokehouse. Their carbines were slung across their backs and each carried a ham in his arms.

"Look at this, sir!" exclaimed one. "The shed's full! Must be fifty of 'em."

"Leave those hams alone!" Jacob yelled, his face reddening. He moved toward the sailor. "We must live off that meat this winter!"

"Get back, boy!" yelled Peck, waving his pistol. "You ain't foolin' me. You got way more'n you need, and besides, nobody slaughters hogs this early! This meat's meant for the rebs! Take it, boys, and *burn the buildings!*"

"My son's telling the truth," said Isaac. "We slaughtered hogs early because of the drought, and those hams are for the whole community. We share our responsibilities – some supply beef, some corn, some flour..."

"You're lyin', you rebel sonofa..."

As Peck drew back to strike his father, Jacob rushed headfirst at the Yankee, butted him in the midsection and knocked him backward off his feet. Two sailors quickly pinned Jacob down. Peck bounced up and began kicking him.

Watching the Federal sailors manhandling his brother was more than Joshua could take. With a guttural scream he charged at Peck.

Peck was already livid at being knocked to the ground by Jacob. In one quick, battle-hardened reaction, he raised his pistol and fired. Joshua grabbed his chest, gasped, and collapsed to the ground. The bewildered onlookers froze in shock, their minds not processing what their eyes were seeing.

Jacob scrambled to Joshua and rolled him over. The front of the young boy's shirt was crimson red. His eyes had rolled back in his head. Mrs. Buckner screamed and rushed to her son's side.

"He charged at me!" yelled Peck. "I warned you, didn't I? I warned you rebels not to interfere with us!"

Jacob glared at Peck. *"You shot my brother. How could you do that? He's only sixteen. How could you do that?"* He started for Peck with both fists clenched. *"Answer me! How could you do that?"*

Peck raised his pistol as Jacob neared him. Isaac stepped in front of his son and wrapped him in a bear hug.

"Jacob, he'll shoot you too! Get control of yourself! We must help Joshua! Sara, get water and bandages. Some of you men move my son into the shade."

Jacob struggled to get free of his father. Peck stood with his pistol raised.

"Better listen to your papa, boy!" growled Peck. "Come at me and I'll shoot you the way I did that whelp yonder!"

Jacob lunged hard at Peck, but his father held him tight. He knew his son's life depended on it.

A woman's scream resounded across the yard and transitioned into a mournful wail. It could mean only one thing. Joshua was dead. Jacob and his father rushed to Sara. She sat on the ground cradling her lifeless son in her arms.

"Tell you what," said Peck. "We'll not burn your place this time, but if we come back and find you're helpin' the rebels, we'll burn you to the ground."

Isaac arose from his wife's side and strode to Peck. As big as the Yankee, his jaw rigid, he stopped inches from Peck's face and glared at him eye to eye.

"Mr. Peck, I...forgive you...for killing my son." He strained to calm his shaking voice. "I pray that God will forgive you too. But threats mean nothing to us, for we have no fear of death. Perhaps it would be best if you leave now."

Not sure what else to do, Peck ordered his men to form ranks and march back to the longboat. Jacob and his father looked on in a trance as the sailors filed into the boat and pushed off. The neighbors, still in shock, moved Joshua's body inside.

He *must* awaken from this nightmare, Jacob thought. No human could act this inhuman, not even in war.

The Amish had never helped the Confederates or anyone else except local people in need. They had greeted these men peacefully and tried to make them welcome. How could his father forgive these murderers? The episode had awakened feelings in Jacob that he never knew existed - feelings of hatred and a thirst for revenge so intense that it made him sick to his stomach. He knew he must...

"Jacob, this was your fault," said Isaac. He rested his hands on the fence and stared at the ground. "You have sinned against God and the church and your sin has cost your brother his life."

The words struck Jacob as hard as a crippling blow to the stomach. His face contorted and he spun toward Isaac. "Father, how can you *say* that? How can you blame *me* and forgive...?"

"Violence begets violence, Jacob, you should know that. Had you not attacked Mr. Peck, your brother would be alive."

Jacob was shaking now. "But Father! They would've burned us down...!"

"You traded Joshua's life for a few buildings? You're guilty of a terrible sin, son."

Jacob broke into tears. "I *loved* Joshua! We were trying to defend our home!"

"*God* was our defense, but you refused to have faith in Him and He forsook us! You must forgive Mr. Peck, and you must ask God to forgive *you!*"

Chapter Two

Isaac Buckner nudged the reins but the old mare needed no prompting. She knew what to do as well as he did. Right on cue she turned off the main road and halted the black, box-like buggy in its usual spot near the barn.

Jacob stepped to the ground and helped his mother down. Isaac stayed on the driver's seat, staring into space as if in a trance. Finally, with a shake of his head, he joined his family as they headed for the front yard.

Buggies, all black and box-like, were filling the drive and lining the main road in front of the house. Family groups carrying wicker baskets with white cloth over the contents disembarked and silently made their way into the yard.

They had come from the cemetery. Joshua's burial services were over, and it was time for the healing to begin.

"Place the food on these tables," said Sara, struggling to be a good hostess. "There's water and fresh tea on that table under the oak tree. We'll eat shortly."

"We're grateful that you're here to help celebrate our son's glorious ascension," announced Isaac, composing himself. "Joshua lives now in a better place." He inhaled, fortifying himself. "We thank our Lord for the strength and wisdom to forgive those who...played a role in taking him from us at such an early age. Now it's time to put that behind us."

Heads nodded and people began to converse and move about. Sara motioned everyone to the tables.

Jacob and Amy stood a short distance apart so as not to attract attention. They had spoken only once, briefly, since the shooting. When Isaac mentioned forgiving those involved in Joshua's death, Amy subtly rolled her eyes toward Jacob in a way that told him she wished to meet in private.

Amy sat with her family near one end of the row of tables. Jacob sat quietly near the other end. Dishes of chicken, fish and pork were passed around along with fresh corn, snap beans and other vegetables. On a separate table was a wide variety of breads, pies, cakes, and jellies.

Jacob tried not to glance at Amy but found himself doing so several times. He also noted a lack of conversation directed his way by others at his table. Of course, he had just lost his brother and wasn't noted for his conversational skills in the first place. Still, he suspected it had to do with his role in Joshua's death.

A half-hour passed. People went to the dessert table and returned with pie or cake. Others visited the privy or saw to their horses.

Jacob arose and ambled around the house to the back yard. With a bucket placed beside the well just for that purpose, he drew water and carried it to their mare, still standing harnessed to the family buggy. While the horse drank, Jacob busied himself unhitching her, all the time wondering if Amy had seen him slip away. Soon he noticed her coming around the far side of the house.

They ignored each other as Amy moved on toward the privy. Jacob led the mare to her stall inside the barn. From a peg he took down a curry-comb and began brushing the animal. Five minutes passed.

"Hello, Jacob," said Amy. She stood in a doorway on the back side of the barn.

Jacob spun around. "Amy! How nice to see you! Did you get enough to eat?"

The feigned surprise was a habit formed to make their meetings seem accidental, though by now everyone knew the truth and weren't surprised to see them together occasionally. That was acceptable as long as they showed proper discretion.

"I didn't have much of an appetite," said Amy. "We call this a celebration, but it's hard to eat on such a day. Your brother was a sweet, kind boy and I'll miss him."

"As will I," said Jacob softly, growing emotional.

Amy came to him and put her arms around his waist. "I know it's hard. I saw your look when your father, you know, mentioned forgiving the ones responsible, but I'm afraid he's right, Jacob. Even if we can't forget, we must forgive and move on."

"He was talking about *me*, Amy, not the Yankees! He holds *me* responsible!"

"I was afraid of that..."

"Does he think I was *trying* to get Joshua killed? I was defending our home! Yet he forgives those murdering mongrels and blames me, his own son! *They* were wrong, not me! It hurts, Amy, it hurts bad."

"I understand, Jacob. Losing Joshua was hard enough but...well...like the Bible says, we must forgive those who trespass against us..."

"I can't look at it that way, Amy! I've said it all along, the strong prey on the weak! Our *weakness* killed Joshua, not me. I'll never bow to those murderers!"

"What...do you plan to do?"

"I don't know. I'd like to patch things up with Father, but...I just don't know.

* * *

"Jacob, I must talk to you."

Isaac's voice, clear and firm, came from the study where he had retreated after supper. It was two days since Joshua's funeral. Jacob had looked for a chance to talk with his father man to man, but hardly a word had passed between them.

Jacob arose from the kitchen table and glanced toward his mother. She sat with her eyes down, nervously kneading a dish cloth through her hands. Jacob knew then that this talk would not be an exchange of pleasantries.

Bookshelves lined one wall of the study and a desk sat against another with a small table in the middle flanked by two rockers. On the table were a coal oil lamp and an ashtray. His father came here every night after supper to read and smoke.

Isaac sat in a rocker with a Bible in his lap, staring out the window. "Sit down, Jacob," he said, gesturing toward the other rocker. He laid his pipe in the ashtray.

The elder Buckner looked tired to Jacob, and there seemed to be a hint of conciliation in his voice. The strain of the last few days, Jacob thought. Perhaps this was an opportunity to reach some sort of understanding. He sat down in the rocker.

"The elders have met and discussed the...the situation, Jacob." Isaac nervously fingered his pipe, lifting it, putting it down again. "We all agree that you committed a terrible sin by opposing our visitors, the worst committed by someone in our community in anyone's memory. You violated the laws of God, you transgressed against your family and friends, and worst of all, your actions caused the death of your brother."

Isaac's voice had turned grim and contained no conciliatory tone. It was clear that the elders had directed him to have this talk with his son.

"But Father..."

"Please don't speak until I'm finished, Jacob!" He lifted his Bible and held it out. "This is the word of God, and in Matthew 5:39 He states: *'Whosoever shall smite thee on the right cheek, turn to him the other also'!* You chose not to do that and now Joshua is gone! You broke God's rules and Joshua's life was the price we all paid!"

Mr. Buckner pursed his lips and fell silent. Jacob's face flushed.

"I didn't see those *Yankees* turning the other cheek," he said, his voice bitter. "What punishment did *they* receive, Father? Did they lose a brother too?"

"That's between them and God, Jacob. We're praying for them as we are for you, but unlike them, you're Amish. If you were a church member you'd be shunned, but even so, your actions were so severe that the elders have decreed that you must repent promptly or leave our community. You and I have discussed rumspringa but now you don't have a choice, and I concur. You must leave, Jacob, and return only if the elders approve. We pray that time will reveal to you the seriousness of your actions."

The very air in the room seemed to turn toxic. Isaac set his jaw and looked out the window. Jacob stared at the floor, his gaze intensifying.

He was being *told* to leave. His only other option was to go before everyone, admit his sins and ask to be forgiven. He wasn't prepared to do that. So be it. He had considered leaving anyhow and was fully prepared to do so if that's what they wanted.

He arose and turned to leave the room. "You're wrong about one thing, Father," he said. "As of this moment, I'm no longer Amish."

* * *

The sun rose over the Mattaponi, its rays casting long shadows among the trees along the shore and sparkling like diamonds on the rippling blue-green waters. Marsh grasses swayed to the touch of a gentle morning breeze as a lone egret deftly trod the shallows in search of breakfast. Two ospreys circled overhead, their orange, brown and white plumage bright against the clear blue sky.

Jacob had told his mother Sara the previous night that he was leaving. He knew no one else would speak to him, not even Amy, for her family would prevent it. Sara had kissed him, bid him Godspeed and broke into tears. He promised to write and to try to return in a year. In reality, he had no plans to return.

This morning as he prepared to leave, he found a cloth bag in the kitchen next to his coat. It contained ham, bread, a jar of apple butter, a wooden figurine and a note from his mother. Wrapped in the note was $20 in Confederate bills, money she had earned by selling eggs and baked goods in West Point.

The figurine was part of a three-piece set carved a decade earlier by Isaac. It was of a woman – Sara - gazing skyward. Two smaller figures meant to be Jacob and Joshua had been carved to fit snugly on each side in her protecting arms. Prophetically, the figure of Joshua had been broken years earlier. His mother's note read:

> *My dearest Jacob,*
> *Enclosed is $20 for your use. Also enclosed is the figure of me that your father carved. Please carry it with you so that each time you look at it, you may know that I am thinking of you and love you more than life. The figure of you will remain in its place atop the cook stove so I may see it as I work. Each day I will pray for your safety as I await the day when the two figures shall be united again.*
> > *Go with God, my son.*
> > *Your loving mother*

A queasy feeling flashed through the dark confusion of Jacob's mind like a streak of lightening. He suspected that she knew he wasn't planning to return and was trying to strengthen the bond between them. It made him realize the seriousness of his actions; he might never see her again, or his father, or even Amy. He felt sick.

But to stay would mean living a lie, and the real Jacob Buckner would suffocate under the weight of the lie. His intuition had led him to that conclusion long ago but he could never bring himself to make the decision. Now events had made it for him.

With the bag over one shoulder and a blanket roll over the other, he slipped out the back door and paused for a long last look across the marshes to the river he loved so much. A moment later found him on the main road headed west, his lanky strides quickly taking him away from the only home he had ever known.

A tall, trim figure emerged up ahead, and Jacob quickly recognized the figure as Amy. She broke into a run toward him. He dropped his bag and blanket roll as she drew near, her eyes filled with tears, her arms hungrily reaching for him.

"Jacob, oh Jacob! I couldn't let you go without seeing you!"

He received her in his arms and they kissed, long and tenderly. Her hair cover slipped from her head to her neck and still they held each other.

"I wanted to see you, too, but your father, you shouldn't have come!"

"I can't help it. When I heard the elders had told you to leave, I just had to see you," said Amy, tears rolling down her cheeks.

"I'm glad you did, Amy. I wish you were coming with me."

"Oh Jacob, you know I love you, but my family, the church - there's just...too many things holding me here. Better that you go and I'll wait for your return."

"Amy...I may not return."

"Don't say that, Jacob. I had those feelings too. You'll return, I know you will. You'll join the church...we'll be married...we'll have a family. I...know you'll return."

"I love you, Amy. I'll write, but I must go now. It's best to do this quickly."

Jacob took up his gear to leave. Amy clung to him as if trying to possess him, but at that moment he didn't want to be possessed. He wanted to leave, to close that door and get on with what he must do. He pulled away and headed down the road. The sound of sobs slowly faded away behind him.

He crossed the Mattaponi a mile upriver on a horse-drawn ferry, then took another across the Pamunkey. At the latter, he met a farmer taking a wagon load of produce to the market in Richmond and hitched a ride with him.

* * *

Jacob had never seen anything like Richmond. The city stretched along the north bank of the James River at the fall line and extended back to envelop a series of low, rolling hills. Tall smokestacks rose skyward from factories along a canal that ran parallel to the waterfront. So large and so many people, all of them in a hurry, but that was to be expected of the capital of a nation at war, he supposed.

When the farmer reached his destination, Jacob helped him unload and then set out for a better look at the wonders unfolding around him. He made his way west along Broad Street, up a hill, and then south down 10th Street.

A six-foot cast iron picket fence blocked his path. It encircled a square block known as Capital Square, which sat on a hill and contained the capitol building and other facilities of the Virginia Government. He went around the left side of the fence and proceeded south on 12th Street, stopping frequently to marvel at the majestic capitol building. It dominated the landscape with its wide portico and pillars the size of the smokestacks down along the river.

He was moving downhill through a warehouse district. That should lead him to the waterfront, he figured. He was curious for a look at the James River and how the waterfront here compared with the one in his small town of West Point.

Richmond seemed a mixture of military camp and city under siege. Citizens and soldiers mingled on the sidewalks, scurrying about, buying toiletries, household goods, clothing, all as if the stores were about to close. Army officers on prancing horses shared the streets with whip-cracking teamsters driving four-horse supply wagons. Well-dressed black coachmen tended fine carriages while their owners, ladies in lacy bonnets and silk dresses, bargained with surly shop owners over the inflated price of flour and linens. All exuded an undertone of nervous anxiety.

The number of people, the shops, the bustle of activity fascinated Jacob. The streets were *paved with cobblestone*, not oyster shells like at home. Less appealing was the trash and smelly garbage piled along the streets and in the alleys.

Three soldiers in grey uniforms approached on the sidewalk. All wore beards of varying lengths and kepi hats cocked low on their foreheads.

"Hello," said one wearing corporal's stripes. "You look lost. Can we help you?"

"I'm all right, thank you," said Jacob, feeling awkward and self-conscious. "Just new in town and, you know, seein' the sights." He put a hand over his scar.

"You lookin' to enlist?" asked another. He was nearly as tall as Jacob and more muscular. "We're in the Fifteenth Virginia Infantry. If you're int'rusted, we can direct you to our camp." The man looked Jacob up and down. "Where you from, anyhow?"

"West Point, east of here." He felt their eyes gawking at him. "Uh, I was raised as...as Amish. Don't have much interest in soldiering...but thanks anyhow."

"Amish? Guess that explains the strange clothes. You're the people who refuse t'fight. I noticed that scar and figured you'd been wounded and was lookin' t'get back in the action. Ya'know, you could still serve as a cook or sumthin'. 'Fore this party's over, they're gonna make you serve one way or t'other. If you change your mind, just follow Broad Street west to our camp. It's a big one. You can't miss it."

Jacob thanked them and moved on, figuring it was time to shed his straw hat, high-waist pants and suspenders. It wouldn't hurt, either, to grow longer hair and that beard he had wanted for so long, but first he must see about a job. What money he had would go quickly for food and a place to stay.

Interestingly though, the grey uniforms of the soldiers had ignited far different feelings in him than the blue ones worn by the sailors who killed Joshua.

He reached the intersection of 12th and Cary Streets. On the corner was a tobacco warehouse. Ships' masts towering above the buildings told him the waterfront lay just a few blocks away. He proceeded down 12th Street to Dock Street and came face to face with an impressive sight. Supply ships, small steamers and navy vessels lined the docks for blocks.

He strolled along the waterfront and drew abreast of a large, paddle-wheel steamer tied to the wharf. Crates of cargo were being off-loaded down a gangplank to waiting wagons.

"Say farm boy, why ain't you in uniform?" bellowed a beefy deck hand leaning over the steamer's rail. "Don't need t'be scared o'gettin' shot. No Yankee alive could hit such a skinny target!" The other deck hands snickered.

Skinny! Jacob's face flushed. "Somebody's gotta grow all the food it takes t'feed fat boys like you!" With a dry grin, he walked on. The man glared at him but turned away as laughter broke out among his shipmates.

Just past an area known as 'Rockett's', consisting of bars, restaurants and shops selling ship supplies, he came to a boy about his own age sitting on a bale of cotton and leaning against a piling. He was shorter and built thicker than Jacob, and had a thin moustache. He wore what Jacob took to be a uniform and held a fishing pole with a line trailing down to a cork bobbing on the water.

It stirred Jacob's memories and he couldn't help but ask the obvious question. "Catchin' anything?"

"Couple catfish. Nothin' worth keeping," said the boy.

"Why? Were they too small? Catfish are good eatin'."

"Too dirty. Catfish eat whatever's in the water. See all the ships? Whadaya think these sailors are putting in the water?"

"Oh," said Jacob. "No problem like that back home. One o'these ships yours?"

Rockett's Landing on the James. Courtesy, Library of Congress

"Yeah." The boy jerked his fishing line, but to no avail. "Yonder against the far bank. The *CSS Beaufort*, Cap'n William Parker commanding. Where you from?"

"The Mattaponi River near West Point." Jacob glanced over and quickly sized up the *Beaufort*. A small steamer, maybe ninety feet, he estimated. He could see one cannon mounted in the bow and a Confederate flag waving lazily from the masthead. "So you're in the, the Confederate Navy?"

"Yeah. We'll be sailing soon. What's your name anyhow?"

"Jacob Buckner. How 'bout you?"

"Roger Phillips, from Amelia, west of here. Do folks call you Jake?"

"Uhh, yeah, Jake's fine." He liked that idea. It was less Amish-sounding. "You seen any fighting yet, Roger?"

"Naw, but it won't be long. Big Yankee fleet off the coast. Soon as we find out where they're headed, we'll head there too. You in the army?"

"No, I'm not in anything."

"Didn't think so," said Roger. "But you may want to think about it. If they start draftin' fellas, they'll put you wherever they want. Now, bein' from the Mattaponi, you must be familiar with boats and the water and such. You ever thought about the navy? The *Beaufort* could use a few more men."

"Never thought about the military at all," said Jacob. "By the way, you ever hear of a Yankee ship called the *Arapahoe*?"

"Yeah. Shallow draft for her size. She's been raiding up the rivers. Plenty of folks 'round here who'd like to see that ship on the bottom. You one of 'em?"

"Could be. How do'ya like the navy?"

"It's not bad. Had a little problem with seasickness at first. But we get regular food, a place to stay, a uniform, some pay. You're Amish, aren't you?"

"Yeah...at least I was. Does it show that much?"

"Had some Amish neighbors back home. Nice people. Sounds like maybe you, you know, got tired o'that life or had a falling out or something."

"You might say that. Guess I better be going."

"Didn't mean t'pry, but if you want'a serve, come on back and I'll take you to Cap'n Parker. He's a good man. I think you'd fit right in. And you never know, we might just come up against the *Arapahoe* one day."

"I'll think about it."

Jacob visualized the *Arapahoe's* huge size and big guns and wondered just how the tiny *Beaufort* would fare in a confrontation. Not well, he imagined.

He headed up a steep hill that led away from the waterfront. He was told it was called 'Church Hill', after a famous church located there. He was told also that there were boarding houses in that area. Sure enough, it wasn't long before he found one and secured lodging.

For the price he had to pay, he expected more than just 'lodging', but that was all he got. He and three other men shared four bunks in a ten-by-twelve room. The bunks had thin, cotton-filled mattresses so lumpy that they might as well be filled with rocks. The room had no heat or blankets and the privy was far out in the back yard. Jacob was glad he had brought a blanket roll with him.

He was still awake when the first light of dawn filtered through the curtains. As if the mattress and cold night weren't enough, one of his roommates needed a good scrubbing with lye soap and another snored like a runaway locomotive, but no matter. He couldn't have slept even if he had brought his own bed and had a room to himself.

It was his first night ever away from home. In the largest city he could imagine, sharing a room with three other men, and he still felt alone. The snoring from the next bunk couldn't replace the soft snoring of his parents down the hall. He longed to go to the kitchen for a glass of milk. He missed falling asleep to the calls of whippoorwills and frogs and the reassuring glow of the moon rising over the river.

He had no job, little money and clothes, facing a possible military draft, cold and hungry and agitated by obnoxious roommates. He lay in his bunk and stared at the dark ceiling, wondering if he had made a mistake.

He must stop thinking like that, he told himself. He must stop feeling sorry for himself and think rationally.

He had left the self-sufficient Amish cocoon he had known all his life and for the first time was realizing the value of money. To make it on his own would require money. Money would restore the security he forfeited when he left home. He must find a job.

For some reason his mother entered his thoughts. He was worried about a job when she no doubt had shouldered an unbelievable burden of chores now with both of her boys gone. But at least the crop season was over. The harvests were in, the canning done, the hogs butchered and the hams hung in the smokehouse.

The hams! The thought brought the whole ugly episode flooding back - the *Arapahoe*, Alonzo Peck, the scuffle, the gunshot. He would never forget that day. Every detail would live in his mind forever.

Roger Phillips had said that the *Arapahoe* should be on the bottom. He would love to help put her there. She was probably raiding a farm or town at this moment. He would also love to face Peck again, this time perhaps with a gun and with men who, like him, didn't believe in turning the other cheek.

He viewed war as illogical and counterproductive. It didn't excite him nor would he ever wish to be involved. But in truth, war had walked into his barnyard one day and killed his brother, and now he was involved whether he liked it or not.

He knew now what he must do. He wouldn't wait to be drafted nor would he look for a job. The perfect job had been staring him in the face all along.

He would join the Confederate Navy. If he must fight, he would fight against the men who killed his brother.

The rising sun's rays gleamed off the state capitol building high on its hill as Jacob dressed and headed for the waterfront. He must go and see Roger Phillips.

Chapter Three

Roger Phillips stepped into the Captain's cramped cabin and saluted. "Beg pardon sir, I have a man here who wishes to join the ship's company."

Captain William Parker, his large size overflowing his canvas-covered camp chair, looked up from the portable desk astride his lap and returned the salute. To one side sat a rope cot supporting a thin cotton-filled mattress, and to the other a washstand with a tin basin nestled in a hole through its top.

"We're not int'rusted in fellas simply out to avoid the infantry, Mr. Phillips," said the Captain. "Does this one actually have experience aboard a ship?"

"Yes sir, well...I'm not sure, sir." Roger's eyebrows lowered, then rose again. "But he grew up near water and seems eager. I kind of recommended you to him, sir."

"The question is, are you recommending *him* to *me*? Do you know him well?"

Now Roger blushed. "Well, not exactly, sir. I met him on the, the dock while I was fishing. But he seems nice. Knows all about catfish."

The Captain grimaced and cleared his throat – it sounded more like a growl. *Raised near water and knows about catfish*, he thought. Ridiculous. But then there was the man who claimed he belonged in the navy because his ancestors had arrived from Europe by ship. Perhaps he thought everyone else had sprouted wings and *flown* over. The Captain gazed out a porthole and sighed. If he had interviewed that man, he might as well look at this one too, he figured.

"All right, show him in."

William Harwar Parker, a bull of a man with a walrus moustache and a voice to match, presented an imposing figure. He had joined the U.S. Navy at fifteen and put in twenty years of service that included the Mexican War, numerous voyages abroad, and two stints as instructor at

Captain William H. Parker, CSN. Courtesy, Naval Historical Center

the U.S. Naval Academy. He resigned at the start of the war and began a new career in the Confederate Navy.

Roger ushered Jacob in. "Sir, this is Jake Buckner. He wishes to sign aboard."

The Captain looked up to see a tall, thin young man, not long removed from boyhood, carrying a straw hat the same color as his hair and wearing ill-fitting trousers, a home-made cotton shirt, and hand-stitched leather shoes. His tight suspenders, clearly designed for a shorter person, gave him a high waistline and a crotch that looked exceedingly uncomfortable.

Eager to look military, Jacob stretched his bony frame stiffly erect and promptly bumped his head on a rafter. What started as his first salute quickly transitioned into a head massage. So much for first impressions, he thought.

"Careful, son. No need to kill yourself just yet! This boat wasn't built for tall fellas like you. I'm Captain William Parker. Tell me about yourself. You look like, you know, some kind of farmer or something. Where you from?"

"West Point, sir, on the Mattaponi River. My family is... is Amish."

Captain Parker's jaw dropped. Raised near water and knows catfish, but he's *Amish*? He shot an angry glance at Roger, punctuated by a few mumbled words. Didn't Roger know the Amish wouldn't lift a finger against the devil himself? How many other details had his midshipman left out, he wondered.

He had served aboard ships as large as 74 guns, mused the Captain. He had expected adjustments when he joined the Confederate Navy, and the one-gun *Beaufort* with its tiny cabin, rope bed and canvas-covered chair was a *major* adjustment. But an Amish crewman? Why not just fly the white flag?

Captain Parker's baffled expression wasn't lost on Jacob and he knew that if he wanted to be accepted, he had best swallow his shyness and speak up. "Sir, I don't share my family's beliefs, and I have a score to settle with the Yankee navy. I want to fight and I want to fight *them*. I will not disappoint you, sir."

The Captain eyed Jacob. This fella needed some meat on his bones, but what he had looked solid, likely from hard work. It seemed a little unusual, though, for one so young to harbor a grudge so strong.

"What's the nature of this 'score' you have to settle, Mr. Buckner?"

"I'm afraid it's personal, sir."

The Captain clasped his hands across his chest. Well, everyone was entitled to a personal life, he supposed. At least he didn't give some lame, half-cocked answer.

"So you agree to serve the Confederacy - and to obey my orders?"

"Yes sir, as God is my witness, sir."

"Very well, Mr. Buckner. I may regret this, but I'll give you a try. Welcome aboard. Show our new man around, Mr. Phillips, while I prepare his papers."

* * *

"Jake, this is Master's Mate Calico Sam McClung, captain of our gun crew. Sam, this is Jake Buckner, our newest crew member." Roger noticed McClung glaring at Jacob. "Jake was Amish, but he gave that up."

"Un-huh," said McClung. "I thought you people was against fightin'."

"The Amish are, but like Mr. Phillips said, I'm not Amish anymore."

"Uh-huh. Well, you know, sometimes a fella don't have time to sort out his feelins'. Sometimes men's lives ride on quick action. How do we know you can kill a man if, let's say, he's tryin' to kill one of us? How do you yourself know?"

Jacob studied McClung, a fortyish veteran balding on top with long salt-and-pepper hair on the sides braided into a pigtail in back. The man's attitude irritated him, but the last thing he needed was to make an enemy of the first man he met.

"I don't, Mr. McClung. That's something nobody can know unless they've faced it, and that goes for everyone on this ship. Folks will be watching me, but I'll be watching them too. After all, *my* life may depend on what *they* do."

Over the course of the day, Jacob met most of the forty crew members and made sure each knew of his Amish background. After meeting Calico Sam McClung, he wanted to get that issue on the table right up front.

Some shrugged, some raised their eyebrows, and a few openly questioned his ability and willingness to fight. Jacob responded as best he could, but he got the feeling he would be watched and likely held to a higher standard.

That night, lying on his newly assigned bunk below deck, surrounded by his just-acquired comrades, he found himself in a cold sweat. He had no relatives or ancestors who had fought in a war. There was no family tradition of serving in the military. His only family tradition having to do with fighting was to turn the other cheek - and that practice had been drilled into him since birth. Suppose it surfaced at a critical moment? Suppose it caused him to freeze up, or second-guess himself? Suppose it cost a life?

He must simply do his best, he told himself. One thing for sure, if there was ever a rumspringa that tested Amish traditions, this promised to be it.

* * *

The colorful days of autumn faded into the blustery days of winter along the James River. The *Beaufort's* crew fell into a daily routine of intense training amidst persistent rumors of imminent action. Gun drills were followed by swabbing the deck, equipment maintenance, clear-for-action exercises and more gun drills.

Captain Parker assigned Jacob to the gun crew as a rammer, the person who rammed the powder-and-shell charge tightly down the barrel once the loaders had inserted it. The eighteen men who manned the ship's thirty-two pounder had to function as one, in limited space and often under hectic conditions. The Captain felt that the tall and lanky Jacob could operate most efficiently out in front of the gun where he had more room. It was a simple but critical job - and dangerous, for the rammer would be in the line of fire should the gun discharge prematurely.

Jacob adapted as best he could to his new environment. He found himself alone in a violent world, living in crowded ship's quarters with forty men most of whom did not accept him, and breathing the stuffy smell of unwashed bodies, stale bilge water and inefficient toilets. But surprisingly, he found similarities to his old world, such as strict rules, regular duties, matching dress and strong emphasis on teamwork.

A highlight of Jacob's new career came when he received his uniform and shed his Amish clothes. He also helped his situation by growing longer hair and the full beard he had wanted for so long, and by December his soup-bowl haircut was a thing of the past. It would take a bit longer, though, for the beard to thicken enough to hide his scar, for his beard was thin and light-colored like his other hair.

* * *

"Sir, ready for your inspection, sir!" Jacob stood at attention on the foredeck beside the ship's thirty-two pounder. The man leaning against the rail ignored him. "Sir, the gun..."

"I heard you, sailor!" said Calico Sam McClung. "I'll be with you shortly."

Jacob waited at attention. Five minutes passed. Scattered raindrops turned to a cold, steady rain. Calico Sam sauntered under the overhang of the ship's superstructure and gazed out over the water, ignoring Jacob. Ten minutes passed. The rain grew heavier, splattering on the river's surface and rattling down on the tarpaulins covering the ship's lifeboats.

Sam McClung, a surly, pig-tailed veteran, had served in the British Navy during the Crimean War and earned the Crimean Medal. His nickname arose from a skin pigment condition that gave him mottled splotches of varying shades. The condition had grown worse over the years from exposure to sun and salt air.

Sam did not want Jacob on his gun crew. Others harassed the young recruit from time to time, but McClung stayed on his back constantly and assigned him a steady flow of extra duties.

Fifteen minutes passed. Jacob's narrow-brimmed hat, acquired as part of his new uniform, dripped water in his face and beard that found its way down his collar, but what bothered him more was that he had just cleaned and polished the gun and now it was unfit for inspection.

"All right, Buckner," said McClung as the rain slowed a bit. "Let's see just how an Amish boy prepares a gun for inspection."

"But sir..."

"You *did* state that the gun was ready for inspection, did you not?" Without waiting for an answer, Sam ran his finger down the barrel. "This gun's *wet!* Why ain't it covered? Why ain't there a tompion in the muzzle? You're going on report! Now dry and polish this gun! There'll be another inspection in ten minutes!"

"But sir, it's still raining. You just said we should cover it and...?"

"I gave you an order, sailor! You're bordering on insubordination! There's navies where that would get you another scar!"

"Aye-aye, sir!"

Jacob grabbed a rag and went to mopping the gun. He was quickly learning that in the navy, duty came first, with personal dignity a distant second. He had determined to take whatever was thrown at him and employ any means necessary to get through it. That included an old Amish practice he had always despised, but which under current circumstances would serve as a useful survival weapon. He would turn the other cheek. Where Sam was concerned, that required a maximum effort.

* * *

Christmas passed and January arrived. Seven inches of snow, the season's first, blanketed the fields and forests along the James. The crew manned shovels and brooms to clear the *Beaufort's* deck so that drills could continue. Rumors that they would soon go into action grew stronger by the day.

In his rare idle moments, Jacob managed to write a few letters to his mother Sara, and though Isaac wouldn't approve, Sara occasionally wrote her son also.

It seemed things were going well at home. The men had cut plenty of firewood. The fall crops had been good. A decent supply of fish was salted away. However, a black bear had killed two of their sheep before being killed by a local hunter. Jacob hoped his mother wasn't being selective in what she told him.

He also wrote Amy but heard nothing in return. It disappointed him, though it didn't surprise him. Amy would never go against her parents' wishes, but he knew her heart and her thoughts were with him. He missed her.

* * *

Eight bells sounded across the decks of the *Beaufort*, struck sharply by the quartermaster of the morning watch. It was 8:00 a.m. and the morning watch was being relieved by the forenoon watch.

Normally the morning watch retired to a hot breakfast, but today they joined the rest of the crew on the cold, breezy foredeck. Captain Parker soon appeared.

"Good morning, gentlemen. A large enemy force, both army and navy, has captured Hatteras and entered Pamlico Sound. Their objective seems to be Roanoke

34

Island." The Captain grabbed his hat as a gust of wind threatened to carry it away.

"We are to sail at noon today," he continued. "We will proceed to Norfolk, down the Chesapeake and Albemarle Canal and thence to Roanoke Island where we will join other Confederate forces. The enemy must be stopped or all of eastern North Carolina and Virginia will fall. *Gentlemen, our mission is critical. We are being counted on to come to the rescue of our country and we must not fail! Dismissed!*"

The tightly drawn ranks exploded with cheers and hats waved in the air, a release of tension accumulated over months of hard training. The men were ready and eager to put that training to work against the enemy.

The outburst startled Jacob but soon he found himself caught up in the cheering, the backslapping, the camaraderie. He too felt pride at being called upon to defend his country, and he was eager to prove himself. Only combat would settle the question he knew others were asking behind his back but that surely burned hotter in him than in the others – the question of his own fortitude.

Only later, after emotions calmed down, did he think about the seriousness of it all. He had seen the *Arapahoe* and the intimidating muzzles of her big guns. He knew that the tiny, one-gun *Beaufort* stood little chance against ships like that. Why would reasonably intelligent men be so eager to face such odds and put themselves at risk of being killed, he wondered, simply in order to kill other men?

Then he realized he was thinking too much like his father. Willingness to risk one's life for a cause was what separated heroes from cowards. Ironically, if a person wished to live in peace, he must be prepared to die. His father didn't think that way, nor had *he* until Joshua was killed. Now he did, and it was time to prove it.

* * *

The *CSS Beaufort* steamed south across the cold and windswept waters of Albemarle Sound under the glimmering light of a half moon. Up ahead steamed the gunboat *CSS Ellis*, commanded by Captain James Cooke, an old friend of Captain Parker's from their pre-war navy days. Following behind, like a ghost in the moonlight, was another gunboat whose identity Jacob did not know.

They had descended the James to Hampton Roads yesterday, taken on coal and other supplies this morning, entered the Chesapeake and Albemarle Canal and emerged onto Albemarle Sound just at sunset. The trip went well until they entered the sound. At that point the wind shifted to the northwest and strengthened to near gale force, causing temperatures to drop.

Jacob leaned on the starboard rail, not feeling well. The narrow Mattaponi had never given him trouble, nor had the broader York, but the crests of the rollers coming down the sound were level with his eyes. Each time the ship rose to a wave and plunged down the far side, the beans and potato cakes he had eaten for supper did a similar roll in his stomach. He fought to retain the food, and with it, his dignity.

But to no avail. He hung over the windward rail, one hand clinging to a cleat and the other to a mooring chock as what had been a tasty supper took leave of him. In the process he learned a valuable lesson. He should have gone to the leeward rail.

"What'sa matter, Amish boy, you miss your mama's cookin'?" yelled Calico Sam McClung, bending over Jacob. "I've seen worse waves on a mill pond! If these ripples bother you then you shouldn't be in the navy!"

Turn the other cheek, Jacob thought. Just turn the other cheek.

"I'm fine, sir." Jacob straightened up and gulped back another heave gaining momentum in his stomach. "I'll...get used to it." He spun quickly toward the rail.

"See that you do, sailor, or this could be your last voyage!"

Calico Sam moved on. Jacob slid to the deck with his back to the gunwale. Roger Phillips made his way down the pitching deck toward him. With him was Henry Stiles, the ship's engineer and one of the few who had befriended Jacob.

"You'll get used to it, Jake," said Roger. "I had the same problem at first." His moustache twitched at the unpleasant thought.

"The seasickness, maybe," said Henry. "I doubt he'll ever get used to Calico Sam McClung. I don't envy you, Jake, being on the gun crew and all. I'd rather be below deck facing the heat of my open furnace, than up here facing heat from him."

"I know Calico Sam well," said Roger. "He just wants his men t'be ready."

"Yeah," said Henry, "except that he takes it too far and enjoys it too much."

Jacob heaved over the side again and slumped back to the deck, wallowing in the helpless self-pity that seasickness brings. He glared up at his friends through watery, bloodshot eyes. They took the hint and moved on.

The *Beaufort* continued steadily south. A large, golden object on the horizon to the port side proved to be Jockey Ridge, a mountainous sand dune that seemed to glow in the moonlight. Ahead lay Roanoke Island, a shadowy mass looming low in the water. The *Beaufort* steamed around the right shore and dropped anchor in Croatan Sound, a two mile wide strait between the island and the mainland. That was where they would make their stand. It was January 31, 1862.

* * *

The Confederate squadron, six converted canal boats and two river steamers, remained at anchor in Croatan Sound for the next week. Gun drills continued, but with only twenty rounds per gun available for the squadron's nine guns, they were not allowed to 'live fire' their thirty-two pounders.

A refugee from the Hatteras fighting reported that the Yankees knew of the squadron's presence and had contemptuously dubbed it the 'mosquito fleet'. That news heightened the men's eagerness to meet the enemy. The next day, Commodore Lynch, the squadron commander, sent two ships down the sound to reconnoiter.

They reported that twenty Union gunboats mounting dozens of 100-pounder guns had entered Pamlico Sound, and their activities - taking on supplies, putting civilians ashore - indicated that they would soon steam north. Another twenty Army transports carried a large force of infantry.

Jacob's heart beat against his ribs as he heard the news. Could Alonzo Peck and the *Arapahoe* be out there? No matter. He must focus on duty. Even *he* knew that the Union force was overwhelming, and that if they didn't slow the enemy until help arrived, they were a fleet of fools on a suicide mission.

Jacob hardly slept that night. Tomorrow he would likely see his first combat. Time after time as he was drifting off to sleep, a cold wave of anxiety swept over him, a realization that the coming day could be his last, that by sundown he could be dead, his flesh cold, his parents and Amy moving on without him.

He feared that dreaded curse that men whisper about - being branded a coward. The thought made him as restless as a trapped squirrel. Many times he spun on his bunk and pulled the blankets tight about him in hopes of finding sleep in their warmth, only to hear the ship's bell sound the passage of another half hour.

Jacob had just fallen asleep when the clanging of the ship's bell again jolted him awake. He bolted upright and winced as his eyes collided with the first rays of dawn. This time the bell wasn't signaling the time.

"All hands on deck! Clear for action!"

A drummer pounded out the frantic, monosyllabic roll that called all hands and sent them running to battle stations. The ship came alive with men scurrying like bees in a jostled hive. The off-duty watches tumbled up from below, tugging at their clothes, flinging themselves at the fire equipment, the capstan, the magazine, wherever duty carried them.

"Take your positions! Prepare to load! Look sharp now!" yelled Sam McClung as the gun crew formed around the thirty-two pounder.

Jacob went to his position in front, removed the tompion from the muzzle and took down the rammer from its rack. The crew came to attention facing south over the ship's bow as they awaited further orders. What they saw froze their blood.

Black smoke covered the southern horizon. A column of Union gunboats was emerging from the channel through Roanoke Marshes and steaming north. The eight small

Confederate ships waited behind a row of pilings and other obstructions placed across the sound earlier by army engineers.

Jacob stood poised beside the gun, gripping the rammer, watching the enemy ships closing. He shuddered as if from a chill, yet sweat beads covered his forehead.

This wasn't real, he thought. He was a farmer and a thinker. He didn't belong here. He belonged in the fields, on the riverbank, with Amy...

White smoke mushroomed from the bow of a Union gunboat, followed by a thunderous explosion echoing across the sound. Jacob's breath froze in his lungs as the 100-pound shell whistled over the *Beaufort*, landed 200 yards astern and sent up a ten-foot plume of water. He tightened his grip on the rammer's wooden shaft.

They weren't even in range of the enemy, yet the enemy could send a shell 200 yards past them? Jacob trembled as McClung barked orders.

"Bearing ten degrees to port! Elevation fifteen degrees! Five pounds powder! Load with shell! Set fuse at eight seconds!"

This was it. In a few seconds he would ram the charge home and stand aside as the gun sent a shell whistling toward the enemy. It would be his first shot fired in anger, his first act of war, the act that would seal his break with the Amish Church. All the hours his mother had spent teaching him Bible verses - 'thou shall not kill', 'turn the other cheek', 'honor thy father and mother' - and he was about to violate all of them. He held the rammer in a death grip and still his hands shook.

Crewmen scrambled to carry out McClung's orders. A dozen men using block and tackle wrestled the gun into alignment with the approaching enemy. A crew member rotated the elevation screw to raise the muzzle. Loaders shoved in a bag of powder and followed with a shell. That was Jacob's signal.

He brought the rammer parallel to the tube and shoved it toward the muzzle, but his shaking hands refused to obey orders and the rammer caught on the muzzle's lip. He quickly adjusted and found the opening. The miscue cost perhaps two seconds, but that was two seconds too long for Calico Sam McClung.

"Look sharp, Amish boy, or you're going over the side!"

McClung inserted a primer in the gun's vent hole, grabbed the lanyard and glanced at Captain Parker. The Captain nodded and McClung jerked the lanyard. The gun roared, spitting flame and smoke. Seconds later the shell crashed into the water just off the enemy's starboard side.

"Son of a...!" exclaimed Calico Sam. "We didn't lead her enough! Reload, and this time lead her more! Let's show these sons-of-Satan a thing or two! Buckner, we have a moving target! Once the gun is aligned we must fire quickly, understand?"

"Aye, sir!" shouted Jacob.

The enemy was drawing closer. The people who killed Joshua were drawing closer. This was what he had wanted, thought Jacob, the reason he had joined the navy. He *must* do it right. He gritted his teeth and waited while his comrades completed the loading sequence. As the charge went in, he moved the rammer toward the muzzle...

"Hold your fire!" yelled Captain Parker, spinning the ship's wheel to port. As the *Beaufort* executed a sharp turn, a shell exploded where the ship had been.

Jacob glanced at the Captain in amazement. Other Confederate ships were simply backing away from the obstructions, putting distance between them and the enemy.

It all proved what Jacob had feared. The discrepancy between the two fleets was too great. The twenty Union gunboats mounted at least fifty 100-pounders versus nine thirty-two pounders among the eight Confederate ships.

Captain Parker and his friend Captain James Cooke had opposed fighting from behind the row of obstructions. They favored attacking the Union ships one at a time as they emerged from the narrow channel through Roanoke Marshes, but they were overruled by Commodore Lynch and the other captains.

Jacob waited while the gun was realigned, then brought the rammer quickly toward the muzzle and focused on inserting it properly this time...

Suddenly a deafening roar, blinding flame and smoke, and Jacob tumbled backward against the rail. He raised his hands to his face but couldn't see or feel them. He blinked and looked again. He saw only a red blur of blood.

"Buckner, what the hell are you doing?" yelled Calico Sam as he rushed to Jacob. "You knew we were ready to fire!"

"But...sir...I never rammed it! I was about to when the Captain..."

Suddenly Jacob realized that his rammer was gone. The gun's discharge had ripped it from his hands and sent the splintered pieces flying into the sea.

"Then why didn't you say something? Didn't you see me insert the primer?"

Stunned, staring at his numb, blood-covered hands, Jacob couldn't answer. It was his fault. He had been too busy watching the other ships. Each crewman was expected to speak up if he had not successfully completed his task.

McClung wrapped Jacob's hands in rags. Miraculously, he had received only cuts and burns, though some were deep. Had the rammer been fully inserted in the gun, he would have lost both hands and likely more. Captain Parker ordered him below deck and called Henry Stiles from the engine room to take his place.

The battle did not go well for the Confederate fleet. Ammunition ran critically short. The CSS *Forrest*, her captain lying wounded, threw her propeller shaft while taking evasive action. A lobbed shell penetrated the CSS *Curlew's* deck and exited through her bottom.

Reduced to six ships and almost no ammunition, Commodore Lynch ordered a night retreat across Albemarle Sound to Elizabeth City, which had a fortified harbor and a canal leading to Norfolk by which they could receive ammunition.

Physically, Jacob rested comfortably during the crossing, but emotionally it was another story. His baptism of fire could not have gone worse. He had botched two firing attempts and but for a piece of good fortune, would have been maimed or killed.

He had wanted to make Joshua proud. They were always making each other proud while growing up, doing things for each other and praising each other. They fed off each other's praise. It helped them get through their daily chores and cope with the strict rules and discipline laid down by their father.

But he had disappointed Joshua and caused everyone on board to lose what little confidence they had in his ability to fight. Certainly it was his first combat, and no one had done well against such overpowering force, but the fact remained that he had failed and he could see no legitimate excuse for his failure.

Clearly being a warrior did not come easily for him, his nerves had told him that. Perhaps he wasn't cut out for war. Perhaps his Amish teachings ran too deep. Or maybe he was simply a coward.

He could imagine what his father and others would say if they heard him say that. He could just see the pitying looks and the silent 'I told you so' nods.

But to quit now meant living with failure for the rest of his life. He couldn't do that. Whether his problem stemmed from his background or his backbone, he must find out. Either way, he must find out.

Chapter Four

"Captain Parker, beg your pardon sir, but could I speak with you?"

Jacob stood at the Captain's door, saluting as best he could with bandaged hands that looked more like paws. The *Beaufort* had just dropped anchor in the Elizabeth City harbor, ten miles up the Pasquotank River from Albemarle Sound.

Captain Parker looked up from his lap desk. "Mr. Buckner! Come on in, son." He returned the salute. "I was finishing my battle report. Thought I'd best get it done; I'm sure I'll have another to write in a day or two. How're your hands?"

"A little stiff and sore, but they'll be fine, sir. Guess I was lucky."

"Indeed, Buckner. I've seen men *killed* in mishaps like that. I've talked with McClung about it. We mustn't let it happen again."

"With all respect, sir, it was my fault, not Mr. McClung's."

"Actually he agrees with you, but I don't. True, part of the blame is yours, but part is his too. A gun captain must be constantly aware of all conditions involving his gun, first and foremost being its readiness to fire. He should have known that you hadn't rammed the charge."

"It was my responsibility to inform him of that, sir, but I was distracted."

"Which is why you must share the blame, but I'm sure you'll learn from it, so let's put it behind us. Anything else?"

"I wish to return to duty, sir. I can replace these bandages with gloves and still handle the ramrod, and the ship will be better served if Engineer Stiles is taking care of the machinery. I'm asking for a chance to redeem myself, sir."

Captain Parker thumped his fingers against the desktop and gazed out the porthole at the Elizabeth City harbor. The last of the squadron's six remaining ships had just arrived and dropped anchor.

This boy's hands would surely be a detriment in battle, he thought, and what if it caused him to become flustered and suffer another case of nerves? It didn't take much to upset a ship's efficiency. But his spirit couldn't be faulted. Seeing combat for the first time was nerve-racking enough for anyone and must have been terrifying for this Amish boy. Yet here he was, asking for more.

The Captain spun his chair away from the window. "This will be a hard fight, Buckner. This harbor is a natural trap and, frankly, I don't think we should be here. But I commend your spirit, son. If you're up to it, we can use you."

"Thank you, sir. It's very important to me."

"By the way, I like your beard, but remember this isn't a pirate ship. I allow no hair below the collar or beards longer than two inches."

"Aye, sir."

As Jacob excused himself, the Captain spun his chair again and looked down the channel toward Albemarle Sound. Columns of black smoke dotted the horizon. It hadn't taken them long, he thought.

* * *

Captain Parker stood by the rail with one eye on the Union fleet visible on the horizon and the other on a launch making the rounds among the Confederate ships. As the launch approached the *Beaufort*, an officer stood up in the bow.

"Orders from Commodore Lynch," he called out to Captain Parker. "You are to take your gun crew ashore and man the battery at Fort Cobb! Your ship and the rest of its crew are to go through the canal to Norfolk and fetch ammunition!"

The orders incensed the Captain. "But...he's already sent the *Raleigh* on the same mission! That'll leave only four ships! What about the fort's regular garrison?"

"They ran off!"

"I must talk with the Commodore!"

44

"You'll find him at the fort. He intends to command from there."

Command from the fort? A commodore's place was aboard his *flagship*, thought the Captain. Lynch had no illusions of defeating the Federals. He was simply securing an escape route for himself, overland or through the canal. That's why he had brought the squadron here in the first place. It was an act of blatant cowardice.

An hour later, Captain Parker and his gun crew stood atop the rampart at Fort Cobb. There was no sign of Commodore Lynch or anyone else. They watched as their ship, in temporary command of Jacob's friend, Roger Phillips, steamed toward the Dismal Swamp Canal. Roger had been made the ship's first officer for the trip.

The dirt and log fort, on the western side of the channel downstream from Elizabeth City, mounted four good thirty-two pounders but was poorly constructed. Three of the guns pointed straight down the channel and were useless once a ship came abreast of the fort. Only the fourth gun could fire across the river.

Hardly had the *Beaufort* entered the canal headed for Norfolk when a dozen enemy ships came steaming like a tidal wave up the broad Pasquotank. Captain Parker's men quickly manned one of the three guns aimed downriver. They would fire a few shots at long range and switch to the fourth gun as the enemy drew closer.

Calico Sam McClung stood at the gun's breech. "Let's make the first shot count, boys! Target dead on, range one thousand yards! Elevation fifteen degrees! Load with shell! Fuse, ten seconds!"

Jacob had removed his bandages, donned gloves and assumed his position near the muzzle. The veteran McClung glared at him from under lowered eyebrows. His meaning wasn't hard to decipher. The hot-blooded gun captain would be watching his every move, ready to pounce at the slightest slip.

Butterflies traced figure eights in Jacob's stomach. Full well he remembered his last performance. Now his hands were nearly paralyzed, for the gloves rubbing against the raw flesh of his burns caused unbearable pain. He gritted his teeth and gripped the rammer. Pain or no pain, he *must not* fail.

The gun's elevation screw jammed. A crewman frantically applied a wrench. The enemy ships were coming on at flank speed, cleared for action, crews manning their big guns. Black smoke belched from stacks and engines groaned as each raced to be the first to engage the rebel fleet.

"Elevation screw ready!" yelled the man with the wrench.

Jacob was shaking like a leaf now. He sucked in air, gripped the rammer as tight as his hands would allow and inhaled again. Nothing helped.

His critical moment, he thought, the most critical of his young life, and he had about as much backbone as fresh preserves. He prayed for strength.

Ammunition carriers rushed forward with powder and shell and the loaders inserted them. Jacob felt the glare of McClung's eyes on him. He grimaced and guided the rammer toward the muzzle.

The wooden rod went in smoothly. His face white from excruciating pain, he plunged the rammer three times to pack the charge and then extracted it.

"Charge ready!" he yelled. A great weight lifted from his shoulders.

Calico Sam inserted the primer in the vent hole. "Prepare to fire!"

The crew turned away and covered their ears. McClung pulled the lanyard and the gun roared. The shell exploded fifty yards short of the lead enemy ship.

"Reload! Maintain elevation!" yelled Sam. "Let them come to us!"

A jet of white smoke exploded from the foredeck of the lead ship. A loud clap echoed across the water followed by the whistle of an incoming shell.

"Get down!" screamed McClung. The men ducked low and held their breath as the whistling rapidly grew louder and higher in pitch.

The impact knocked Jacob against the wood-and-dirt rampart. He staggered to his feet. The shell had exploded on the opposite side of the gun and flung crew members in every direction. Some struggled to get up. Others lay bloodied and unmoving, their faces relaxing in death. McClung was crumpled in a heap against the gun carriage, blood streaming from his head.

Captain Parker lay spread-eagled on the fort's dirt floor twenty feet away. Jacob rushed to his side.

"Sir, are you all right? Can you get up?"

"I...don't know. I think I'm...I don't know. The gun...we must..."

"Just lay still, sir! I'll take care of it!"

Jacob rushed back to the gun. Sam McClung had come to but was mumbling something about the Crimean War and Russian artillery. He had been thrown head-first against the gun. Jacob tore off a piece of shirt, wrapped the cut on McClung's head, and moved him out of the way as another shell whistled toward them.

"Get down!" Jacob yelled. Only half-a-dozen men were able to respond.

The shell exploded on the side of the rampart away from the crouching men and did no harm. Jacob peered downriver. The lead enemy ship was within five hundred yards now and closing fast.

Jacob's mind exploded with rage. *There they are, right in front of me! The people who killed Joshua!* Blinded by blood lust, he was barely able to think. Then habits engrained through months of training took over.

"Man the gun!" he screamed. "You and you, bring up powder and shell! You four help me turn the gun! Bring it to bear on that lead ship!"

The turntable jammed. Frantically the men threw all their strength into it. Slowly the gun moved. "A little more! Lead them!" Jacob sighted down the barrel. "That's it! Now load! Do it carefully if you wish to see home again!"

Like a man possessed, Jacob rushed to the muzzle as the charge went in, rammed it home, then rushed back to the breech and inserted a primer. He again sighted down the barrel and then pulled the lanyard. The gun thundered, the shell hurtled on its way and exploded just off the enemy ship's port bow.

"Reload!" yelled Jacob, upset for having missed. "We must lead them more!"

"No! The enemy will be abreast of us by then!" came the weak voice of Captain Parker. He leaned unsteadily against the rampart. "Use gun number four!"

They rushed to the fourth gun and were joined there by an eighth man, John Stillwell, who had regained his senses. Jacob gave him a fifteen-second lesson in ramming and pronounced him the new rammer.

The enemy ships were charging directly at the beleaguered rebel squadron, but some targeted the fort in passing. Shells screamed overhead. One exploded ominously near the magazine, another in a marsh beyond the fort. Yet another sent one of the guns crashing from its carriage. Jacob knew they could be killed at any moment, but that seemed unimportant now.

"Ready!" he yelled as Seaman Stillwell completed his job. Jacob inserted the primer, checked the sights and pulled the lanyard. The shell flew over the target and exploded in the sea beyond.

"Reload!" Jacob barked again, seething with frustration now. "Another shot before they get past us!" Furiously he spun the elevation screw to lower the muzzle.

The skeleton gun crew was working in sync now, shouting and encouraging each other, eager to score a hit. They raced through the loading procedure as the closest ship drew abreast of them. This time Jacob pulled the lanyard at a range of barely a hundred yards. The shell pierced the steamer's hull and exploded within her, igniting a secondary explosion. The clearing smoke revealed a gaping hole in the ship and dead men in the wreckage. Cheers erupted from the gun crew.

"Her boiler blew! She's done for! Good work, men!" yelled Captain Parker. "But her crew will be putting ashore now. We must retreat or be captured!"

"Sir, we can get off another shot!" pleaded Jacob.

"No! We must gather our wounded and retreat while their focus is on our squadron. We cannot help our comrades. We must think of fighting another day."

Four of the men had been killed and six wounded, including three who could not travel and had to be left to the enemy. Captain Parker and the eleven remaining men gathered their canteens and side arms and quickly set off overland.

Dazed and exhausted, the men marched with heavy hearts. The dead and wounded left behind were comrades they had lived and trained with for months, and they knew that any of the wounded who lived faced a prisoner-of-war camp.

In the Elizabeth City harbor, the enemy gunboats were making short work of the rebel squadron. Their flagship *Seabird* was sinking, her crew captured. The *Fanny* billowed smoke after being set afire by her crew and abandoned. The *Appomattox*, visible in the distance, steamed for the canal. Only the *Ellis*, under Captain Parker's friend James Cooke, still resisted but she was surrounded and being boarded by overwhelming numbers. A panorama of total defeat covered the horizon and the men knew they could do nothing about it.

Captain Parker led them a short way inland and then turned north toward the canal. He knew the enemy ships were too big to enter the canal, and he hoped to find the *Raleigh*, the *Appomattox* and his own *Beaufort* waiting there.

Jacob had seen comrades killed. He had narrowly escaped death himself. He had fired his first shots in anger and had seen men who were his enemy, the same enemy that killed Joshua, blown to pieces by one of his shots. All those things were part of his baptism of war, but he knew now that none were necessarily enjoyable. He had lost his Amish innocence and was physically and emotionally spent. He prayed that...

"Mr. Buckner, a word please," said Captain Parker, coming up beside Jacob.

"Yes sir, Captain. Do you need help? Are you feeling all right...?"

"I'm fine, Buckner. This isn't about me, it's about you. I want to tell you what a fine job you did. I've rarely seen such courage and leadership. You likely saved some of these men's lives. I plan to give you special mention in my report."

Jacob looked at his shoes. "That…isn't necessary, sir," he mumbled. "You and Master's Mate McClung were hurt, so the rest of us just…"

"You were hurt too, son, yet you took charge and the men responded to you. That's a rare quality in any situation, let alone battle. You would deserve recognition even if you *hadn't* disabled that Yankee ship and I plan to see that you get it."

"Thank you, sir" said Jacob, nodding. He didn't know what else to say. As the Captain returned to the front of the small column, Jacob realized for the first time that once he took charge of the gun, he had lost all thought of his injured hands.

His head still bandaged, Calico Sam McClung edged up to Jacob. "One hit in three doesn't deserve special mention in any report of mine, Buckner," he sneered.

McClung's words stung but Jacob didn't answer. Experience had taught him not to risk this man's blistering tongue by speaking unnecessarily. And for someone who had never fired a gun in his life – any gun, let alone a thirty-two pounder in battle – he didn't think one for three was all that bad.

He agreed that he didn't deserve special mention. What he did was sheer lunacy propelled by hatred for the enemy, and only God's mercy had allowed him to live. He had only done his job. Among the Amish, that was expected. Only slackers drew special mention.

* * *

"Captain Parker, Seaman Owens is bleeding again, sir," said Jacob. "His leg needs a new bandage. Could we stop a few minutes?"

The Captain nodded. "Captain Simms, have the men fall out, and if you will, please go to that farmhouse for permission to refill our canteens. Any food they can spare would be welcome also."

"Right away, Captain."

They were following the canal north toward Hampton Roads. Their party had grown to fifty men with the addition of remnants of the *Fanny* and *Appomattox* crews. The former ship had been set afire and abandoned in the Elizabeth City harbor. The latter had attempted to enter

50

the canal only to find that she was two inches too wide to pass through the locks, and had been scuttled to avoid capture. Captains Tayloe of the *Fanny* and Simms of the *Appomattox* were among those joining the group. Captain Parker was the senior officer present.

"Sir, do you think the *Raleigh* and *Beaufort* are in Norfolk?" asked Captain Tayloe, a young man rated as a passed midshipman but serving as a captain.

"Most likely, yes," said Captain Parker. "Mr. Buckner, how is Owens?"

"We've re-bandaged his leg, and he seems all right," said Jacob. "But Seaman Brown of the *Fanny* was shot while swimming ashore. He's very weak, sir."

"Captain Parker, the folks at the farmhouse will give us water," reported Captain Simms as he returned. "They're also gathering what food they can spare, and they've sent their daughter to fetch a doctor who's delivering a baby nearby."

"Excellent! As soon as the doctor arrives, direct him to Seaman Brown," said Captain Parker. "Then have him look at Owens and our other wounded."

They devoured a small quantity of cornbread and cabbage provided by the nearby family, but the sparse meal did little to fill the exhausted men who had walked twenty-five miles with nothing to eat since leaving Fort Cobb. With Seamen Brown and Owens left behind in the doctor's care, they soon got underway again.

They approached a group of shacks beside the canal. The Captain recalled from an earlier trip that the shacks marked the halfway point between Elizabeth City and Hampton Roads. He also remembered that there were canal locks a little further on. He dispatched two men to examine them.

The scouts were hardly out of sight before they came running back. "Captain! A ship just beyond the locks! It looks like the *Beaufort*, sir!"

Indeed it was the *Beaufort*. Standing on her foredeck and wearing a big smile was Roger Phillips. The rest of the crew lined the rail.

"Ya'll ain't hungry, are ya?" Roger called, his moustache twitching playfully. "We just ate, and we're kind'a full, so mess won't be for a couple of hours yet..."

"How'd you like t'be keel-hauled?" growled Sam McClung. "If we go another five minutes without food, you're gonna find out!" The others seconded the motion. They knew Sam was joking, but were hungry enough to go along even if he wasn't.

The fifty starving men were soon placated, but the onslaught decimated the ship's stores. An hour later the *Beaufort*, with the additional men lounging on her deck, headed up the canal toward Norfolk where more supplies waited.

Jacob and Roger stood by the rail, watching the canal's shoreline slip by.

"Sorry to hear about the casualties," said Roger. "We lost some good men. You were lucky not to have been hurt again."

"We never had a chance," said Jacob. "I'm glad you and the others weren't there. Most likely we would have lost the ship...and suffered more casualties." He had grown fond of this country boy who liked to fish.

"I heard you were a hero," said Roger.

"Wish everyone would quit saying that."

"From what the fellas are saying, it's true, but it must have been hard for you, considering your...you know...your upbringing."

"Yeah..." nodded Jacob, staring at the passing bank. So hard that he would never forget it, he thought. "By the way, you were supposed to take the ship up the canal to Norfolk. Why were you waiting at those locks?"

Roger glanced about and leaned toward Jacob. "Before we left, the Captain ordered me to wait at those locks until I saw either him or the enemy. He knew what was about to happen, and he knew we were powerless to stop it."

"But...Lynch *ordered* the Captain to send the ship to Norfolk..."

"Yes, but no timetable was given. The Captain knows more than one way to skin a cat."

They lapsed into silence. Jacob could tell Roger had something on his mind.

"Jake, let me ask you something." Roger leaned forward with his elbows on the rail. "Don't answer if you'd rather not, but...since you're Amish, I always figured you got your scar in an accident, but after how you did in battle, I wonder now if it was in a fight. Just how *did* you get it?"

Jacob watched a moccasin slide from the bank into the water. He wished he could escape Roger's question that easily, for it embarrassed him to talk about that day. Still, Roger was his best friend. Maybe it was time to talk about it.

"A little of both," began Jacob. "I was ten and...my brother Joshua was eight. We were in the hayloft horsing around and ended up mad over something, I don't remember what. Anyhow, Joshua pushed me down and I got up and lunged at him, but he dropped down and I flew over him and out the loft window."

"My God, Jake, how far was it to the ground?" exclaimed Roger.

"Oh, ten or twelve feet, but our wagon was parked under the window. I hit the side of it and split my jaw open. Joshua ran for our mother, and she patched me up. Joshua told her I lost my balance. He never said anything about our fight."

"You could have been killed, Jake."

"If Joshua hadn't ducked, we *both* would have gone through that window and who *knows* what might have happened."

"And your father never found out?"

Jacob shook his head. "Amish children are taught that it's a sin to lose their temper. If Father had found out, we'd have been punished. But the accident, and knowing what could have happened, punished us more than anything he could have done." Jacob put his hand to his beard-covered jaw. "This scar became our permanent reminder and bound us together. We truly became our brother's keeper."

A seaman came up and told Roger that the Captain wanted to see him. The interruption suited Jacob, for he didn't want to get into Joshua's death and the role his temper had played. He had no desire to relive how he had failed as his brother's keeper.

He stood silently by the rail as the forests and fields slipped past to the rhythmic chugging of the ship's steam engine. He felt good about having explained his scar to his friend, something he had never done before with anyone, not even Amy. He wasn't sure why it made him feel good; it just did.

The canal traversed the great Dismal Swamp. For thirty miles the sharply defined shoreline gave way to vast reaches of flooded forest dominated by heavy, vine-entangled undergrowth and cypress trees, each of the latter with its colony of knobby roots sticking up like knees. Subtle movements in the thickets and reddish brown water betrayed the presence of native residents – beavers, catfish, moccasins, muskrats. Jacob glimpsed a black bear through the trees, there for a meal of fresh fish but shying away from this floating island crowded with humans.

The swamp was beautiful, Jacob thought, a strange but fascinating world compared to his world along the Mattaponi. It felt good to be alive. He gazed up at the heavens and silently thanked God for having survived his first brush with that other strange world, the one with guns and blood and violent death.

* * *

A crowd gathered as the *Beaufort* eased into her berth. Word had spread that she was coming upriver, her Confederate naval ensign waving and her deck crowded with seamen, many wearing bandages.

Richmond was electric with rumors and the citizens rushed to every possible source of news the way a starving man rushes to food. They were eager to quiz these grizzled, bloodied men who were just back from a terrible battle in North Carolina, reportedly a devastating defeat for the Confederacy. The mooring lines were not yet secured when questions began flying at anyone who would answer.

"Has North Carolina really fallen?"

"Just the Outer Banks and the sounds."

"We heard that the enemy's advancing up through the canals..."

"The canals are blocked. By the time they clear 'em, we'll be ready."

"But our fleet was destroyed!"

"Well, *we* survived, and the *Raleigh* and maybe the *Ellis*, but the other five are gone. No question we have plenty of work to do."

"What's the situation in Hampton Roads?"

"The enemy controls the entrance, we control most of the rest."

"We hear Richmond will be under siege within days..."

"Don't know about that."

"This new kind of ship that's supposedly being built – when will it be ready?"

Captain Parker intervened. "Those are just rumors, sir. No more questions, please. The men are tired and hungry, and we must get our wounded to a hospital."

Jacob stood to one side, watching and listening. When he first came to town, he had gotten the feeling that Richmond was a city apprehensive about its future, already mentally under siege and concerned about coming under a physical one.

That feeling appeared to be growing stronger. The euphoria was wearing off. People were beginning to comprehend the long odds and painful sacrifices that likely lay ahead, and they hungered for news, any news, that would contradict their fears. They had gotten precious little encouragement today.

With the ship secured, Captain Parker granted shore leave to most of the crew. Roger Phillips and Henry Stiles, accompanied by two other crewmen, came up to Jacob as he stood by the rail. Henry had volunteered to move from ship engineer to loader on the gun crew, replacing a man who had been killed at Fort Cobb. He claimed he was tired of being stuck below deck and missing all the action.

A savvy, dependable veteran of four years in the pre-war navy, Henry was a muscular man in his early twenties, clean-shaven with chocolate brown eyes and an ear ring in his left ear. He had a reputation as a rounder with a good sense of humor.

"Say Jake, how 'bout coming along?" said Henry. "We're headed over to the shops on Broad Street."

"Thanks," said Jacob, "but my left hand is still bothering me some, so I think I'll take it easy today, maybe write a letter or two. Ya'll have fun."

Jacob was pleased that they had asked. It was further evidence of the change in the crew's attitude toward him. The events at Fort Cobb had speeded up a process that his Amish background and shy nature otherwise would have prolonged, but as much as he would enjoy going uptown, he wanted more to write his mother. He had not received or sent a letter since before the expedition to Roanoke Island, and he sorely missed her.

He went below, took his small sea chest from under his bunk and returned to the deck. He knew a spot in a corner near the transom where he could be to himself and still enjoy a view downriver. It wasn't ideal, but it was the closest he could come to the banks of his beloved Mattaponi.

He settled against the gunwale, took paper and pencil from the sea chest and put the chest on his lap as a desk. He gazed downriver for a moment, pondering what to say. The late-day February sun at his back stretched the shadow of the *Beaufort* far downstream, distorting it like a political caricature. His father would likely call that anti-war symbolism, he figured. He began writing.

Aboard the CSS Beaufort at Richmond,
March 1, 1862

My Dear Mama,
I pray that this finds you well. The men must be preparing for spring planting and it should be a good one, what with the snows of this past winter. Did the livestock come through the winter all right? I hope there were no more bear incidents.

I know Father would not approve, but I have grown a full beard. It covers my scar and makes me look more manly, if I do say so myself. Our captain warned me that he does not allow beards to exceed two inches, so you needn't worry about me looking like Methuselah.

Much has happened since I last wrote you. I have been to war, Mama. We took our ship to North Carolina and fought two battles against the Yankee ships. The fighting was like nothing I ever imagined. They beat us bad. I suffered injuries to both hands and my left hand is still sore, but I am all right, so you mustn't worry about me.

It grieves me to tell you, Mama, but I have killed men. We suffered casualties and I had to take charge of our big gun. I fired three shots, one at close enough range that I saw it kill several men. They were part of the same enemy that killed Joshua, yet it gave me no pleasure.

It must be done. We cannot allow murder and stealing in the name of war. I know Father will never forgive me but I pray that at least you and Amy will understand.

Please ask Amy to write me. I know she probably will not, because of the rules, but just one letter from her would be like a gift from heaven. I miss her terribly. Tell her I think of her every waking moment and often even dream of her. I hope she is well. I long for the day when I will see her again, and of course, my dear mama as well.

The sun is setting and I must close for now. I remain your adoring son,

Jacob

Chapter Five

A big supply wagon rumbled away from the dock and another promptly took its place. Workers transferred provisions to two-wheeled push carts and rolled them up the gangplank to the ship. Wagons from the Richmond Arsenal stood by to transfer munitions. Men aboard a barge alongside the ship shoveled anthracite coal through a chute to storage bins below deck. Nervous anticipation pervaded the scene as tangibly as that of a bride and groom standing before the alter.

The *Beaufort* had been ordered to sail again, this time under circumstances that many said could change the course of the war.

"The rumors were true!" exclaimed an excited Roger Phillips. "We've built a new type of ship, one covered with iron! The Captain had orders not to talk about it, but no matter now. We've been ordered downriver to join her squadron!"

"What's the ship called?" asked Jacob. "Is she finished?"

"The *Virginia!*" said Roger, his moustache twitching as it always did when he was excited. "She's being tested. We're to support her in an attack on Hampton Roads!"

Henry Stiles walked up and overheard the conversation. "Holy...! The enemy keeps a powerful squadron in Hampton Roads – the *Minnesota,* the *Cumberland*, the *Congress*...! The *Minnesota* alone mounts *fifty guns!*"

"Well, apparently the *Virginia* is just as formidable," said Roger. "They took the lower part of the old, burned-out *USS Merrimac*, built a casemate on top and covered the whole thing with enough iron to withstand hundred-pound shells."

"When do we leave?" asked Jacob, beginning to share the excitement.

"Soon as we finish taking on supplies."

The *Beaufort* steamed out of Richmond at dawn the next morning - March 6, 1862. With her steamed the *Raleigh,* the only other member of the former Mosquito Fleet still in Confederate service. Three ships of the James River Squadron - the *Patrick Henry,* the *Jamestown* and the *Teaser* - would follow shortly.

* * *

Hampton Roads was a no-man's-land. Areas to the south around the Elizabeth River and Portsmouth were controlled by the Confederates while northern portions from Newport News to Fort Monroe were under Union control.

At noon on March 8, 1862, the 275-foot, 3,200-ton *CSS Virginia* steamed out of the Elizabeth River and headed across the six-mile wide harbor. With her main deck just inches above water, only her casemate could be seen from a distance so that the ship resembled a large floating coffin. The *Beaufort* and the *Raleigh* were with her. Waiting were five large ships of the Union Flotilla.

The *Virginia* headed first for the twenty-four gun frigate USS *Cumberland.* The two exchanged withering broadsides as they closed on each other, but shells from the *Cumberland* simply bounced off the *Virginia's* iron plates, while those fired in return penetrated the *Cumberland's* hull and exploded among her crew, causing heavy casualties. The results weren't long in coming.

"She's slipping under the waves!" yelled Sam McClung.

The Confederate behemoth next prepared to advance against the forty-four gun *USS Congress,* which was being kept busy by the *Beaufort* and the *Raleigh.*

"Men, make sure our gun is secured and hold tight for some hard turns!" yelled Captain Parker from the wheelhouse. "She has more firepower but we're faster! It's time we lived up to our 'mosquito' nickname!"

Jacob had hoped never to experience anything worse than Fort Cobb, but that was nothing compared to this day. Guided, in his opinion, by what must have been a divine hand, Captain Parker repeatedly spun the ship's wheel first one way and then another, sending the *Beaufort* zigzagging to avoid the enemy's massive shells, any one of which could have sunk the tiny *Beaufort.*

"Charge loaded and rammed!" yelled Jacob.

"Primed and ready!" responded Calico Sam. He pulled the lanyard and the shell roared on its way. A section of the *Congress's* forward rail exploded skyward.

The *Beaufort* fired round after round with telling effect on the beleaguered Federal ship. Then an enemy shell exploded just off the *Beaufort's* starboard rail.

"I've taken shrapnel in the arm!" yelled Calico Sam. "I'm bleeding like a pig! Buckner, take over while I get it bandaged!"

Jacob rushed to the breech of the gun and again pressed John Stillwell into service as rammer, as he had at Fort Cobb.

"We're coming up on her stern!" exclaimed Jacob. "Reload and aim at her water line! We'll try to damage her rudder head!"

A moment later Seaman Stillwell signaled all was ready. Jacob sighted the gun, ordered an adjustment and pulled the lanyard. The shell exploded on the big ship's transom near the water line, sending up a shower of debris.

The captain of the *Congress* abruptly discovered that his ship wouldn't steer properly. With the *Virginia* bearing down on him, he ran his ship aground in hopes that the *Virginia's* twenty-two foot draft would keep the rebel giant away. To his surprise, the *Virginia* maneuvered to within a hundred yards and opened a deadly fire. The *Congress* lost a hundred crewmen in an hour and soon struck her colors. The other Union ships withdrew to the protection of Fort Monroe.

That night, a stranger arrived in Hampton Roads, a mysterious stranger resembling a cheese box on a raft. The next morning when the *Virginia* set out to finish off the fifty-gun *USS Minnesota*, which had run aground the previous day, she found the tiny cheese box on a raft guarding the big wooden warship as a bulldog would guard its master. It was the *USS Monitor*, similarly armor-plated but much smaller than the *Virginia*. A four-hour slugfest at close range ended in a draw, for neither vessel could harm the other. Both ships withdrew to safe waters.

Thus ended the battle of Hampton Roads, the first battle between "ironclads". Jacob and his comrades took pride in the role they had played and came away with an unmistakable feeling that theirs had been a front-row seat to history being made.

Two months later, with Confederate forces evacuating Hampton Roads in the face of advancing Union forces under General George McClellan, the Confederate Navy attempted to move the *Virginia* up the James River to safety in Richmond, but they discovered that her twenty-two foot draft prevented it. Consequently, on the night of May 11, 1862, after a career of only two months, the *Virginia* was run aground by her crew off Craney Island in Hampton Roads and burned to the keel.

With the fall of Hampton Roads, the *Beaufort* and the *Raleigh* joined the James River Squadron in Richmond. The squadron played a key role in Lee's victory over McClellan by preventing the Union Navy from advancing upriver to the city. The victory ushered in a period of relative inactivity for the men of the *Beaufort*.

* * *

Jacob found himself in surroundings as foreign to him as the inside of a Jewish synagogue, and not nearly as reverent. Tobacco smoke hung in the air of the dimly lit room like a stinging, suffocating fog. A constant clamor flowed from the men crowded around the tables. The smell of beer and spirits permeated the room so strongly that Jacob feared getting drunk just from inhaling.

He and his friends halted inside the door of the tavern to let their eyes adjust, for the transition from bright sunlight made it difficult to find their way to an empty table. A man wearing a soiled apron - he dripped sweat into the pitcher of beer he carried - pointed them to a table toward the back.

"Ya'll want beer?" he called after them.

"Yeah!" exclaimed Henry Stiles eagerly. "A couple pitchers and three mugs."

It was a warm summer day and the three had been walking around town, visiting shops, taking in the sights. Jacob had bought stationary, but the other two seemed more interested in the ladies. The three settled into chairs around the table.

"Did'ja see that one in the clothing store?" exclaimed Roger. "Just beautiful! And her perfume! A real treat after living with sailors who bathe once a month – at best."

"You noticed her smell? I was too busy noticing her breasts," said Henry. "But I liked the redhead in the apothecary shop better. She smiled at me."

"She was just jealous of your ear ring," quipped Roger. "Say, Jake, tell us about Amish girls. Are they pretty? I'll bet they're good cooks."

Jacob nodded and cleared his throat. The smoky air irritated him. "They're pretty but in a natural way. No jewelry, makeup, fancy clothes, hairdos. None o'that is allowed. As for cooking, one of the keys to Amish society is equal division of labor. Cooking and housekeeping fall to the women, and they're *very* good at it."

The waiter arrived and deposited beer and mugs on the table.

"I see you writing letters, Jake," said Roger. "You have a girl back home?"

"Name's Amy," nodded Jacob. He thought it best not to explain that he was actually writing his mother. "She's beautiful. I miss her."

Henry raised his mug. "All right, fellas, the first toast goes to Amy!"

The boys clinked mugs and took a long swig, except Jacob, who took just enough to hide the fact that beer was new to him. Indeed, his only prior taste of alcohol was when he and Joshua found a bottle of Mrs. Detweiler's cooking wine and drank it dry despite its sour taste, unaware that she had thrown it out. They spent that day throwing up and the next one in the privy, suffering from an upset stomach, headache, and stark fear that their parents would find out.

The beer tasted worse than that spoiled wine, in Jacob's opinion, plus he was having a problem with its resemblance to horse urine. But he must put up a good front if he wished to fit in. Maybe the beer would at least soothe his irritated throat.

"Well, dang me if it a...ain't some'a my shipmates!" The badly slurred voice came from Calico Sam McClung. He pulled a chair from the adjoining table – its occupant had gone to the privy – and wedged himself between Roger and Henry. "Mm...mind if I sit?"

By the time the question was asked, it had become academic. They made room for him and quickly discovered that several hours in the tavern had mellowed Sam's sour disposition, but not his obnoxiousness.

"So, how...how's my boys?" he asked as he helped himself to their beer. "You're a good bunch'a boys, an' don'chu let no...nobody tell you diff'runt!"

"Thank you, Sam," said Henry, winking at the others. "You certainly seem full of, ahh, good spirits today!"

"I feel good! Got me a ga...good gun crew, I do, now that Amish boy here has learned his head from his hi...hind sides." He took a swig of beer. "How you doin', Amish boy? We showed them Ya...Yankees down in Hampton Roads, din'ed we?"

"I'm fine, and yes sir, we showed 'em," said Jacob with a touch of irritation. People in this condition disgusted him. They reminded him of the people - most had smelled of alcohol - that had harassed him back home when he was growing up.

"Then drink up! Why ain'chu drinkin' up?" blurted Sam. "You 'fraid o'gettin' sick agin like you did comin' through thu...thu canal that time?"

"It was the sound, not the canal," said Jacob, his irritation growing.

"He got seasick in the *canal*, boys, I swear he did, pu... pukin' his guts out!"

"You're *mistaken*, Mr. McClung!" said Jacob, his jaw hardening. "I got sick in the sound! There was a gale blowing!"

"Say mister, that's my chair!"

The man came up behind Sam. He was a big man and wore the soot-stained coveralls and heavy boots of a foundry worker, probably from nearby Tredegar Iron Works. He had a rose tattoo on one bulging forearm and a coiled snake on the other.

Sam twisted around and glared up at the man, then turned back to the table. "That so? I don't see no...no name on it, do you, boys? It was jus'...sittin' empty."

"Yeah, but it was over here in front'a *my* beer!" said the ironworker. "Can't a man go for a leak? Git outta my chair, sea dog!"

"Give him the chair, Sam," said Henry. "There's others."

"Then let hog face find one! I'm com'table right wha... where I am!"

Like a lighthouse beacon flashing a warning, the ironworker's glaring eyes circled the table. Suddenly, with a sound like a hissing snake, he sucked in breath and jerked the back legs of Sam's chair upward, dumping Sam on the floor.

The man took his chair and started for his table, but a yell from a comrade sent him spinning back toward Sam just as the latter lunged for him. In Sam's hand was a naval dirk, a dagger-like knife from the Crimean War that he always carried. The worker deflected Sam's thrust and grabbed the wrist holding the dirk.

Jacob and the others vacated their chairs as the two struggling men landed on top of their table and rolled to the floor. The man's three friends at the other table arose and moved closer. A circle formed around the fighting men.

Jacob sensed that a general melee was in the offing. "Stop!" he yelled. "Stop it now! Give up the knife, Sam! You fellas, help me separate them!"

To Jacob's relief, two of the men grabbed their big friend and wrestled him off Sam. As they pulled him away, it became apparent that they had acted for a reason.

The dirk was planted in Sam's chest nearly to the hilt. Blood poured from the wound. Wearing a strange expression, Sam looked at Jacob and tried to say something. Jacob rushed to him and placed his ear close to Sam's mouth, but to no avail. The latter's eyes had frozen in place. Calico Sam McClung was dead.

* * *

Captain Parker was not happy. "So you're telling me it was Sam's fault?"

"Yes sir, Captain, that's the way we saw it," said Jacob.

"Sam took that big worker's chair and the man just wanted it back, sir," said Roger, his thin moustache twitching nervously.

"Sam was drunk, Cap'n, and he pulled a knife on that fella," added Henry. "I hate t'say it sir, but it was a clear case o'self defense. I would'a done the same thing."

The Captain frowned and exhaled, more like a sigh of resignation. "Very well. If the constables are satisfied, I guess I am too. If you will, Mr. Phillips, please draw up a statement describing what happened and have everyone sign it. I'll put it in my report, and that should be the end of it."

"Right away, sir," said Roger.

"But let me tell you something," gritted the Captain. "How many times have I warned you about going to places like that? Now we've lost a good man. We lose enough good men to the enemy without losing them in stupid incidents like this! I expected more from all of you, especially you, Mr. Buckner, given your background! This whole thing makes me sick!"

"Sir, it wasn't Jake's fault," said Henry. "He wanted to return to the ship, but we talked him into coming with us. He's not much of a rounder, sir."

"That's something to be proud of, not ashamed of, Mr. Stiles! You should all learn from him, and Mr. Buckner, I hope you've learned something as well."

Jacob nodded. "I feel terrible, sir. We should have acted quicker...grabbed Mr. McClung when he first pulled the knife. But we didn't, and now he's dead. He was a valuable asset to the ship, sir. He taught me a great deal."

Jacob spoke sincerely, for he had come to realize that all the harassment and hard work he had endured under Sam had been for his own good, designed to tear him done and rebuild him in a different mold. It had taught him teamwork. It had given him confidence. It had enabled him to do things he never thought himself capable of doing. He owed the quick-tempered, veteran master's mate much.

"Well, you seem to have learned well, Mr. Buckner, at least I hope you have because I'm giving you a new job," said the Captain. "You will replace Mr. McClung as our gun captain, effective immediately."

"But sir, I..."

"No buts, Mr. Buckner. Just do the job and stay away from taverns."

* * *

The summer's hot, dry weather stubbornly persisted in central Virginia as August gave way to September. The cheerful chirping of birds at dawn gave way to silent stillness by mid-morning. The big oaks and maples along the James curled their leaves before noon. Cotton-ball clouds came and went, only teasing at rain.

Night approached and still the stifling air hung like a wool blanket. After another long day of sweating through drills and chores – the Captain demanded the same schedule regardless of weather –most of the men came up on deck after supper, hoping to catch an elusive breeze off the river.

They lounged about on boxes or along the rail or leaning against the ship's superstructure. Two men sat cross-legged on the deck, concentrating on a serious game of checkers. Columns of blue-white smoke curled lazily upward from those who had broken out pipes and tobacco bags.

"Jake, I like that new loading process," said John Stillwell, one of several gun crew members sitting with Jacob. He had been made the new rammer. "With the powder man comin' up on the right and shell carriers on the left, they don't get in each other's way, an' the faster they get their job done, the faster I get mine done."

It had been a week since Jacob took over as gun captain. Much of the day had been taken up with gun drills, cleaning the weapon and discussing techniques.

"I think it'll work well," nodded Jacob. "We'll run through it a few more times in the morning, then try a full clear-for-action drill in the afternoon. I'll bet we've lowered our time by fifteen seconds. By the way, how's your kid sister's fever?"

Jacob had never been in charge of anything, let alone men who were older and more experienced. It made sense to him to adopt policies that reflected how *he* would like to be treated. He knew firsthand how belittling it was to be yelled at and he figured that was the last thing these veterans needed, so he preferred to discuss rather than yell and demonstrate rather than tell. Taking a cue from Amish custom, he also showed an interest in the men's personal lives.

"Sis worried us for awhile," nodded John, "but she's pullin' out of it now."

"Good. Be sure and write her," said Jacob. "Letters can be strong medicine."

"Say Jake, how's that gal o'yourn?" asked Henry Stiles. "Amy, I think it was. Have you heard from her lately?" He had removed his ear ring and was polishing it.

"She's fine, but she doesn't write much. Her parents won't allow it. Say, doesn't that thing bother you?"

"Naw, and besides the ladies like it. Her parents won't allow her to write you? But ya'll plan t'git hitched, don'cha?"

Jacob inwardly cringed. He had opened a door he preferred to keep closed. He had no desire to get into details of why he left home, but he knew he must share things if he expected the men to do the same.

"It's complicated," he said. "She's a church member and I'm not, and since, you know, I turned my back on all that, her mother and father don't want her having contact with me until I decide whether to return."

"That must be hard. Are you plannin' t'do that, to go back?" persisted Henry.

"We have things to work out, but one way or the other, we'll be married."

Jacob could see Henry pondering the issue and braced for more questions.

"Good for you. Sounds like you got your sights set on the target," said the salty veteran. "But you should write her even if she can't write you, let her know you're thinkin' about her. Like you said, letters can be strong medicine."

Jacob nodded, relieved at being let off so easily. Actually he had written Amy several times without receiving an answer. He had stopped for fear her parents were intercepting his letters and perhaps reading them, but Henry was right. He shouldn't give up so easily. Amy meant too much to him.

Their relationship had become much stronger over that last summer before Joshua was killed. Strolls through the fields, relaxing on the riverbank, quiet talks in the hayloft -

they had become integral parts of each other. He must write her and show her parents and anyone else reading the letters just how much Amy meant to him. Perhaps the sentiment would reach her even if the letters didn't.

"Jake, let me ask you something," said Henry, interrupting Jacob's thoughts. "Some of us have wondered why a quiet Amish fella like you gets so worked up at the very *sight* of Yankees. I had a friend like that in the old navy, real quiet 'till you got him mad. There are rumors that you've got some kind of, you know, grudge against Yankees, something deeper than most of us…"

Out of the frying pan and into the kettle, thought Jacob. He had never told anyone about his 'grudge' since leaving home, but now he was gun captain and soon would likely lead these men in battle. They had a right to know.

"My little brother was murdered by a Yankee raiding party," he said calmly. "In our barnyard in front of me and our parents. He was sixteen."

Deathly silence. The group stared at Jacob, uncertain how to respond.

"That's awful, sir," ventured John Stillwell. "They're savages, I tell you, pure an' simple! This ain't the first story like that I've heard. Death to 'em all, I say!"

"I'm real sorry," said Henry. "Didn't mean t'stir up bad memories."

"It was the *Arapahoe*, wasn't it?" asked Roger Phillips, standing nearby. "You asked me about that ship the first day we met…"

Jacob nodded. "A dozen sailors under a man named Alonzo Peck. They were cleaning out our smokehouse, and I tried t'stop 'em. Joshua rushed t'help me, and Peck shot him dead. I'll never forget that son-of-a-dog! I still see his ugly face in my sleep. Every time I look down our gun, I pray he's out there on the receiving end."

"After the other things that you've, you know, told me, Jake, that explains a lot," said Roger. "You considered yourself your brother's keeper, and you feel you let him down. Now you're trying to make up for it."

Jacob broke into an embarrassed grin. Roger had come close to the truth.

"Well, that may be," he said, "because there's one thing you can know for sure. If I ever come face to face with Alonzo Peck, I'll kill him."

Chapter Six

The spring of 1863 found the men of the *Beaufort* in the throes of boredom. The previous summer the James River Squadron, including the *Beaufort*, had helped defeat McClellan. Now they guarded the river approach to Richmond even though fighting had moved north to the Rappahannock. The men welcomed even occasional false alarms as a way of livening up an otherwise monotonous routine.

They spent off-hours lounging about the ship, writing letters home or going into town - especially the latter. Clashes involving sailors grew more frequent and serious. Incidents of the Calico Sam McClung type generated a steady stream of injuries and even deaths. Prostitution and associated maladies proliferated.

But the blossoming of spring opened a new avenue of activity for two young midshipmen aboard the *Beaufort*. They went fishing.

"Got one!" yelled Roger Phillips, giving his line a jerk. The manila string went taut and zigzagged across the water twenty feet from shore. "These fellas are *hungry!*"

"Eating and mating, that's all they care about right now!" exclaimed Jacob as he played a fish of his own. The annual run of shad and herring was underway.

"Can't say I blame 'em," said Roger. "But it just shows how sex will get you in trouble if you're not careful!"

"I wouldn't know about that," said Jacob. "Watch out, he's running! We'll get tangled! Move to the left!"

The two friends were on the bank opposite the city, upriver from the ship and just below the rapids marking the fall line of the James. They needed only hand-held lines and hooks baited with bread dough to catch the hungry, migrating fish.

"Dadgummit, he got off!" exclaimed Roger. "Don't matter, it looked like a shad. Can't stand all those bones."

"Yeah, I'll take a herring any day," said Jacob. He swung his fish onto the bank. "A beauty, over a pound I'd say!" He removed the hook, pulled a stout cord holding a dozen herring from the water's edge and slipped it through the fish's gill, then returned the string of fish to the water.

"Whoa, got another one!" hollered Roger a moment later.

"That'll about fill our line," said Jacob. "We'll salt 'em down and have the galley cook 'em for breakfast. Haven't had salted herring since I left home."

"Maybe Henry can join us," said Roger. "Most of the other veterans don't like fish. Reminds 'em too much of the navy and not enough of home, I guess."

"Reminds me more of home," said Jacob. "I was practically raised on fish."

"Me too. We lived near the Appomattox River. Nothing like salted fish and hot biscuits on a cold morning."

They curled their lines and sat on the bank. Richmond lay across from them, its busy streets sloping upward from the river's edge to the hill where the pillared facade of the capitol building gleamed in the morning sun. It dominated the city much the way the ancient Parthenon dominated Athens.

Jacob gazed at the sprawling city and shook his head. "Ya'know, these people live right here, yet most of 'em pro'bly never fished a day in their lives."

"Yeah," said Roger. "They view things different from us country boys."

"At one time I had thoughts of living here," said Jacob. "Now I'm not so sure. So many people, so closed in, things costing so much..."

"It sounds like maybe you, you know, miss home...your old ways and all..."

Jacob watched a piece of driftwood swirl around a rock and bob downstream. Roger's comment surprised him. He wasn't aware of any feelings of homesickness.

He missed Amy and some aspects of Amish life – the close family ties, being self-sufficient - but he wasn't the same person who left home eighteen months ago. He had a full beard and a reputation as a leader and fighter. He had embraced firearms and even taken men's lives. Turning the other cheek' was just a phrase. He was as far removed from Amish life as he could imagine, and had grown comfortable with his new life.

"Oh, Amish ways have their advantages and disadvantages," he said. "But I feel I'm doing what I should be doing."

"I'm glad you're not homesick," Roger said. "Would you ever consider, you know, making a career of the navy? I plan on doing that."

"Pro'bly not. When this war ends and Amy and I get married, she'll likely not want me in the navy."

"Well, let me ask you something more personal, Jake. You said awhile ago that you didn't know about, uhh, sex and all. Does that mean...that you've never..."

Jacob nodded. "The Amish abstain until marriage. Amy and I discussed it and decided that's what we would do."

Roger cleared his throat. "Well, you know, I never did anything either until I came to Richmond. Oh, there was this daughter of the foster parents we stayed with and we fooled around some, but were always afraid to, you know, take the final step. Now, there's this place I know of uptown where..."

"I appreciate it, Roger, but I'm not much interested in that. Did you just say you stayed with folks who weren't your parents?"

Roger nodded. "I don't talk about it, but my parents died when I was ten and my two sisters and I went to a foster home." He grimaced. "It was...a bad time for us." He turned and pulled up his shirt. Deep scars criss-crossed his back.

"Roger! Your foster parents did that?"

"Just the husband of the first couple. His name was Hector, and his wife ended up leaving him. He kept me locked in the tool shed at night and my sisters next door in the carriage shed. I guess he figured we'd run off. We were the only 'slaves' he could afford."

"That's awful! What happened? Did you finally run off?"

"Yeah. One night when I was sixteen – Jenny was fourteen and Rachel twelve – it all came to a head. We were locked in the sheds, and I heard Hector next door with my sisters. He was ordering them around, they were crying. I looked through a crack and he was...on top of Jenny, having his way with her. Rachel was cowering in a corner with her hands over her eyes."

Jacob shook his head. "Roger, I'm sorry. I didn't know."

"Well, it's not something we brag about. I'd heard that going on before, but all of a sudden I couldn't take it anymore."

"What'd you do?"

"I yelled at him but he ignored me, so I grabbed an old plow handle from the corner and broke out of the shed. He heard me and came busting out of the other shed still buttoning his pants. I was waiting and caught him in the stomach with the plow handle. When he doubled over, I broke the handle across his back. He went down like a sack of potatoes and I grabbed my sisters and ran."

"Hope you killed him. Where'd ya'll go?"

"Well, there was a family that use'ta come by to visit. I think they knew what was going on. Anyhow, that's where we went. I didn't kill Hector, but he was laid up for awhile and never came after us. Guess he was afraid of the law – or me. A year later I joined the navy. My sisters still live with those folks."

Jacob had heard of things like that but never dreamed it had happened to his best friend. He was speechless but impressed that Roger - calm, gentle Roger - had taken such action at such an early age. It gave him new respect for his friend.

* * *

The *Beaufort's* drummer beat out a staccato roll intended to be reveille. The ship didn't have a bugler, for theirs had been wounded at Fort Cobb and had not returned. It was 6:00 a.m. and dawn was breaking on a warm May morning.

An hour later the men gathered for breakfast, except the morning watch still on duty. Some of the older veterans arrived late. Reveille from a drum simply did not ignite the same urgency in them as a bugle.

Jacob and Roger sat with Henry Stiles. All looked forward to enjoying the herring caught by the former two the previous day.

Grace was said after which the three friends kept their seats expecting to be served their special dish – after all, they were junior officers - while everyone else went through the chow line. Then they noticed that those going through the chow line were returning with stacks of herring and hot biscuits. The staff had acquired a supply of the fish from a local fishing boat. The boys filled their plates and enjoyed the meal anyhow, except Roger who swore that *these* fish were much *smaller* than the ones they had caught. The late-arriving veterans, who like most old salts did not enjoy fish, regretted getting out of bed.

After breakfast, the quartermaster of the morning watch announced that a shipment of mail had arrived from the depot. It was the first mail the *Beaufort* had received in two months. It seemed that their mail had been mistakenly routed to Beaufort, North Carolina, a town on the coast occupied by Union forces.

Roger and Henry each received a letter which they quickly opened and began reading. Jacob was handed two, both marked West Point. Certain they were from his mother, he quietly arose and headed for his spot near the transom.

He looked casually at the handwriting. The top one was his mother's, but the bottom one had gotten wet and smeared. He held it up to the sunlight and looked again. The name could be that of his mother, but...

It wasn't his mother, it was Amy Unger.

His heart pounding, Jacob sat down on the aft deck against the rail. He laid aside his mother's letter and tore open the one from Amy. He could barely hold his shaking hands steady enough to read the words:

April 10, 1863
Dear Jacob,

I have wanted to write you for a long time and could not, but my father has given me permission to write this one letter. I pray it will find you well. I have worried about you since the day you left, and especially after your mother told me that you had gotten hurt.

Jacob, it saddens me that you have embraced a lifestyle so foreign to our ways. To bear arms in anger, to seek revenge rather than forgive, and to go so far as to kill other men are all things that do not please our community nor, I fear, do they please God. Your eternal salvation rests on you acknowledging your sins, asking our Lord for forgiveness, and turning to Him for guidance.

I have agonized and prayed for weeks over how to tell you these things, and also how to tell you, Jacob, that I plan to marry Crist Webber. He is a devoted member of the church and respected by everyone. Though older than me, he will provide the stability and spiritual sustenance that you and I never could achieve in our relationship, but that I must have if I am to raise a family.

We will marry this Saturday. Please understand and forgive me.

For your family's sake, I pray that you will change your ways and return home. The capacity of God to forgive is great if you will only turn to Him.

Do not expect to hear from me again, but please know that I will be praying for you.

Amy

There are times in everyone's life when the unthinkable happens, and now was such a time for Jacob. The shock and agony he felt was second only to that following the death of his brother. He let the letter slip to his lap and stared out at the river as the cool morning breeze blew across his face and through his hair.

Why? They both knew they had things to work out. They *always* worked things out. They had *agreed* to work things out. His stomach churned. All purpose and direction had been ripped from him. He felt confused and lost, and reread the letter with the sick feeling of hopeless longing.

Suddenly he realized that the stains on the envelope were tears. It had been no easier for Amy to mail this letter than it was for him to receive it. She had not wanted to end their relationship but for some reason felt she must.

Tears of his own mixed with Amy's on the paper. He sat for a long time, gazing out over the river, trying to put it all in some kind of logical perspective, but unlike most problems he had faced, the answer to this one came quickly.

It was the church. The church had pressured Amy into not loving him. Her father no doubt added to the pressure until finally her affections were redirected to a church member, someone who met the approval of the church *and* Mr. Unger. Based on the date of the letter, she and Crist Webber were already married.

Jacob could feel no animosity toward Crist Webber. He remembered him as a man of about forty, a devout church member who had never married. He was quiet and not particularly handsome, a hard worker who lived alone on his farm. Shy and retiring, he most likely had been 'recruited' as a suitable match for Amy.

Still half in disbelief, Jacob laid Amy's letter aside and opened the one from his mother. It contained the same news he had just read and made him glad he had opened Amy's letter first and gotten the news directly from her. In soothing words only a mother could evoke, she assured him that God had other plans for him, that perhaps both he and Amy were better off, and that even though it was hard, he must listen to God's guidance and get on with his life.

The letter contained an easily detected undercurrent of subtle hints that he had lost Amy not because of anything Amy had done, but because he had betrayed Amish beliefs and embraced violence and the like. Jacob would have pointed out that Alonzo Peck and the Yankees weren't exactly faultless, and that the Bible contained many examples of God ordering ungodly people killed. Strange how the Amish favored benevolent self-sacrifice, yet self-sacrifice that involved honor or glory was frowned upon as self-promotion. He couldn't figure why one must exclude the other. It seemed to him that both were needed.

He had always known that working things out with Amy would be hard. She had chosen the Amish life and he had not, and he could never live in their community unless he changed his mind It was a problem that defied solution. It pained him to think about it, but his mother was right; it was time to move on. He had made new friends and a new home in the navy, and he must look there for new purpose and direction in his life.

He headed along the deck toward the gangplank with no particular purpose in mind. He might seek a quiet spot along the river, or head into town and wander among the shops. As he passed the galley, Roger and Henry were just emerging.

"Why, hello Jake. Where'd you disappear to?" asked Henry.

"Oh, back there by the transom, just...readin' my letters."

"You all right, Jake?" asked Roger. "You don't seem like yourself."

"I'm fine. Just been...doin' some thinkin'. You said yesterday that you plan to make a career of the navy. I think I'd like to do that too."

* * *

Jacob walked along Dock Street to 17th Street, turned right and entered the heart of the city. He passed small shops, warehouses, and the market where he had helped the farmer unload his wagon. He turned right again, this time on Broad Street, and headed up Church Hill past the boarding house where he had spent his first night. Atop the hill stood historic St. John's Church where Patrick Henry delivered his 'Liberty or Death' speech. Its steeple towered above the surrounding houses.

He continued past the church, gazing at the numbers on the houses, and was about to cross over to the next block when he was startled by a voice.

"Can I help you? Are you looking for someone in particular?"

The young woman was kneeling beside a rose bush. Her well-kept yard held a variety of plants and flowers interlaced with brick walkways.

"Uhh, yes ma'am," mumbled Jacob. "A friend gave me a name and address..."

"What's the name?" The woman slipped her silk bonnet to her neck. She was in her mid-twenties with brown hair, hazel eyes and a smooth almond complexion.

"Jessica. That's all I know." Inwardly, he hoped he was *talking* to Jessica.

"Oh. They're in the next block. You're a sailor, aren't you?"

"Yes ma'am."

"Why do all you young men want those girls? Don't you know you could catch a disease and take it back home to your girl friend?"

"*Those* girls?" asked Jacob. "Is there more than one Jessica?"

"Your friend didn't tell you? That's a code name. You ask for Jessica and you get whatever girl happens to be free at the time." Her friendly expression turned to a frown. "Seems to me a handsome boy like you could get a nice girl of his own!"

Jacob couldn't remember being called handsome before, certainly not by a girl this pretty. It must be his new blond beard or his navy tan, he figured. He puffed himself up, trying to fill out his loose-hanging clothes.

"I *had* a nice girl, but she up and married another fella."

"I see. So you plan to drown your sorrows with a harlot. I declare, sometimes men act like they don't have a brain a'tall!" She returned to her roses.

"Uhh, what's your name?" asked Jacob.

"Lydia Schenk. What's yours?" She busily trimmed her roses.

"Jacob Buckner. The fellas call me Jake. You live here?" He was trying hard to prolong the conversation.

She nodded. "I run a small flower shop in back. So what ship are you from?"

"The *Beaufort*," said Jacob. "You have a German name, like mine. My folks are Amish, but I gave that up. They live on the Mattaponi River near West Point."

Lydia carefully removed a dead, thorn-covered shoot from the rose bush. "Do tell. You don't *look* Amish."

"It's the uniform and full beard. It don't pay to look Amish in the navy."

"Well, I was born Amish too, from near Lancaster up in Pennsylvania."

Jacob stared at Lydia. "Really? I didn't know there were others in town!"

"Oh, there's quite a few, even one of the 'Jessica's' down the street. Most of us came here on rumspringa and decided not to go back. You must have made a similar decision, being in the navy and all."

"There were things I never could accept, and then my kid brother was killed by a Yankee sailor. My folks don't believe in settling scores, but I do."

"You're a brave young man. From what I can see your girl friend is making a big mistake. Take my advice and move on - just not to the next block. I must finish my chores, but it's been nice talking with you. Come by again sometime."

* * *

The heat of summer arrived, compounding the lethargy induced by inactivity. Daily drills continued until the crew could practically perform their duties while asleep. To bolster morale and keep the men out of town, Captain Parker encouraged games such as cards or checkers. Those who were off-duty sometimes went to an empty lot near Rockett's to engage in lawn bowling.

Jacob mostly kept to himself. Sometimes he thought of Amy, but that grew less frequent as time passed. He kept up his correspondence with his mother and toyed with writing Amy, but concluded that it was not a good idea. Lydia Schenk had seemed nice, but she was a good five years older than him and a sophisticated city girl. His shyness prevented him from initiating another visit.

It was late July and awakened early by the heat, Jacob was up before reveille. He stood near the transom watching the sun rise and awaiting the call to breakfast. Roger approached down the rail.

"I just came from the Captain and something's up!" he exclaimed. "There'll be a formation before breakfast. Sounds like we may be finally going into action."

Sure enough, ten minutes later the drummer sounded assembly and the crew formed up on the foredeck. Even the morning watch, still on duty, was ordered to fall in. The men snapped to attention as Captain Parker appeared. For the first time in memory, he wore his dress uniform complete with sword.

"Good morning. I have been aware for some time of navy plans to establish a floating academy here on the James River, aboard the *Patrick Henry*. I have been appointed superintendent of that academy and will leave the *Beaufort*. Gentlemen, you are the best crew I've ever had the pleasure of commanding. I have no doubt that you will continue serving our country well, as you have in the past. That is all."

The crew stood stunned, staring after Captain Parker as he retreated down the companionway. Most of them had never served under anyone else. They viewed him as a mentor, a protector, even a father figure. Their respect for him had grown to genuine affection.

Slowly they began to mill about and talk softly among themselves. More than one hand covertly wiped back tears.

"My God, who you think will take his place?"

"No one *can* take his place. He's the best commander in the navy."

"Yeah, why else would they pick him to command this new school?"

"We'll pro'bly get some desk jockey who's never been aboard a ship."

"No, Captain Parker thinks too much of this ship to let that happen."

"Listen, fellas!" Jacob raised his voice so all could hear. "This is bad news, but the Captain deserves our support! Let's wish him well!" He climbed atop the lifeboat cradle. "Three cheers for our captain! Loudly now! Hip hip, hooray! Hip hip..."

Like a page from the British Navy of old, three hearty cheers reverberated through the ship as the men gave voice to their affection for their captain. They were certain the Captain heard them, and making their feelings known to him seemed to have an uplifting effect on them as well.

Soon after, Roger came to Jacob and told him the Captain wished to see them.

They entered the small cabin and found Henry Stiles already present. The three took seats in the badly limited space. Jacob wedged his lanky frame between the other two with his knees drawn up nearly to his chest. None knew what the Captain wanted, but they felt certain it had to do with the transfer of command.

"Gentlemen, I'm sure my announcement surprised everyone, but I appreciate the cheer on my behalf. A captain is never sure whether his leaving will be received with sadness or joy."

"The men love you, Captain. They're very sorry to see you go," said Roger.

"I'm sorry to leave them," said the Captain. "But this project is too important and too badly needed for me to refuse the offer."

"This academy, will it be like the U.S. Navy's in Annapolis, sir?" asked Henry.

"Very similar. We'll begin with perhaps fifty cadets. Those who graduate will be ranked as 'passed midshipman', eligible to sit for the lieutenant's exam."

"That's a good idea, Captain, and sorely needed," said Jacob. "But we'll surely feel lost without you around."

"Which brings us to why I called the three of you here," said Captain Parker. "I'd like you to consider enrolling in the new academy."

The three stared blankly at each other. That thought hadn't occurred to them.

"But...why us, Captain?" asked Jacob.

"You're young, experienced, have shown leadership qualities and have said you wish to make a career of the navy."

"What...do we have to do, sir?" asked Henry.

"Well, first I want you to think about it. If you decide to do it, you must submit an application. We anticipate a big response but I can assure you that any of the three of you who apply will be accepted."

"I don't need to think about it, sir," said Jacob. "I wish to apply right now."

"Me as well," echoed Roger. "I can't leave my captain."

"No decision to be made, Captain," said Henry. "Count me in."

Chapter Seven

Drewry's Bluff rose a hundred feet above a sharp bend in the James River eight miles below Richmond. Its heavy guns commanded the river approach to the city. Forts downriver added more guns and provided an early warning system. The channel was obstructed but for a narrow passageway and behind the obstructions waited the ships of the James River Squadron. It was the Gibraltar of the Confederacy. Into this fortress on September 15th, 1863, came the three new naval academy recruits.

As the carriage from Richmond bounced and swayed along the heavily used road, Jacob gazed out at passing farms and plantations, most dating from colonial times. Fields of maturing tobacco grew next to others of corn and wheat. Shoeless darkies, the men wearing sweat-stained hats and the women brightly colored kerchiefs, paid little heed to the passing carriage as they labored among the rows.

Jacob noticed that they worked at a pitifully slow pace. What a contrast between this outdated feudalistic system, where men worked without pay or benefit, and the Amish system where men worked for their own survival. He would wager that no matter who won the war, slavery would not long survive.

Jacob began to have second thoughts as the carriage neared Drewry's Bluff. Did he really wish to spend the next few years in a classroom? He wondered if his eagerness to support Captain Parker had led to a hasty decision. Perhaps he should have studied the issue more closely before deciding.

But if he was to make a career of the navy, the academy was a logical step, he kept telling himself. It would provide the knowledge and credentials needed to be a career naval officer. He would graduate as a passed midshipman, ready to take the lieutenant's exam and join the thin ranks of trained Confederate naval officers.

Most of all, he *needed* the navy. His brother Joshua was gone. His father had effectively disowned him. He was an outcast in his own community. Even Amy had forsaken him. Aside from his mother, the navy was his only family.

"They've constructed a *village* here!" exclaimed Henry as the buggy halted atop the bluff between two rows of buildings. "Is this for us?"

"No, it's for the permanent garrison. Our quarters will be aboard our school ship, the *Patrick Henry*," said Roger. He had been given an advance tour. "We'll come ashore as needed to man the big guns."

They walked along the crest of the bluff past a dozen heavy-caliber guns mounted in stout dirt-and-timber emplacements. In an open area behind them, a company of marines wearing white cross-belts was being put through close-order drills by a sergeant. Construction crews busily strengthened breastworks and ammunition storage bunkers near the gun emplacements. Half a dozen gun crews stood at their assigned guns, receiving instruction from officers of an artillery unit.

He was about to receive an education like none other, marveled Jacob, one that would flow from classroom to battlefield and back again, where knowledge was as likely to come from battle experience as textbooks - and he was among the very first recruits. The more he thought about it, the more his excitement grew.

"This place is a fortress," said Henry, looking around. "No Yankee ship will *ever* force its way past here."

"I agree," added Jacob. "But why are some of the gun emplacements empty?"

"We'll ask the Captain," said Roger. "That's the *Patrick Henry* below us."

At the bottom of the steep slope, a pier jutted into the river. Moored to it was a large, side-wheel steamer 250 feet long, twice the length of the *Beaufort*. She had been fitted with a tall, square-rigged mast on the foredeck for use in teaching cadets the art of sailing. The aft deck had a much smaller mast, giving her an unbalanced look. Jacob and Henry gazed in awe at the big ship.

"She's our home for at least the next two years," said Roger. "How long we're here depends on how we progress."

CSS Patrick Henry before conversion to school ship. Courtesy, Naval Historical Center

CSS Patrick Henry Post-Conversion. Note foremast and recital room structure. Drawn and signed by Cadet J. Thomas Scharf. Courtesy, Naval Historical Center

The boys descended the stepped walkway to the pier, eager to inspect their new home. Captain Parker waited at the gangplank.

"Welcome aboard, gentlemen," he said cheerfully. He was now ship captain *and* academy superintendent, and the unique arrangement agreed with him.

"Good to see you again, sir," said Roger. "Have any other students arrived?"

"Only a few. Most have further to travel than you. Come, I'll give you a tour."

They walked to the deck area between the paddlewheels where construction was progressing on recital rooms. It was here that the cadets would be quizzed on the day's lessons. A number of sailors mingled about.

"These men are part of the regular crew," said the Captain. "They'll run the ship. The cadets will be called upon only as needed."

"I see four guns," said Jacob. "That doesn't seem enough for a ship this size."

"Very observant, Mr. Buckner. We had to remove our six eight-inch guns to make way for the refitting. They're in Richmond being put on land carriages and will be placed up on the bluff. Perhaps you noticed the empty gun emplacements."

"Yes sir," nodded Jacob, "but doesn't that leave our defenses weak until the guns return?" It seemed to him more logical to bring the *carriages* to the *guns*, which would have minimized their time out of service.

"Again correct, Mr. Buckner. We'll be vulnerable for another three weeks. By the way, no cadet is to discuss matters such as this when away from the ship."

They viewed the recital rooms, wondering how much future suffering lay in store for them in those rooms. Next came the sleeping deck, where fifty closely-placed bunks had been set up. With the cadets added to a regular crew of 100, the ship would be crowded. Jacob resigned himself to the fact that there would be no quiet, secluded spot like the one near the transom of the *Beaufort*. He suspected also that he could forget fishing for awhile.

The tour concluded with visits to the magazine, the engine room, and the galley. The boys marveled at the two boiler fireboxes – each large enough for a man to stand up in - and the galley, which could seat a hundred men at a time.

By month's end, most of the new cadets were present, arriving from all over the South. Since the curriculum required a minimum of two years, they were all rated as Second Classmen. The next year, those who passed would be seniors, or First Classmen, and a new group would enter as Second Classmen.

Instruction got underway by late September. The core courses were Gunnery, Seamanship and Navigation, with such topics as Naval Tactics, Steam Mechanics and Infantry Tactics also important.

* * *

"Mr. Buckner, imagine that you're the Officer of the Deck. You're under full sail, close-hauled in a stiff wind, and the ship begins to gripe," said Charles Graves, Instructor of Seamanship. "What is meant by 'griping' and how do you correct it?"

Jacob stared empty-eyed at the instructor, for he had failed to finish reading the day's material. He was having a hard time getting interested in how to handle a sailing ship when the navy was rapidly converting to steam. He could only guess at the answer and hope to get lucky.

"Sir, I believe that...'griping'...refers to a ship's timbers creaking and groaning when under too much pressure. I would correct it by easing off on the sails."

"A logical guess, Cadet Buckner, but a guess nonetheless," said Mr. Graves. "Perhaps you should read the assignment, uhh, more closely next time. In this case, 'griping' does not refer to 'complaining', but rather the tendency of a close-hauled ship to veer up into the wind. You did, however, manage to stumble upon the correct solution. You would indeed ease off the sails."

The instructor's eyes surveyed the room, looking for his next victim. The students held their breath and tried their best to become invisible.

"Mr. Stiles, let's see if *you* managed to read the assignment. Suppose that..."

A heavy caliber gun thundered in the distance, echoing along the river.

"All hands on deck! Clear for action!"

The ship's bell clanged frantically. A drummer beat a fast roll accompanied by the sound of running feet.

"Class dismissed!" announced Mr. Graves, but the cadets were already out the door and rushing to their assigned posts.

"Ya'think it's a drill?" asked Roger, nearly stumbling over Jacob and Henry as they and a dozen other cadets hurried down the ship's gangplank on their way to their assigned gun, an eight-inch rifled Columbiad atop the bluff. Jacob had been made gun captain. The other cadets rushed to other guns along the crest. The guns aboard the *Patrick Henry* were being manned by the ship's regular crew.

"I dunno, but old man Graves was about to light a match to my butt, so I'm grateful no matter what it is!" exclaimed Henry.

Eight-Inch Columbiad Atop Drewry's Bluff - a gun manned by Confederate Cadets. Courtesy, Library of Congress

No sooner had they reached their gun when a loud report rumbled upriver, accompanied by the telltale whistle of an incoming shell. This was no drill. The earlier shot had been a signal from downriver that enemy ships were approaching. Jacob and his crew crouched behind breastworks as the shell exploded on the slope below them.

Jacob gazed downriver. An enemy ship was steaming toward them, belching a dense column of black smoke. Other columns indicated more ships coming.

Jacob couldn't wait to fire. Rifled Columbiads were renowned for accuracy as well as distance, and with six guns absent, the sooner they opened fire the better.

"Powder and shell!" he shouted. He grabbed a fistful of friction primers from a box. "Remove tompion! Make ready with sponge and rammer! Load!"

The big enemy ship came on at flank speed, cleared for action, gun ports open. Jacob inserted the primer and sighted down the barrel.

"Five degree left! Elevation ten degrees!" he yelled. Men heaved on the tackle to swing the gun into compliance with his orders. "Ready!" he shouted.

Suddenly Jacob remembered he must await the battery commander's order to fire. He nervously watched and waited as the enemy ship closed to within 1,000 yards. He noticed that she had no paddlewheels...

A screw steamer...single smokestack...three schooner-rigged masts...a long, slim hull with a row of gun ports – could it be?

Henry Stiles called out. "Sir, isn't that the...?"

"Commence firing when ready!" yelled the battery commander.

Jacob knew what Henry had been about to say and he was right. The ship was the *Arapahoe!* Jacob lunged for the lanyard, but his urge to fire quickly gave way to an even greater urge to score a hit. Remembering the disciplined calm Captain Parker always displayed in action, he methodically checked the gun again, aligned the sights and adjusted for the enemy's forward motion. Then he gritted his teeth, said a prayer and pulled the lanyard.

The great gun thundered and bucked against its restraining tackle as the 200-pound shell whistled toward the *Arapahoe*. Jacob followed the shell's arching trajectory across the clear sky. It ran as truc as if guided by divine hands and exploded on the enemy's forward deck. The impact flung crew members in all directions, some never to rise again. A cheer went up along the bluff.

Other guns commenced firing. Shells rained down around the *Arapahoe*. Geysers gushed skyward as if the river itself were erupting. The *Arapahoe* turned cross-channel to bring her broadside guns to bear on the bluff.

"Prepare to receive a broadside!" yelled the Confederate battery commander.

"Hurry! Reload!" yelled Jacob, eager to fire another shell. But before the order could be obeyed, the enemy ship's big guns spewed a wall of smoke. "Get down! Get down!" he yelled.

A dozen shells exploded on the bluff in unison, turning it into a maze of flying dirt and shrapnel. But the shells landed well below the crest and did only minimal damage to the Confederate gun emplacements, which were along the top. Either the *Arapahoe's* gunners had miscalculated or were unable to elevate their guns enough to bear on the top of the bluff.

The Confederate guns continued to pummel the enemy. From the bluff, the explosions resembled a massive charge of buckshot ripping into its target.

The *Arapahoe* fired another broadside, and again the shells landed low. That settled the issue. She could not raise her guns enough to bear on the bluff's crest.

Swirling water appeared under the *Arapahoe's* bow. Her captain, recognizing his ship's untenable position, had reversed engines and was backing downriver. Jacob sent her a parting shot as his comrades cheered her departure.

Jacob was sorry to see the ship go. Despite missing six of their biggest guns, they could have sent her to the bottom if only given more time.

He prayed that Alonzo Peck had been a casualty, though he preferred to achieve that in a more personal encounter. At any rate, the enemy had received a hard lesson that would likely prevent another attack on Drewry's Bluff any time soon. His next chance to encounter the *Arapahoe* probably would have to wait until he had left the academy and gone on duty elsewhere.

* * *

As the year 1863 wound down, the cadets were introduced to a phenomenon that they found most disagreeable – mid-term exams. The Christmas holiday, which began at the completion of exams, would not be a happy one for two cadets from Virginia, one from South Carolina and another from Georgia. They had been found lacking and put on probation for the spring semester.

"It was close," said Henry, not known for his academic skills. "I did all right in Seamanship, Gunnery and Naval Tactics, but Navigation involves too much math. Never was good at that. And why must I know about steam or infantry tactics?"

"I'm the other way around," said Jacob. "I did all right in Steam Mechanics but had trouble with Seamanship. *Steam* is our future, not sails."

"Don't forget, we sometimes go on joint missions with the army, like we did at Roanoke Island," added Roger. "So we need a knowledge of infantry tactics."

"Yeah, but missions like Roanoke Island we can do without," said Henry.

"Well anyway, I'm looking forward to our time off," said Roger. "I'm going to see my sisters in Amelia. They're young ladies now. In fact, Jenny's engaged. Can't wait to put the fear of God in the future groom. What do ya'll plan to do?"

"I'm from New Bern, North Car'lina, and I'll go for a quick visit," said Henry. "Haven't seen Ma and Pa since this war began. You going home, Jake?"

"Naw, I'll pro'bly stay around town. I need some time to myself."

"What about your girl?"

"She...moved on awhile back."

"I'm sorry, Jake...I didn't know," said Henry. "That must be hard..."

"I knew something was wrong, but I figured it was none o'my business," said Roger. Suddenly his face brightened. "Say listen, you could come with me and meet my sisters! Rachel's seventeen now and not spoken for - and she's a real looker!"

"That's tempting, Roger, maybe next time. Nothing against you or Rachel, it's just that I wouldn't be very good company right now."

"Say, what about me? I'd *love* t'meet Rachel!"

"Forget it, Henry!" said Roger.

* * *

Jacob lounged in his bunk in the crew's quarters below deck. With half the regular crew and nearly all the cadets away, the *Patrick Henry* seemed deserted.

He welcomed it. Three months of studying, recitations and gun drills, from 7:00 a.m. to 10:00 p.m. six days a week, had taken its toll. He looked forward to time to reflect and recharge himself. He had thought about looking for a quiet spot along the banks of the James, but with the ship half-deserted and colder weather setting in, his bunk seemed a more logical place to reside.

He hoped Roger, Henry and the other cadets enjoyed their time away. He knew he should make more friends among the others. They would become fellow officers and having friends in those ranks would not be a bad thing. He vowed to do a better job of getting to know them, but the regimen left little time for socializing, something he didn't do well in the first place.

At least he had Roger and Henry. He valued those relationships. They had grown closer since joining the academy - studying together, helping each other. The strengths of one seemed to counterbalance the weaknesses of the other.

Jacob thought about what Roger had endured as a boy. He couldn't imagine growing up without parents or being beaten or seeing his siblings treated as Roger's sisters had been treated. He had a strained relationship with his own father, but as far as he knew, they still loved and respected each other.

For all the faults he found with the Amish community, it made him proud that rape and incest were not among them. Amish youth were taught strong morals and respect for family members from the time they were born.

But despite everything, Roger and his sisters seemed to have turned out well. He would indeed like to meet Jenny and Rachel – especially Rachel.

91

He found himself drifting toward an afternoon nap. That was all right, that was what he needed. But thoughts of Rachel kept energizing him. She must be a handsome girl, he figured, given Roger's general features. Soon imagined images faded in favor of a more defined one – of Lydia Schenk.

He thought back to that day months ago when he and Lydia met. Though she was older and more inclined to city life, they still had things in common – an Amish background, no family in town. He wondered if she had gone home for the holidays or perhaps even moved back to Pennsylvania. He wouldn't be surprised if she were married or engaged by now, as pretty as she was.

But what if she was alone for the holidays? No one should be alone on Christmas. Perhaps he should go and see. It couldn't do any harm, and besides, it would do him good to get off the ship for awhile.

Cadet Midshipman James Morgan, CSN. Morgan: Recollections of a Rebel Reefer

Twenty minutes later found him headed down the ship's gangplank toward a buggy that stood by the dock. The driver had just unloaded some Christmas boxes sent to crew members and was preparing to head back to town. Two other cadets, two of the few who were still around, waited to jump aboard.

"Say Buckner, how 'bout coming along with us?" hollered James Morgan, a cadet from New Orleans. Like Jacob, he was captain of a big gun up on the bluff. "We know a place near Rockett's that's open even today. We'll celebrate a little and return to the ship before dark."

"Is today Christmas? I thought that was tomorrow,"

said Jacob. "Actually, I'm on my way to visit a friend in town, but I'd love a ride."

James Morgan had always impressed Jacob as being mature and intelligent. The son of a wealthy Louisiana rice farmer, he had a youthful face, medium build and close-cut hair. He had attended the U.S. Naval Academy for a year before the war and had seen action in several battles since joining the Confederate Navy. The other cadet, Palmer Saunders, was a Virginian who remained aloof and said little. Jacob was not well acquainted with him.

Jacob left the others at Rockett's, but not before they had hired the driver to meet them there in three hours for the return trip to the ship. He ascended Church Hill past St. John's Church, and soon stood before Lydia Schenk's well-kept yard.

The rosebushes had been cut back now and their bases mounded up with pine needles. He followed the brick walk to the door and reached for the knocker just as Lydia peered through the curtains, a quizzical look on her face.

Jacob felt hesitant. He wasn't sure whether he was welcome or if Lydia even remembered him. He waved and smiled awkwardly. Through the curtains he saw her lay aside a feather duster and straighten her hair. The door swung open.

"Well, if it isn't my jilted sailor friend!" smiled Lydia. She quickly ran her hands down the buttons of her work dress to make sure all were fastened. "Your name is Jacob, isn't it? Don't tell me you've forgotten where 'Jessica' lives!"

"Oh, no, ma'am, that's not it," said Jacob, blushing. "Just remembered our talk and wondered how you were doing and, you know, thought I'd come by..."

"Well then, I'm glad you did. Please come in, but I must look a fright!" She led Jacob into the parlor and motioned him to a seat beside her on the sofa.

"Uhh, with all respect, ma'am, you could never look a fright."

"Why thank you, Jacob. But one thing, you mustn't call me 'ma'am'. I'm not *that* old. My name is Lydia. So, did your shipmates abandon you on Christmas?"

"Most of 'em, but I felt like being alone anyhow. I'm a cadet at the new naval academy down at Drewry's Bluff, and the classes are hard. I needed a break."

"So you're to be an officer. How wonderful, Jacob! But tell me, you wanted to be alone and yet you came to see me. Should I be flattered or insulted?" She flashed her hazel eyes and gave Jacob a puckish smile.

Jacob blushed a deeper red. "I surely didn't mean to... to insult you. I just wondered - well, since you have no family in town, I thought you might be alone, like me. But if you *prefer* to be alone or...or if you're expecting other company..."

"You're wondering if I have a romantic interest, aren't you? Sadly, I don't. I was engaged to an army lieutenant, but he...got himself killed at Gettysburg."

"I'm sorry. I know how hard it is to, you know, lose someone that close. I still haven't gotten over my brother's death."

Lydia nodded with a weak half-smile. "My fiancé was the reason I didn't go back to Lancaster. My family didn't... approve of me marrying a soldier..."

"Just as my family didn't approve of me becoming one."

Lydia smiled more freely now. "Guess we're just a couple of Amish outcasts," she said. She laid a hand on his arm.

"Yeah, I guess that's it," Jacob said. He covered her hand with his.

"It's hard this time of year, isn't it Jacob? I'm glad we found each other."

"I am as well. I'm used to having a lot of people around at Christmas. Coming and going, visiting each other, elaborate meals..."

"Tell you what; my ex-fiancé's parents gave me a ham and some trimmings for Christmas. I told them they'd best use it themselves, but they insisted. I haven't entertained in a...a long time, Jacob, and it surely won't be elaborate, but if you can stay, I'd love for you to have dinner with me and visit for...for as long as you can..."

Jacob's bashful nature urged him to decline. But Lydia's warm, inviting smile pushed him in the other direction. "Well, I've had only navy food and male company for months now, so your invitation is very appealing. If it's all right, I'll accept."

"Wonderful! By the way, your blond beard is *very* becoming. It almost hides your scar. Did the scar come from battle, or perhaps your ex-girlfriend?"

"Nothing so exciting. Just a boyhood accident. Fell from a hayloft."

* * *

"What happened to you yesterday, Buckner?" asked James Morgan, leaning on the ship's rail at the top of the gangplank. "We waited an extra hour for you at Rockett's, but had to leave so the driver could get back home before dark."

"Sorry," said Jacob as he came up the gangplank. "My...friend invited me to stay for dinner and, you know, time got away from us. I bunked down on her...her sofa and caught a ride this morning. Appreciate you waiting, though."

"So, time got away and you slept on her sofa, huh?" smiled James. "She must be a, uhh, most 'accommodating' friend. Someone you've known for a long time?"

"Kind of," said Jacob, embarrassed and eager to get past this conversation. "She used to be Amish, like me, so we had a lot to...to talk about..."

Chapter Eight

"Well, I think Jenny could have done better, but she seems to love him and I guess that's the main thing," said Roger.

The three boys were together once again aboard the *Patrick Henry*. They sat in the mess hall, having just finished an evening meal of dried beef and potatoes.

"What's the matter with him?" grinned Jacob. "Is he weak between the ears?"

"There was a boy back home that wet himself every time a girl spoke to him," said Henry. "Fella couldn't understand why the ladies stayed clear of him."

"Oh, this fella's handsome enough, and smart, but he's not in uniform," said Roger. "He has this cough and claims it's consumption, yet he seems healthy as a mule."

"Say, I couldn't help but hear you fellas discussing girls - my favorite subject," said James Morgan, leaning over from the next table. "Why don't you ask Buckner how he spent Christmas?" He departed with a chuckle.

Wonderful, Jacob thought. Like a fish on a griddle, he grimaced and braced for the heat he knew was coming. He also vowed to look elsewhere among the cadets for new friends.

"Sooo, tell us, Jake, just how *did* you spend Christmas?" ventured Henry.

"None a'your biz'ness." That was like dumping blood in shark-infested waters, and Jacob knew it the moment he said it.

"I'm sure it didn't involve a *girl*, did it?" asked Roger. "Not after you turned down a chance to meet my sister *Rachel* because you wanted t'be *alone...*"

Jacob's seat was growing warm. "It wasn't like that, fellas. There's this lady...I met her last summer and...well anyway, she used to be Amish..."

"A lady? Reminded you of your mother, did she?" asked Henry.

"Well, she's at least twenty-five, and..."

"Twenty-five? The poor decrepit thing!" said Roger. "And you'd rather spend time with such an old woman than my seventeen-year-old sister? I'm disappointed, Jake. Her name wouldn't be 'Jessica', would it?"

"Her name is Lydia if you must know, and I stayed clear of 'Jessica' – all of 'em!"

His tormentors' faces, stoic until now, broke into laughter. Jacob shook his head. Such harassment had to be expected if one left himself open to it.

Roger wiped away his laugh-induced tears and tried to reestablish a straight face. "So...you're saying that this 'Lydia', uhh, made you forget all about 'Jessica'...?"

"Yes, but not the way you think. We just, you know, kept each other company on Christmas. It got late, so I slept on her sofa that night."

"You spent the night?" exclaimed Henry. "We need t'have a serious talk!"

Roger nodded. "Yeah, Jake. We're glad you weren't alone on Christmas, but there are certain dangers. Let us know next time and we can tell you what to do..."

"Exactly," added Henry, grinning. "But only if you share *all* the details."

Henry swerved as a cold biscuit flew past his ear.

Jacob knew their remarks were harmless, even well-intended, but he found it interesting how they had so eagerly jumped to the juiciest of conclusions. Such was human nature, he figured.

He had never appreciated the Amish practice of not allowing young couples too much time alone, but now he did. To put oneself in a situation that created the wrong perception was to have people believe that perception.

* * *

The message from Captain Parker had arrived in a sealed envelope marked 'open in private'. Jacob's first reaction was to wonder how he was supposed to comply with that order aboard the crowded *Patrick Henry*. Yet it must be a serious matter, for the Captain had never before communicated in that way.

Curiosity ate at him as he hurried down the gangplank and along the dock to where crates of supplies awaited transfer to the ship. In the shadow of the ship's bow, he leaned against a crate and tore open the envelope:

> *Cadet Buckner,*
> *You are requested to volunteer for a secret mission to be conducted by joint army and navy forces to include a select group of cadets, all under the command of Commander John Taylor Wood. The mission will involve risk and require you to be absent from the academy for at least a week. If you accept, please report tonight at 2200 hours to Recital Room #2 for a briefing. Under penalty of dismissal from the Academy, you are to say nothing to anyone regarding this matter.*
>
> *William Parker, Captain*

Jacob's heart thumped as he approached the recital room. A steady stream of thoughts had buzzed through his mind like swarming bees since receiving the note. A secret mission involving risk, a select group of cadets, under penalty of dismissal - he couldn't imagine what this mission involved, but clearly it was serious.

Several cadets were already in the room when Jacob entered, including Roger and Henry, and he seated himself next to them. The group grew to eight with the addition of his 'friend' James Morgan, as well as Palmer Saunders, the other cadet with whom he had shared a buggy ride into town on Christmas Day.

Jacob noticed that nearly all of those present had done well in their studies. The one exception was Henry, whose grades were below average. Jacob concluded that Henry must have been picked because he was more experienced than most.

"Gentlemen, let's get started," said Captain Parker, standing in front of the room. With him was a bearded, thickly-built officer in his early thirties. "I'd like to introduce Commander John Taylor Wood," continued the Captain. "Commander Wood is to head up the mission and will explain it to us. Commander Wood?"

John Taylor Wood was the nephew of Jefferson Davis and the grandson of Zachary Taylor, and had served as gunnery officer on the *CSS Virginia*. In tones as calm as if planning an afternoon tea, the Commander explained that the mission was part of a large-scale attack on Federal forces occupying New Bern, North Carolina.

"Liberating New Bern will ease pressure on Eastern North Carolina," said Wood. "Our mission is to capture one or more of the gunboats stationed there and use them to support General George Pickett, who is to attack the city with a division of infantry. You cadets will serve as our junior officers for this mission and be joined by seventy-five sailors and marines from the James River Squadron."

Cmdr. Wood paused. "Will Cadet Henry Stiles please raise his hand?"

Henry's hand went up. Now it dawned on Jacob why they had picked Henry.

"Cadet Stiles is from New Bern and knows the harbor well," said Wood. "He scouted it at Christmas and will act as our pilot. Each man will receive a revolver and a cutlass. We go to Richmond in the morning and board a train there."

It was nearly 11:00 p.m. when the cadets exited the recital room. Too excited to sleep, they lingered along the rail on the deserted main deck.

"What can we expect, Henry?" asked Jacob. The others gathered to listen.

"New Bern is heavily fortified," said Henry. "I don't think Pickett has enough men, so they're counting on us to capture a gunboat or two and supply some heavy artillery. We might just end up spelling the difference in this fracas."

Faces lit up. To go on such a mission and to play such a role! After months of hard study, the cadets relished the prospect.

"Did you see any gunboats when you were there?" asked James Morgan.

"Yeah, I went down through the marshes in my old rowboat and saw several in the harbor," nodded Henry. "But chances are those men have been sitting around so long that they've gotten careless. If we do this right, I think we can pull it off."

"What'll we do for boats when we get there?" asked Jacob.

"We're taking four cutters from the James River Squadron with us. They'll be loaded on flat cars in Richmond," said Henry.

* * *

Morning revealed many a face that had not slept well as the chosen cadets gathered on the dock near carriages that would take them to Richmond. Later that day, Captain Parker announced to the rest of the academy that the missing cadets were away on a 'special training mission'. Only the faculty knew the whole truth.

In route to Kinston, N.C., the embarkation point, the train stopped at several towns along the way for fuel. Curious crowds gathered to gaze at the strange sight of boats lashed to flatcars with armed sailors, marines and cadets perched in them.

At one stop, a group of pretty teenage girls from a nearby school were in the crowd. The girls' attention was drawn to a group of young men in uniforms of a type they had not seen before.

"Who are you and where are you going?" inquired one girl.

"We're cadets from the Confederate Naval Academy on our way to capture the Yankee navy!" yelled Roger. Then he remembered their orders not to discuss the mission, and wondered if he had given away too much to these girls.

"Ohhh, do bring back trophies! Lots of battle flags!" squealed an especially attractive young lady.

Roger relaxed; he was safe.

"All right, but you must promise to reward us with a kiss for each flag!" yelled Henry, beginning to see possibilities here.

"Agreed!" hollered the girls, waving and cheering as the train pulled away.

The train reached Kinston at 2:00 a.m. of the second morning. From there, the Neuse River would carry them the sixty miles to New Bern. Cmdr. Wood rested the group a few hours and then ordered the four boats unloaded and launched. They set off downriver at mid-morning. Jacob and Roger were in a boat commanded by Lt. Benjamin Loyall, Wood's second in command. James and Henry, the

100

latter acting as pilot, rode in the lead boat with Cmdr. Wood.

They rowed all day and into the night with little sign of life along the river. Occasionally the boats flushed a flock of wild ducks and the frantic beating of their wings never failed to startle the men, most of them rowing while deep in thought.

Jacob was no exception. He watched the forests and marsh grasses slipping by and listened to the rhythmic swishing of oars and gurgling of the river currents, and it reminded him of his days on the upper reaches of the Mattaponi. For a brief while, he lost himself in the simple enjoyment of again being on an unspoiled river, where nature remained in control and wildlife abounded.

"We're nearing New Bern! No talking! No cocking of weapons until ordered!"

The sharp message, delivered in a loud whisper and passed down the line from boat to boat, slashed through the moment and quickly brought Jacob back to the harsh reality that he would soon see battle again.

He had tried to suppress thoughts of the *Arapahoe* and Alonzo Peck, for the odds of either being in these waters were remote. Still the chance existed, and the closer they got to New Bern, the stronger those thoughts became. He could only hope, he thought. He rested on his oar and fingered the handle of his Colt pistol.

At four in the morning, Cmdr. Wood, with Henry Stiles beside him, led the boats into a side creek off the Neuse River just short of the New Bern harbor.

While three of the boats remained hidden among the marsh grasses, Wood took his boat out into the harbor. The men rowed silently as Henry directed them on a pass up the harbor and back again, searching for a gunboat that would make a good target. But darkness and a cold, dense, February fog thwarted their efforts.

"Dawn is coming up fast, sir," whispered Henry. "When this fog burns off, we'll be spotted for sure."

"Rest oars!" ordered the Commander. "Listen! Hear that?"

The twenty sailors and marines sat quietly, letting the boat drift. Through the fog-shrouded silence came the muffled rumble of gunfire, like distant thunder.

"That's Pickett! He's attacking!" exclaimed Cmdr. Wood. "We must find a target quickly or our mission will fail!"

"We have time for one more pass up the harbor, but then we *must* return to the creek or be spotted," said Henry.

"Very well. Careful with the oars, men, and no talking," said the Commander. "Take us in a little closer, Mr. Stiles. I'd rather be spotted than miss an opportunity."

The men bent to their oars and the thirty-foot cutter glided silently through the fog. Using only a compass and the fast-running tide to guide him, Henry put the boat on a course that he estimated was no more than 300 yards offshore.

"I don't dare go any closer in, sir," he whispered. "We're in a dangerous area."

They proceeded slowly up the harbor. The brightening dawn had penetrated the fog for a distance equal to the length of the boat, but still they could see or hear nothing that would betray the presence of a ship. Only the distant barking of a dog and the even more distant rumble of Pickett's attack disturbed the silence.

The fog grew brighter. A buoy slipped past and got Henry's attention.

"We're further out than I thought, and near the upper end of the harbor!" he whispered. "The channel here is too narrow for a ship to safely anchor. We must come about and move closer in. With your permission, sir, I'll inform the coxswain!"

The order passed down the cutter to the coxswain, who promptly swung the tiller to starboard and sent the boat in a half-circle to port. It brought them fifty yards closer in. The Commander urged silence as they started back down the harbor. Every eye strained into the thinning mist.

A squealing seagull came side-wheeling through the fog fifty feet over their heads, its bright white feathers clearly visible. The fog was lifting.

"Commander," whispered Henry. "Coal smoke, bacon cooking - I smell a ship!"

Barely had he spoken when the hazy outline of a large side-wheel steamer emerged looking like a ghost ship in the fog. She rode at anchor a hundred yards inshore from them, her topgallant spars visible against a patch of blue higher up.

"My merciful God!" whispered Cmdr. Wood. "Lay into the oars – quietly now!"

One glance at the towering enemy ship was all the motivation the sailors and marines needed, and the cutter shot ahead. Within minutes, the big steamer had faded into the thin fog with no sign of an alarm having been given.

Cmdr. Wood and his men reached the creek to find the others in a clearing on shore with their cutters moored nearby. Wood briefed everyone.

"We think it's the *Underwriter*," said the Commander. "Those of you who were at Roanoke Island and Elizabeth City may remember her - a side-wheel steamer, four guns, a crew of about seventy. We move against her tonight."

Only an order to maintain silence prevented the young cadets from breaking into cheers. The veterans on the other hand, many of whom had been with the Mosquito Fleet, remained more reserved.

Jacob, Roger and Henry were in the latter group. They glanced at each other as Cmdr. Wood paused and took a sip of coffee handed to him. Henry wanted to share something with the others and could hold back no longer.

"She's the ship that fired on us at Fort Cobb and killed four of our shipmates!"

"Are you *certain?*" whispered Roger. "There were a dozen ships there."

"Positive! I don't forget profiles, and I got enough of a look to know!"

"Then we have a debt to settle," said Jacob grimly.

"We'll be boarding her in the dark and there'll be close quarter fighting," continued the Commander, "so I want every man to tie a strip of white cloth around his left arm. Our password will be 'Sumter'. If there are no questions, be ready to depart at ten o'clock tonight."

They spent the day cleaning firearms, sharpening cutlasses, writing letters home. The veterans remained somber. They knew that capturing a ship at night in hand-to-hand fighting would be difficult, especially against a battle-hardened crew. The younger men chatted confidently about the coming fight, what they would achieve, and how they would boast of it to lady friends.

Jacob suspected that the chatter reflected nervousness, an issue he could identify with. But listening to it increased his own nervousness so he retreated to the creek bank and sat alone, gazing out over the marsh grasses to where the Neuse River snaked its way through the wetlands toward the New Bern harbor.

Distant firing rumbled across the marshes. Pickett's troops must be wondering when the artillery support they had been promised would arrive, Jacob figured.

It occurred to him that failure to capture the *Underwriter* would mean some of those men would die who otherwise might live. That was the gist of this matter, not personal glory, not bragging to girl friends, not even Alonzo Peck. Those young sailors and cadets who were so busy laughing and bragging now would likely be singing a different tune before this night ended.

* * *

"Our heavenly Father, as we go forth into harm's way, we commit ourselves to thy hands. We ask that you protect us and keep us safe, and should we fall, we pray that you will take us into thy heavenly arms. And if it be thy will, we ask thy blessing upon our efforts. In Jesus' name we pray, amen."

Cmdr. Wood's 'amen' was echoed by dozens of kneeling men. The Commander got up and looked at his watch.

"Ten o'clock," he announced. "Make sure your strip of white cloth is firmly pinned. Do not cock your weapons until ordered. You may proceed aboard the cutters, but remember, we must maintain *strict silence!*"

The men filed down the bank and into the waiting boats. The calm February night was clear and cold, moonless but with bright starlight.

A young sailor with blond hair stood in line in front of Jacob and Roger. He turned to them. "Does my...my white cloth show in the dark?" he asked nervously.

"Yes, clearly," said Roger. "And so does your head. I'd get a hat if I were you."

"Oh! Yeah, thanks." The boy pulled out a grey wool cap and put it on.

"I think the four of us should stick together and protect each other's back," said James Morgan. He and Palmer Saunders were behind Jacob and Roger.

"Good idea, but it won't be easy. There'll be a lot of confusion and only the stars to see by," said Jacob.

Palmer Saunders gazed up at the twinkling sky. "I expect some of us will be up *among* those stars before sunrise tomorrow," he said.

Jacob and Roger glanced at the solemn young man, a veteran at only seventeen. Rarely had they heard him speak a complete sentence, let alone anything so profound, and they knew all too well that he likely spoke the truth.

It occurred to Jacob that those who were talkative earlier had grown quiet and now the veterans were doing the talking. He had noticed that pattern before. As battle drew closer, emotions tended to progress from calm confidence to nervous anticipation to petrifying horror. The veterans had reached the nervous stage, while the ex-talkers found themselves engulfed in horror - simple proof that combat brings everyone face to face with his own mortality.

The four cutters emerged from the creek and proceeded up the harbor in two columns of two. The stars receded behind thin clouds and the night grew darker. Only faint lights from the town aided Henry Stiles as he estimated his bearings. He laid a course in the general direction of the anchored *Underwriter*. The group of small boats made its way slowly and quietly through the harbor's black waters.

A bell, barely audible, sounded in the distance like a ghost beacon in the night. Henry counted four peals. He pulled out his pocket watch. Two a.m. - four bells on the midnight watch. With unbridled astonishment he realized that it must be the bell on the deck of the *Underwriter*, sounding the time.

He altered course toward the sound. The cutters pulled cautiously in that direction, the men tense, weapons ready, straining to see through the dark night.

After what seemed hours, Henry again pulled out his watch. Two-thirty. He cupped an ear. The bell sounded again, five peals, not 300 yards ahead.

"Boat ahoy!" came a voice through the night. Hearts jumped into throats. Cmdr. Wood offered no response.

"Boat ahoy! Boat ahoy!" came the challenge again, more urgent this time.

Still Cmdr. Wood did not respond. The *Underwriter's* bell began clanging frantically. Shadows rushed about her deck as the big ship cleared for action.

"Give way, boys, give way!" yelled Cmdr. Wood. No need for silence now.

The cutters sprang forward through the darkness. They must close quickly on the *Underwriter*, for a single shell from her big guns could splinter the small boats.

A flash and a bang announced the first shot. A high-pitched whine rent the air as the shell passed over Jacob's head. Others followed on its heels, but all flew high. The cutters had gotten under the guns' field of fire.

Now came a barrage of musket and pistol fire from the *Underwriter's* deck. To Jacob's left, the coxswain in Cmdr. Wood's boat slumped over. Before anyone could grab the tiller, the cutter veered into the *Underwriter's* paddlewheel housing. Jacob knew that Henry, James and the others in that boat would find it difficult to board over the paddlewheel and would be sitting ducks for the armed sailors on her deck.

Frantically he boated his oar and scrambled to the bow where Lt. Loyall stood holding a grappling hook, looking up at the *Underwriter's* rail.

Jacob was beside himself. "We must board quickly, sir, or those men...!"

"Open your eyes, Mr. Buckner! There's an anti-boarding net up there!"

Startled that Lt. Loyall knew his name, Jacob quickly recovered and peered up through the dim light. Heavy cord netting stretched from the rigging down to the gunwale and prevented entry to the deck. The winking flash of starlight on cutlass blades and carbines betrayed Union sailors rushing to engage Cmdr. Wood's men as the latter attempted to board over the paddlewheel.

Consumed with a blood lust that surprised him – he had to be insane, he told himself – Jacob leaped forward, bounded off the cutter's bow and catapulted upward to where he could just grab the bottom strand of netting.

For a moment he dangled there, kicking and flailing as if on the end of a hangman's rope. A vision flashed through his mind of being shot by one of those carbine-carrying sailors while he hung there.

He found a foothold on a protruding ledge just below the gunwale. Holding onto the ship's rail, he pulled his brass-hilted cutlass from its scabbard and began hacking at the netting. The other two cutters were up now and exchanging fire with the Union sailors, providing a semblance of cover for him.

After what seemed an eternity of frantically cutting away the netting, Jacob managed to open the boarding gate and clear the way to the deck. But the activity had gotten the attention of a Union officer. He yelled an order and a dozen men took up positions across from the gate.

Aided by the ship's rigging, Lt. Loyall and his sailors and marines clawed their way up to the open gate. Lt. Loyall was the first one through, but nearsighted and without his glasses, he tripped and fell as he stepped onto the deck. A barrage of gunfire meant for him cut down the four men directly behind him. They lay on the deck, three wounded and writhing like freshly beached fish, another already frozen in death.

Lt. Loyall righted himself and directed his men to fan out and push forward. A short distance away, Cmdr. Wood's men had managed to scale the paddlewheel housing and were pouring onto the deck. Jacob saw Henry Stiles locked in a cutlass duel with a Yankee sailor.

The night erupted with blood-curdling yells and screams, the flash of pistols, and clash of cutlasses as the fighting became hand-to-hand. The Southerners forced the Union sailors back along the deck toward the stern quarterdeck. The cadets led the way, and leading the cadets was none other than the young Palmer Saunders.

"Roger, to your left!" yelled Jacob as a Yankee sailor raised his cutlass.

Roger met the blow with the barrel of his pistol and then fired the pistol into his enemy's chest. The man collapsed to the deck. Roger glanced toward Jacob and fired again. A sailor aiming a pistol at Jacob's head grabbed his shoulder and retreated.

"Never mind me, Jake, watch your front!" yelled Roger.

Their strength increasing as more men climbed to the deck, the Southerners relentlessly pressed the Federals, who retreated up to the quarterdeck or down the companionways to steerage, the wardroom, anywhere that offered a possible escape.

Palmer Saunders, using his empty pistol as a club, reached the steps leading up to the quarterdeck. Blocking his way stood a veteran Union sailor, a giant of a man brandishing a heavy cutlass that resembled a Roman short sword. The young Saunders swung his pistol at the big Yankee's knees.

The cagey veteran nimbly retreated up a step. Before Palmer could draw his own cutlass, the man raised his big cutlass and brought it down in a powerful wood-chopping blow to the top of Palmer's head. The young cadet collapsed to the deck.

Jacob grabbed an empty musket from a dead sailor and rushed to Palmer's aid. Wielding it like a club, he swung the musket at the big man, but the latter fled across the quarterdeck and joined a group of his comrades who were jumping off the stern and swimming for shore. Other Union sailors were flinging their weapons to the deck and raising their hands.

"*The ship is ours!*" yelled Cmdr. Wood. A rousing cheer went up.

Jacob rushed back to where Palmer lay on the deck. Roger was already there, cradling the seventeen-year-old in his arms. James Morgan joined them.

Roger looked up, his hands and clothes covered with Palmer's blood. "Get a light. I think he's...dead."

Henry Stiles came up with one of the ship's lanterns. The light revealed a split in Palmer's skull nearly down to his ears. The horrible wound left no doubt that the young man had died instantly.

Jacob remembered Palmer's grim prediction that some of them would reside among the stars before morning. He doubted that the young man had imagined himself in that category.

In addition to Palmer Saunders, the battle had cost the South an engineer, a marine and three seamen, plus eighteen men wounded. The Confederates counted nine Federal dead and eighteen wounded, and had captured another nineteen. The coxswain that had died in Lt. Loyall's boat, causing it to hit the paddlewheel, had been firing a pistol from each hand and steering with his knees when he took a ball in the forehead.

Eager to aid General Pickett, Cmdr. Wood gave orders to get the *Underwriter* underway quickly. But an engineer returned from the engine room with news that the furnaces were out and it would take an hour to raise steam pressure. While the engineers worked, Jacob, Roger, Henry and James gathered by the rail.

"Henry, I saw you and a fella fightin' tooth and nail with cutlasses," said Jacob. "How'd that come out?"

"He was an old acquaintance from my prewar navy days..." Henry swallowed hard. "I had to kill him."

Their conversation stopped abruptly at the sound of incoming shells. Alerted by the *Underwriter* crewmen who had reached shore, nearby Union forts were firing on the ship. One of the shells struck and splintered a paddlewheel.

Under enemy fire, the ship now inoperable, Cmdr. Wood faced a decision.

"Burn her!" he ordered. "Remove our dead and wounded and set her afire!"

Ten minutes later the men were safely back in the cutters. Flames rose up through the *Underwriter's* hatchways and out the gun ports. The Union wounded and captured sat huddled in the boats. The enemy dead had been left behind.

"Well, looks like Pickett is on his own," said Jacob as they pulled away.

"There's been no firing recently," said James. "His attack may have failed."

"That means Palmer and those others died for nothing," said Roger solemnly.

"Well, at least we destroyed the *Underwriter*," said Jacob. "That helps settle the score for those fellas who died at Fort Cobb."

The men traveled back up the Neuse to Kinston and the waiting train. While the boats were being loaded, the cadets bought a supply of cloth of varying colors. Once aboard the train, they busied themselves making 'battle flags', and by the time the train reached the town that housed the girls' school, there were a large number of 'captured' flags on hand, all of which appeared suspiciously crude.

The young ladies were summoned. The cadets brought out their hard-earned 'war souvenirs', reminded the girls of their promise and demanded satisfaction.

"But can't the Yankees sew better than *that*?" asked one skeptical young lady.

"Their mothers don't like 'em, so they have to do it themselves," said Henry.

After a round of laughter and denials - and just enough resistance to satisfy everyone's conscious - the kissing began. Only the whistle signaling departure time enabled Cmdr. Wood to get everyone back aboard the train. Even then, Henry nearly succeeded in smuggling a young lady on board.

As they steamed north toward Richmond, Jacob pondered some things.

With Pickett's attack clearly audible, why wasn't the *Underwriter's* furnaces lit and its boilers at full pressure? The town was under attack. Shouldn't the ship have been ready to move either out of danger or to help repel the attack? And if her captain saw no danger, why were the anti-boarding nets in place?

None of it made sense. He must remember to ask Captain Parker about it.

Chapter Nine

"Cadets, atten-shion!" growled Captain Parker.

Assembled in rows of ten across the *Patrick Henry's* main deck, fifty cadets snapped to attention in a single, unified click of heels.

"We are here to honor those who so admirably represented the Academy in the recent capture and destruction of the Federal gunboat *Underwriter*," said the Captain, his deep voice cutting the quiet stillness as his breath turned white in the cold morning air. It was one of those rare occasions when he wore his dress uniform, sword at his side. "Please come forward as you are called."

"Cadet Jacob Buckner..."

Jacob stepped from ranks, moved briskly to the front and drew up at attention to Captain Parker's right.

"Cadet Daniel Lee...Cadet James Morgan...Cadet John Northrop..."

The cadets came forward and formed a row to Jacob's right.

"Cadet Roger Phillips...Cadet Thomas Scharf...Cadet Henry Stiles."

As Henry stepped into place at the end of the row, Captain Parker turned to face the seven cadets.

"Your gallant actions have brought praise to you and the Academy. You captured and destroyed the most powerful gunboat on North Carolina waters. That same gunboat inflicted casualties on us at Roanoke Island and Elizabeth City. I am proud to announce that the Confederate Congress has passed a resolution recognizing and thanking you for your deeds. Gentlemen, you are heroes. You are to be congratulated!"

A roar arose from the assembled cadets. Captain Parker called for order.

"Most regrettably, eight cadets went forward but only seven returned. Cadet Palmer Saunders was killed while leading the attack. His bravery and unselfish sacrifice

111

must never be forgotten. We grieve at the loss of a friend and comrade, and we extend our condolences to his family. May he rest in eternal peace in the arms of God. In honor of him, let us bow our heads in a moment of silence..."

For the next moment, the silence was broken only by the hissing of steam from the boilers and lapping of waves against the ship's side.

"Classes will resume at 0800 hours. Cadets dismissed."

* * *

As Jacob ascended the hill toward St. John's Church, the bell high in the church steeple began a slow, methodic toll, announcing high noon. He had passed this way and heard the bell before, but today, for some reason, he stopped to listen.

Each strike of the clapper brought a low, mournful wail that reverberated seemingly without end, hanging in the air and never quite fading away before being replaced by the next strike. It was beautiful but sad, Jacob thought, not at all like the crisp clang of the school bell at home, or the farm bells used to alert neighbors.

He was drawn down the walkway to the church door, found it unlocked, and stuck his head inside the sanctuary. He saw no one, which wasn't surprising since it was Saturday. Rows of oak pews stretched across the cavernous room. Stained glass windows rose nearly to the ceiling. Ornate brass candelabras flanked the pulpit with matching sconces hanging from the walls. A large pipe organ sat in the far corner.

Jacob had never imagined such things in a church. It struck him as a strange way to worship God, for he had always been taught that God frowned upon such lavish displays. The Amish simply rotated services among members' homes.

As boys, he and Joshua had endured countless longwinded sermons in someone's great room or yard, trying to appear attentive while awaiting the meal. The only entertainment came when their father nodded off, which always brought a chuckle. Only through endless repetition did they absorb what they were taught.

Now, as he wandered in awed silence down the aisle between the rows of pews, gazing at the cross on the wall

112

behind the pulpit, the Holy Bible on a table in front of it, the stained glass window with the haloed image of Christ, he felt a certain peace, a deep reverence, a strange presence, and he began to understand why people would come here to worship. The world outside may be at war, but not here.

He removed his hat and sank into a pew. He savored the peace and quiet, the chance to be alone and reflect on things the way he used to on the river bank. But somehow there seemed to be another dimension now, like he wasn't alone at all.

Roanoke Island, Fort Cobb, Hampton Roads, the *Underwriter* - so much killing and so many close calls, he thought. Captain Parker had called him a hero, when in truth he was fortunate just to have lived. The moment of silence on the *Patrick Henry's* deck might as easily have been for him as for Palmer Saunders.

But it had been his choice to forsake Amish ways and follow a different path, a path he had felt strongly about and *still* felt strongly about. Yet he wondered if it was the *right* path. What if he were killed without learning the answer?

He gazed again at the image of Christ on the stained glass window. A peculiar feeling came over him, a strange mix of fear and reverence that set him to shaking as with a chill. He fell to his knees and rested his arms on the pew in front of him. Tears rolled down his cheeks as he realized he was in the presence of the Almighty. He wiped his eyes and stared at the image. *Why have I been allowed to live? Am I following the right path? How am I to know?* He lowered his head and prayed for wisdom and guidance.

* * *

For the third time, Jacob reached for the doorknocker. Lydia seemed to have a knack for getting him to relax and unwind and he needed that right now, so he had come hoping for a quiet visit with her. But she was either busy or not home – or perhaps she didn't wish to see him. He banged the knocker again, louder this time. No response. He had turned to leave when the door opened.

"Jacob, I'm so glad to see you!" Lydia's hair was covered with a towel and she busily secured a robe around her midsection. "I've been hoping to talk to you! There are stories all over town about an Amish boy who was a hero in the capture of that enemy ship! Was that you?"

Jacob felt awkward. Lydia obviously had been bathing. She stood before him only one layer removed from nakedness.

"Well, people get things mixed up, but I suppose they *could* mean me. I'm closer to being Amish than any other sailor I know of, but..."

"I heard you hacked away some netting and were the first to board..."

"No, the first fella was killed and the next three wounded. I feel bad, because I cleared the way for them. I surely don't deserve to be called a hero."

"Don't be such a ninny! I'm told you went up the side when everyone else was standing around sucking their thumb!"

"Well, things *were* kind of hanging in the balance, and it had to be done and done quickly or a lot more fellas would have died. I'm grateful that God enabled me to do it and yet survive, but a hero..."

"You're a *hero*, Jacob, whether you like it or not, and I'm proud of you. I just wish you'd be more careful." She put her arms around his waist, reached up and kissed him on his cheek, his scratchy beard notwithstanding.

Jacob blushed. He didn't consider himself a hero, but being perceived as one clearly had its advantages.

"Was the fighting as bad as I've heard?" she asked.

"It was terrible, Lydia. I saw men, some of them friends, killed right in front of me. Their blood turned the deck red."

"What an awful experience - and you raised as *Amish!*" She laid her head against his chest. "Strange how you've changed so much from the old ways and yet retain some of that deep Amish faith. That's very unusual and I love it..."

"Well, the more death I see, the more I'm drawn to faith. Sounds hypocritical since I've done some of the killing, but I can't help it."

"It's only natural, I suppose." Lydia led him into the parlor and a seat on the sofa. "When I lost my lieutenant I had the opposite reaction - I questioned God. I mean, he was a good man and I prayed hard for his safety, and then to have him killed…"

"Questioning the Almighty isn't a good idea," said Jacob. "When Joshua was killed, I blamed those who did it. Some would claim the Yankees were merely doing God's bidding, but in my opinion they were doing the devil's bidding. I joined the navy to give them what they deserve."

"So you have a vendetta; you view *yourself* as doing God's bidding, being his warrior. That's why you fight so hard…"

Jacob stared blankly at Lydia. He had never thought of it that way. There was no question he carried a vendetta, and it didn't take Alonzo Peck to incite him. *Any* Yankee would do. But was that doing God's work? Was that why his life was being spared? It was a comforting thought but one he seriously doubted.

"It's no secret that I hate Yankees. I've killed them and will kill more if I can. I consider it defending our country against murdering thieves. If that happens to please God, then so much the better."

"And what if it doesn't?"

"He has the power to stop me any time He wants."

Lydia cradled the side of Jacob's head in her hand. "That's what I'm afraid of, Jacob. Losing my lieutenant was enough. I don't want to…to lose another friend…"

Jacob gazed at her hazel eyes, her auburn-brown hair hanging loose in damp ringlets, her alluring figure, the latter covered by a robe but minus the usual camouflage of petticoats. She was indeed beautiful, he thought.

He felt a strong urge to kiss her, but Amish rules governing single couples had prevented him from spending much time alone with girls, other than Amy, and he was hesitant. He found himself as nervous as in his first battle. Lydia sensed as much.

"It's all right, Jacob. We're not Amish now."

She brought him to her and they kissed, a gentle embrace at first but growing in meaning. When finally their lips parted, she smiled an admiring smile and laid her head on his shoulder. Jacob knew they both had taken a big step in burying the heartbreak each had suffered.

"So, you questioned God," said Jacob. "Did He, you know, answer you?"

Lydia smiled. "Only recently. He told me you were special, and that I should hang on to you. I told Him I already knew that."

* * *

Jacob tapped on Captain Parker's cabin door and waited.

"Enter if you wish," came the deep, raspy voice.

Jacob opened the door and stepped in. The captain's cabin, several times the size of the one on the old *Beaufort,* contained three upholstered chairs arranged in front of a mahogany desk. The Captain looked up from the desk.

"Why, Cadet Buckner! I was about to send for you, but that matter can wait. Please have a seat. Did you have something?"

"Nothing important, sir." Jacob sat in a chair. "Just a couple of things about the *Underwriter* mission that puzzle me, and I'd like to ask you about them."

"Very well. What is it?"

"Well, that night in the harbor, we could clearly hear Gen'rul Pickett's attack in progress, yet the *Underwriter* wasn't cleared for action. The ship's furnaces were banked, there was no steam pressure...wouldn't you think they'd be ready for action, sir, what with a rebel army on their doorstep?"

"That does seem strange, but remember, they had no reason to think we had naval forces in the area."

"But if that's true, why were their anti-boarding nets deployed?"

Captain Parker rubbed his chin. "That *is* strange. It almost sounds like they knew we were there and *wanted* us to attack, and were so confident about defeating us that they didn't bother to fire up the furnaces."

"My thinking exactly, sir."

"Well, it may be true, but don't rule out incompetence. There are questions about Captain Westervelt. A friend tells me he's accused of deserting his ship and crew early in the attack. Of course he'll never be punished. His body was found floating in the harbor. It appears he drowned while trying to swim ashore."

"Guess that solves the mystery. It sounds like what folks call 'poetic justice'," said Jacob. "Thank you for your time, sir." He got up to leave.

"You're welcome, Buckner, but don't rush off. As I said, I was about to send for you. There's a matter of utmost importance I'd like to discuss with you."

"Yes sir?" Jacob sat back down.

The Captain frowned. "It's no secret that the war isn't going well for us. The Mississippi's in enemy hands, our army in Tennessee is retreating, the blockade is choking us, and now this fella Grant is taking command of Lincoln's army here in Virginia. He's a real fighter. I think Lee will have his hands full with him."

The information wasn't news to Jacob, but the Captain was concerned and that disturbed him. He leaned forward. "What can I do, sir?"

"We want you to volunteer for an important mission, a dangerous one," said Captain Parker. "The Union Navy is growing stronger and more aggressive here on the James. If Grant pushes south toward Richmond as we think he will, then an advance up the James by their navy will likely be part of that push."

"We'll be ready, sir. They've tried that before. But what about this mission?"

"They've tried it before but now they have entire *squadrons* of ironclads, and we've seen firsthand how ineffective large-bore guns are against ironclads. No, we must improve our river defenses." The Captain paused and took out his pipe.

"The British have developed a new torpedo, one that's far more effective," he continued. "A supply of them is to arrive aboard a blockade runner in a few days. A fishing boat will rendezvous with the blockade runner off the Virginia Capes, offload the torpedoes and ferry them up the York River to a point below West Point."

Jacob perked up at the mention of his home town. "I know the area well, sir."

"That's one of the reasons we chose you for this job, son, along with the fact that you've proven yourself time and again." He pulled a pouch of tobacco from his pocket.

"We want you to take a detail and meet the fishing boat on the York, offload the torpedoes and transport them here," he continued. "It will require a boat, a wagon and three or four good men. But it's risky. The York and the roads in that area are closely watched because the Federals have a supply base upriver at a place called White House Landing. Even so, our odds are better there than here on the James. You can pick your own men." The Captain began packing his pipe. "Whadaya think?"

"Tricky, sir. I'm familiar with White House Landing. The ship traffic is heavy, so the transfer must be made at night. What's the name of this fishing boat? Who's the captain? Where do we meet him and on what date?"

Captain Parker smiled and lit his pipe. Jacob had already begun gathering and analyzing details. He knew he had his volunteer.

"His name is Stanley McNulty, from Gloucester. His boat is the '*Grey Heron*', a sixty-foot steam trawler with a screw propeller. He's worked for us before. You'll meet him off Holly Forks Point at midnight on the fifteenth. Know where that is?"

"Five miles below West Point. I've been there a few times. It's fairly remote."

"That's why we chose it. You happen to know anyone there? We need a boat."

Jacob nodded. "Yes, a friend, a Mattaponi Indian named David Two-Feathers. We've fished together many times. He's a crabber and oysterman with a forty-foot workboat, but the Yankees keep taking his catch. I know him well. He'll help us, sir."

The Captain took a draw on his pipe. "Can his boat carry sixty torpedoes that weigh perhaps forty pounds each? That's over a ton of dead weight."

"Should be able to, sir," answered Jacob. He said it with his fingers crossed.

"Excellent. So you're volunteering. Let me know who you want with you..."

"That's easy, sir - Cadets Roger Phillips, Henry Stiles and James Morgan."

* * *

Jacob snapped the reins. "Come on Billy, come on Clyde, hahhh!"

The two big draft horses broke into a trot and the empty hay wagon lumbered down the dirt road. Roger sat next to Jacob on the driver's seat of the big rig. Henry and James sat behind them in the load bed.

Henry leaned forward. "Jake, you really think we'll pass for Amish?"

"Well, we stand a lot better chance now that you've gotten rid of your ear ring and Roger has shaved that mousy-looking moustache! If we're caught out of uniform like this we could be shot as spies."

"It's a tossup between that and having to wear this awful outfit!" said James.

Jacob had resurrected his old clothes, suspenders and straw hat, plus an old coat from a used clothing store, and had secured similar outfits for the others.

"Uhh, fellas, maybe I should have told you sooner," said Henry. "I don't speak Amish..." The others broke into laughter.

"There *is* no 'Amish' language, Henry," smiled Jacob. "But tell you what, if we're stopped, just relax and let me do the talking. And everyone remember, we're on our way to pick up a load of hay for our cattle."

"Can we trust this Indian friend of yours, Jake?" asked Roger. "Not being armed makes me nervous."

"He hates Yankees as much as I do," said Jacob. "I'd trust him with my life."

"We'll be doing exactly that," said Roger. "That's what bothers me."

Jacob nodded. He wasn't concerned about David Two-Feathers. From the Indian settlement upriver from the Buckner farm, David was a frequent fishing companion until he took up crabbing and oystering and moved to Holly Forks Point on the York because oysters and crabs were more plentiful there.

Jacob had visited David just before leaving home. They were standing on the banks of the York, watching rockfish feeding offshore, when Jacob told him about Joshua being killed. David's eyes had narrowed and he swore to track down and kill the guilty party, but Jacob claimed that right for himself. David understood and offered to help if ever needed. Jacob was about to take him up on that offer.

He kept Billy and Clyde at a steady gait. They had passed New Kent Court House and the hamlet of Slaterville, and soon crossed over the Richmond-to-West Point Road. It was an area of thick, barren forests and isolated small farms.

"Should we think about camping soon?" asked Henry, his stomach growling.

"It's only another few miles to Holly Forks Point. We'll be there before dark and set up camp then," said Jacob.

"Things sure seem dead through here," said James. "Not a soul stirring."

"Not much reason to be outside, I guess," said Jacob. "March is my least favorite month. No green showing yet, too early to plant or fish..."

"Jake! Movement up ahead!" exclaimed Roger. "In those hollies to the left!"

Jacob slowed the horses and everyone focused on a stand of holly trees just off the road, painfully aware that the thick, green foliage could conceal a great deal.

"I swear I saw movement," whispered Roger. "Maybe deer or something."

"I don't see any...there! Horsemen!" exclaimed Henry.

"More than one!" said Jacob. "Everyone stay calm."

Four riders emerged onto the road and trotted toward them, carbines at the ready. They wore the blue uniforms and insignia of Union Cavalry.

"Who are you and what's your biz'ness here?" demanded a sergeant.

He'd love to ask this arrogant son-of-a-dog the same question, thought Jacob, but not now. "We're from West Point, on our way to fetch a load of hay for our cattle."

The sergeant steadied his prancing horse. "Four boys like you, all of military age? In a pig's eye! Search the wagon, men. You boys keep your hands in the clear!"

"We're Amish, sir!" said Jacob, trying to appear calm. "We have no weapons. Our religion forbids it. We only wish to go about our business peacefully."

"Amish, huh? Where you plannin' t'get this hay? Is God gonna drop it from heaven?" His men were quietly searching the wagon.

"We prayed and God sent word to us that a man near Holly Forks Point has hay for sale. We have faith that it's true. If not we'll have to slaughter our livestock early. We have only a week's supply of hay left."

"That's a good story but I think you're lying!" growled the man. He leveled his carbine at Jacob. "I think you're rebel spies *posing* as Amish, but we'll find out real quick! What's the name given to the laws of the Amish Church?"

Jacob's eyes sprang wide. That was a wrinkle he wasn't expecting. Roger and the others stared anxiously at him as he frantically searched his memory banks.

"Uhhh, the Ordnung."

"And who founded the Amish movement?"

"Uhhh, that would be, uhh, Jacob Amman...in 1693... in Switzerland. But tell me sir, are you...Amish?"

The sergeant lowered his carbine. "We had Amish neighbors back home and I wrote a school paper on 'em once. But even a lot of *Amish* couldn't have answered that last question, and certainly not a rebel spy. You're free to go, but I'd go quickly. The other patrols around here won't be so familiar with you Amish people."

"God bless you, sir, and may He always be with you," said Jacob, solemnly raising his hand as if blessing the man. He frantically waved his other hand behind his back, cajoling a chorus of 'amen's' from his companions.

The sergeant touched his cap and rode away with his men following. Jacob snapped the reins and started the team at a steady canter down the road. Roger, James and Henry sat speechless, trying to recover after growing faint from fear the sergeant would ask *them* a question.

"Jake, you never really joined the Amish church...and yet you knew those things," said Roger. "Lucky for us you remembered."

"Lucky perhaps. I knew the first one, but had no idea on the second one."

"But you got it right," said James.

"It was strange, like somebody...I don't suppose any of you whispered the answer to me, did you?"

* * *

Night was falling when the big hay wagon lumbered into the yard of a small, dilapidated cabin on the shores of Holly Forks Point. The York River lay fifty yards away through the dim light. A workboat sat tied to a rickety dock.

Jacob brought the horses to a stop, climbed down and walked up on the porch. He halted at the sight of a gun protruding from the partially open door.

"That far 'nuff! What you want?" The voice was void of emotion.

"David! It's Jacob Buckner!"

"Jacob? Who them others? They Yankees?"

"No, they're friends, David. We need your help."

The door swung open and a small man wearing buckskins and carrying a rifle stepped onto the porch. He had dark skin and black hair braided into a long pigtail.

"Good to see you, my brother," he said. He clasped Jacob's hand.

"And you also. I trust you are well," said Jacob. He introduced his friends.

"Why you come, and with such big wagon?" asked David.

"We're in the Confederate Navy, David, on a mission. We need your help."

David studied Jacob. "I see anger in your eyes, brother, same as two years ago. You still fight those who kill Joshua?"

Jacob nodded. "We are to meet a boat tomorrow night – out there. The boat is bringing a supply of a new kind of weapon that will destroy enemy ships. We need you and your boat to help us bring them ashore and load them on the wagon."

"My brother's enemy is my enemy. I swore to help you avenge Joshua and I will, but why you take so long? Not good to keep wounds open. Just make worse."

The next night found Jacob, David and the others aboard David's boat on their way out to the channel to await the *Grey Heron*. David cautioned against light or noise, for Union ships plied the channel regularly. The channel ran east and west, and with the wind southerly, he proceeded across channel to the north side so that any smoke or smell from his boiler firebox would not cross the path of an approaching ship.

The night was pitch black but for faint starlight. David steamed straight out for fifteen minutes, then throttled back and brought the boat to a standstill.

"With nothing to guide you, how do you know where we are?" asked Roger.

"Always know. Woods, river, day, night - no matter. We anchor here."

As the anchor went over the side, Jacob pulled his watch but could not see the hands. "Must be about eleven o'clock, so we've got awhile to wait."

"Tide, wind, enemy ships – I think maybe long wait," said David.

The Indian took a seat on the transom, pulled his Bowie knife from the leather sheath on his belt and began whittling a piece of wood. Seeking heat from the firebox, Roger, James and Henry went forward to the boat's cabin, for the night was growing cold. Two hours passed with no sign of the *Grey Heron*.

Jacob joined David on the transom. David was shorter by several inches, with a sinewy frame that contained no fat. He received his name at the moment of his birth when his father noted that he weighed no more than two feathers.

"David, do you see much of the old river anymore?"

"I go home to Mattaponi when leaves turn, take salted fish, help my people harvest corn, get ready for winter. Then again in spring to help plant."

"Do you...ever see my mother and father?"

"I travel upriver past farm, wave sometimes. You miss them?"

Jacob nodded with a sigh. "I think about them some and, you know, wonder how they're doing. It's hard not seeing them for so long."

"It sadden them when your brother killed, and again when you become warrior, but I think you make right decision...honorable....decision..."

David sprang up and stared downriver into the darkness. "Ship! Mile away!"

"How can you tell?" asked Jacob, following David's gaze. He saw nothing.

"Bow split water. Engine make noise. There!" He pointed into the dark.

Roger, Henry and James came running, looking tense but eager.

"You think it's the boat we're waiting for?" asked Roger.

"Too big," said David. "Yankee gunboat. We move away from channel, closer to shore. You and you raise anchor. You shovel coal. *Must be quiet!*"

"I hear her engine now!" said Jacob. He stood with David by the rail. "That's a big ship, far bigger than the *Grey Heron*! And us without weapons!"

The single double-stroke of a ship's bell danced across the water. Two bells, one o'clock on the midnight watch. Moments apart and further off, a second ship's bell sounded, then a third. They were in the path of an enemy squadron, and apparently the commander had not bothered to coordinate the hourglasses of his ships.

"Three ships! Weapons no good now. We must fight with heads."

As James and Roger wrestled the anchor onto the foredeck, David moved a lever to reverse and nudged the throttle. The boat began to move backward, creating almost no wake as it eased away from the channel and toward the north shore.

The hulking outline of the lead ship came into view moving up the channel. She appeared to be a commercial freighter. The two smaller vessels, which Roger recognized as coastal corvettes probably escorting the freighter, appeared to be veering toward the south shore. They carried perhaps twenty men and two guns each.

"Strange," pondered David. "Why they go toward shore like that at night?"

Suddenly Jacob felt nauseous. "I think they're looking for us," he said.

From their spot near the north shore, they watched the corvettes as best they could as the enemy boats moved toward Holly Forks Point, nearly two miles away. But soon even David lost them in the dark. The larger ship had anchored just upriver in mid-channel to wait for her escorts.

A bright flash split the darkness and a loud boom rumbled across the still water. A second flash and bang followed the first one. It was the guns aboard the corvettes, and the reports came from the direction of Holly Forks Point. They looked on as flames appeared on shore and rose higher and higher, illuminating the night.

David Two-Feathers watched in stoic silence. They were burning his cabin.

* * *

Dawn ended what had seemed an endless night. The small workboat with its crew of four cadets and one Indian rode peacefully at anchor in gently rolling waves just off the north shore of the York.

David had awakened before first light but could find no trace of the enemy vessels. They likely had continued upriver to the White House supply base.

Jacob joined David. They gazed across the water to Holly Forks Point. White smoke rose in lazy columns from the ashes of David's cabin. Smoke also marked what was left of the big hay wagon. The horses lay dead, shot by the Federals.

"I'm...sorry, David. I had no idea it would turn out this way."

"You good warrior and good warriors do honorable thing, but still not always win. No worry about cabin. Not much good no how. Boat main thing. I take you and your comrades to West Point. From there you get ride to Richmond."

"We would appreciate that. What will you do?"

"Go home for while, make sure parents all right. Then we see."

"You know, clearly the Federals knew about our mission and were looking for us. Someone betrayed us, David. I just hope the new weapons didn't fall into enemy hands. But regardless, if you hadn't moved your boat across the channel to the other side, we'd be prisoners awaiting a firing squad right now."

"All matter of how wind blow. Great Spirit with us. Traitor make big mistake, I think. Now you kill him *and* man who kill Joshua. But you must be careful. Hard for even best warrior to watch front and back at same time."

Chapter Ten

Jacob and his comrades had not eaten or slept in two days. Just climbing the *Patrick Henry's* gangplank to her deck proved a chore.

David Two-Feathers had put them ashore on the west bank of the Pamunkey River near West Point. From there they walked several miles before hitching a ride on a lumber wagon headed for Richmond. They arrived in late afternoon.

"I don't know which to do first, eat or sleep," said James Morgan.

"No debate here," said Henry. "It's either eat or die of hunger in my sleep."

Soon all four were seated around a table in the galley. Since it was between regular meal times, they had to settle for potato cakes and boiled turnips, all cold. Even so, each devoured a plateful. As they finished, Captain Parker entered and approached them. They pushed back their chairs and prepared to rise.

"Gentlemen, please keep your seats," he said. "I heard you were here and just wanted to say how glad we are for your safe return. We've been worried about you."

"Thank you, sir," said Jacob. "I'm sorry the mission wasn't successful, sir."

"That was due to things beyond your control, Mr. Buckner. Indeed, I'd like to commend all of you - Mr. Phillips, Mr. Morgan, Mr. Stiles - for a job well done."

"Sir, may I call your attention to my friend, David Two-Feathers," said Jacob. "Without him, we wouldn't have stood even a chance for success. He saved us from capture and a possible firing squad - and in the process lost his home."

"Please note that in your report, Mr. Buckner, and I'll pass it on to the Navy Department. Meantime, all of you are excused from duty for the next twenty-four hours, and I strongly advise you to get some sleep. Mr. Buckner, if I may keep you from your bunk a bit longer, I'd like a word with you in my cabin."

Jacob had intended to speak to the Captain the next morning. Right now it was the last thing he wanted, but such a request couldn't be declined so he dutifully followed his commander up the passageway and across the deck to the aft section. Sailors and cadets saluted but otherwise paid little heed. Most were not even aware of the mission, much less the role played by Jacob and the others.

"Sit down, Mr. Buckner," said the Captain as they reached his cabin. "I'd like to hear your opinions about the mission."

"The enemy knew, sir. They knew about us, they knew about the rendezvous, and they knew when and where it was to take place. Someone betrayed us, sir."

Jacob tried to speak normally, as if he was saying nothing out of the ordinary, but his jaw flexed continuously as he spoke.

"I suspect you're right," nodded the Captain. "We have a report that the *Grey Heron* was fired on and sunk in the Chesapeake Bay. We don't know the fate of her cargo or Captain McNulty."

"Well, if she was fired on, I suppose the sinking could have been accidental," said Jacob. "Perhaps a shell striking one of the torpedoes..."

"Possibly, but the shelling itself was no accident. The question is whether it was a trap or a chance meeting. If a trap, then we have a spy somewhere. If simply a chance meeting, it may be that Captain McNulty was captured and forced to divulge the rest of the mission. Then we may *not* have a spy."

"Sir, remember our discussion regarding the *Underwriter*? You yourself said it seemed like they *knew* we were there and *wanted* us to attack. And remember how the *Arapahoe* attacked Drewry's Bluff at the very time six of our biggest guns were away? Seems to me there's a pattern here, sir, too much coincidence."

Captain Parker turned in his chair and gazed out a window, caressing his thick moustache. "What you say has merit," he said, turning back to Jacob. "I've sometimes had questions myself, like on Albemarle Sound when the enemy so quickly followed us from Roanoke Island to Elizabeth City. They seemed to know where we were going."

Jacob nodded. "Back then, the guilty party could have been any of hundreds of men, but not this time," he said. "If there's a spy, he almost certainly has to be inside the Navy Department or the Academy."

"Well, hopefully we're just being paranoid," said the Captain. "We must keep our eyes open, but right now, you need to *close* yours."

* * *

Classes over for the day, Jacob left the recital room and headed below deck to his bunk. Still tired, he was tempted to take a nap but instead reached under his bunk and pulled out the small sea chest he had used since joining the navy. It contained stationary and the carved figurine of his mother that she had given him.

"Writing home, Jake?" asked Roger. He shed his frock coat and laid it on his bunk, which was next to Jacob's. They had just attended the same class.

"Thought I'd write and tell my mother about seeing David Two-Feathers again. She always liked him. He used to come by and she'd give him cookies or cake."

Roger smiled. "Pro'bly not something Indians get very often. He seems a decent fella, and obviously a good friend."

"We shared a lot growing up. The Indians and Amish are both picked on and that creates a special bond. We accept each other. Both know the other isn't a threat."

"But...Indians don't believe in turning the other cheek, do they?" asked Roger as he sat down on his bunk.

"No, and David and I have had some lively discussions about that." Jacob sat down across from Roger. "The Mattaponi aren't a strong tribe, but if they're pushed, they react. David never understood why the Amish don't do that. He was pleased when I swore to avenge my brother's death, and became a 'warrior', as he puts it."

"He seems a very capable man. Too bad our mission ended so poorly."

"Yeah, the Yankees may one day regret making an enemy of him."

"Well, whadaya think, Jake? Did someone tip off the Yankees ahead of time?"

"The Captain isn't sure. He thinks they may have stumbled on the *Grey Heron* by accident and learned of our mission that way. But if you ask me, they knew in advance."

"That means a spy at work," said Roger. He grew quiet for a moment, gazing at the floor. "Uhh, I don't suppose...I mean, don't get upset, Jake, but...do you ever discuss business with Lydia?"

"Navy business? Absolutely not!" exclaimed Jacob, glaring at his friend. But it was a legitimate question and he shouldn't get mad, he thought. Besides, he always knew Roger to be the suspicious, slow-to-trust type, probably stemming from the way he and his sisters were treated.

"Hope you're not angry," said Roger.

"It's all right. Things like this are unpleasant but if we're to get to the bottom of it, we must question every possibility. My relationship with Lydia is fair game."

"Well, you're my best friend, and I want to keep it that way."

"We've been through a lot together," smiled Jacob. He smacked Roger on the knee. "Remember the day we met on the dock?"

Roger smiled. "You were more interested in fishing than the navy back then. I invited you to join, but I never for a minute thought you would."

"Then I met Calico Sam McClung and thought I'd made the mistake of my life!" laughed Jacob.

"Sam nearly had a heart attack the day you shot yourself with a *cannon!*" said Roger. "It's a wonder you didn't blow your own head off! We all had real doubts about you then."

"I had doubts about *myself*, but things worked out, I guess."

"Yeah," nodded Roger. "Now we're a year away from being passed midshipmen, most likely on a warship. I hope we serve together."

Jacob nodded. "I'd enjoy that."

* * *

"I wondered why I hadn't heard from you for awhile," said Lydia. "I should have known you were off somewhere risking your fool neck again."

"I could have been with another girl..." grinned Jacob.

"Then you'd *really* be risking your neck!"

They were strolling about Church Hill on a beautiful, late March afternoon. A warm sun encouraged jonquils just emerging from flowerbeds along the way. A faint cloak of green, visible only if caught in just the right light, covered the gently swaying branches of willows and crabapples. Songbirds scurried about searching for mates and preparing nests. Spring stood poised on the doorstep of Richmond.

With a gentle hand on her arm, Jacob turned Lydia toward him. "Actually, I've grown too fond of you to even *consider* anyone else, Lydia."

She gazed up at him. "And I you, Jacob."

They longed to embrace but knew they were in public, so instead turned and continued along, arm in arm. A neighbor's rose garden loomed up ahead.

"Oh look!" exclaimed Lydia. "The first rosebud of spring, a bright red one! How beautifully they weather the winters. We humans should be so fortunate."

Jake nodded. "I'll be happy just to *see* another winter."

"Don't go getting all depressed on me, Jacob! It's too beautiful a day for that. We're on the verge of spring, the time of rebirth, of renewal, when everything pops out and grows and multiplies! I've always viewed spring as God's showcase, the time when He's most visible! How could anyone not believe in Him at times like this?"

"Your Amish roots are showing, Lydia."

"I only gave up Amish ways, Jacob, I didn't become an *atheist!*"

Jacob smiled. "I know what you mean. There've been things recently that made me more conscious of *my* faith."

"You've said that before. Not another close call, I hope. Tell me."

"Well, that church up ahead - St. John's? I was on my way to see you a couple weeks ago, and I went inside. Actually, it was like something *drew* me inside. I sat down and...don't laugh, but something came over me, something

131

very strange, like a presence of some kind. I've never felt anything like it before…"

"I'm not laughing, Jacob. Did a voice speak to you?"

Jacob shook his head. "I posed questions, but got no answers. Guess God was too busy to hear me."

"He heard you."

"Then on this mission last week, a Yankee patrol stopped us and began cross-examining me. I had no idea on one of the questions – and I know this sounds strange too – but I swear it was like someone *whispered* the answer to me."

"Uh-huhh," nodded Lydia.

"Later, we were out on the river and because of the direction of the wind, we crossed to the far side, and because we were on the far side, the Yankee ships didn't find us. If they *had* found us, we'd be awaiting a date with a firing squad right now."

Lydia nodded again. "I don't know what you asked God in that church, Jacob, but like I said, He heard you."

* * *

Carbine at 'shoulder arms', the young cadet strode to and fro in measured paces – ten to the right, about face, ten to the left, about face. Like all cadets, he was required to perform guard duty on the dock in front of the *Patrick Henry*.

A figure approached. The young guard continued his pacing but watched the figure from the corner of his eye. He looked different - his dress, his complexion - like a frontiersman, perhaps an army scout. Seemingly ignoring the guard, the figure halted at the base of the gangplank and stared up at the *Patrick Henry* as if he had never seen a ship before, or perhaps not one this large or up this close.

The cadet stepped in front of the stranger and thrust his carbine forward to block his progress. "Halt, sir!" he ordered. "May I help you?"

The stranger glared at this boy standing in his way. His coal black, penetrating eyes sent a chill down the young man's spine.

"Not need help. Here to see Jacob Buckner."

"Uhh, yessir," said the boy, glancing at the man's rawhide-trimmed buckskin and the big Bowie knife hanging from his belt. "Please wait here, sir."

As the boy turned to mount the gangplank, a shout came over the rail from the officer of the deck. "What's the problem, Cadet Bryan?"

"Sir, this gentleman wishes to see Cadet Buckner!"

"David Two-Feathers!" exclaimed James Morgan. By chance, he happened to be serving his turn as officer of the deck. "Cadet Bryan, let that man pass!"

David strode up the gangplank and raised his hand in a peace gesture, but his countenance remained one of stone. James couldn't determine whether he was relieved or distressed at seeing a familiar face.

"Good to see you again! Come with me and we'll find Jake," said James.

"Good. We talk. You too maybe, others maybe," said David.

The unusual procession made its way across the deck. James Morgan in his tailor-made cadet uniform led the way, glancing around and inquiring about Jacob's whereabouts. The dark complexioned, buckskin-clad Indian with the long braided hair and over-sized Bowie knife followed solemnly, keeping his eyes straight ahead yet missing nothing. They left behind a trail of sailors and cadets staring after them.

Their search took them to the recital rooms. Classes were over, but Jacob and Roger sat alone in one of the rooms, textbooks open, reviewing study material. They glanced up as James and David entered.

"David! What on earth brings you here?" exclaimed Jacob. "It must be important to get you this close to Richmond! Good to see you, old friend."

"And you, my brother. I have idea, come to talk."

"We'll leave you two alone," said Roger. He and James turned to leave.

"No. You stay please. See what you think."

James and David took seats and over the next fifteen minutes David laid out his idea. As it unfolded, the eyes of his three listeners grew progressively wider, and they quickly realized that Captain Parker needed to meet David Two-Feathers and hear his idea directly.

They found the Captain in his cabin and explained why they were there. Jacob, James and Roger sat across from the Captain. David preferred to stand.

"I've heard good things about you, Mr. Two-Feathers, and I want to thank you for your recent help," said the Captain. "I regret that it cost you your cabin. I've asked the Navy Department for compensation for you."

David nodded. "Jacob say you good chief, but if you mean money, no need. Cabin not worth anything."

"Well, we'll try anyhow. Now tell me about this idea of yours."

"Bluecoats have big camp on Pamunkey, place called White House Landing. Ships all time come and go, bring food, guns, bullets, all things needed for war. No fort there, only few soldiers."

"Are you proposing an attack, Mr. Two-Feathers?" asked the Captain.

David nodded. "Much activity there now. I think bluecoats attack soon. They have new chief, eager to make war. Better greycoats attack first."

"We've had reports that Grant is preparing to move," nodded Captain Parker. "And we know all about White House Landing. It's a big complex. An attack will involve a lot of details."

"Chief Parker no worry," said David. "Mattaponi take care of details."

"You have warriors who are willing to help?" asked Jacob. "How many?"

David held up all of his fingers. "Bluecoats not friend of Mattaponi. We scout, get details, take care of guards when time come. Together with our greycoat friends, we settle score with bluecoats. Teach them lesson. What you think?"

Captain Parker glanced at the cadets. Jacob spoke for the group.

"We like the idea, sir," he said. "It's an opportunity to strike a blow at Grant's campaign before it starts. They're probably stockpiling supplies at White House for use as they move south. If we destroy those stockpiles, it could upset their plans."

"And if we destroy the docks, it would create a *real* problem," added James.

"It will take a sizable force to pull this off, sir, a hundred men or more," said Roger. "And probably a night attack similar to the one on the *Underwriter*."

The Captain inhaled and nodded. "I'll present the idea to the proper people. If approved, we'll begin planning right away. Meantime, we must keep this quiet. Let's not forget what happened on our last mission."

* * *

When Captain Parker proposed a raid on White House Landing to Secretary of the Navy Stephen Mallory, he got a mixed reception. The failure of the *Grey Heron* mission had not set well with the Secretary. This mission would require a large force and more intricate planning, and therefore involve even more risk.

The Secretary agreed to study the proposal. But the winds of March subsided, April showers came and went, and still nothing was heard from him.

Then in late April a courier arrived with a message ordering Captain Parker to Secretary Mallory's office. The Captain, who counted Stephen Mallory among his close friends, took the liberty of bringing Jacob and David Two-Feathers with him.

"Well, it seems General Grant is on the move and the direction appears to be south," began the Secretary. "That makes a raid on White House more palatable to me. Now any damage or destruction we inflict likely will not be repaired in time to do Grant much good. You may begin your preparations."

"Very good!" said Captain Parker. "Who is to command, Stephen?"

"You are, William, seconded by Major Sam Owens of the Confederate Marines. You'll need some of his boys in this. I suggest you make Mr. Buckner your third in command. Mr. Two-Feathers, can we count on you as well?"

David's eyes flashed fire. "I hunger for chance."

"The Mattaponi have agreed to be our scouts, sir," said Jacob. "They dislike the Yankees and know the area well. We have complete confidence in them. I appreciate your confidence in me also, sir."

The Secretary nodded. "I suggest two companies of marines and one of sailors. This will be an important mission. It could spell the difference between success and failure for General Lee when he tries to stop Grant. I wish you luck."

* * *

Captain Parker lost no time. Two days after meeting with Secretary Mallory, he scheduled a planning session.

"Gentlemen, let's get started."

Small talk died away among the four men gathered in the Captain's office. Major Sam Owens of the Confederate Marines, a veteran of the Mexican War, drew on his cigar and sent a perfect smoke ring drifting toward the ceiling. Jacob and Roger – the latter was to assist Jacob – folded a map they had been studying. David Two-Feathers stood quietly against a side wall. The four would command a combined force of 150 men assigned to the mission.

"Our purpose today is to develop a plan of attack," said the Captain. "I'll start by providing you some background on our objective. White House Landing was formerly part of White House Plantation, home of Daniel and Martha Custis. Daniel died early and left Martha with two small children. She ended up marrying George Washington and together they raised her children. Martha's great-granddaughter is now Mrs. Robert E. Lee." He hesitated for effect.

"The Landing is at the navigable limit of the Pamunkey, several miles above West Point," he continued. "The Federals expanded it to a supply base two years ago during McClellan's Peninsula Campaign. The mansion had a historic connection to both of our countries, yet the Yankees burned it to the ground. That just shows how insensitive these people are, gentlemen. Now, Mr. Buckner, tell us what you and Mr. Two-Feathers have learned about the base."

"Yessir," said Jacob. "The landing stretches for a quarter mile along both shores. Wharves jut into the river every hundred yards on both sides, with warehouses built in fields behind them."

White House Plantation, Pamunkey River - ancestral home of Mrs. George Washington and Mrs. Robert E. Lee. Courtesy, Library of Congress

"They make bridge across river, where water grow too shallow for ships," added David. "Use to move supplies and soldiers from one side to other."

"There are dozens of vessels of every description," said Jacob. "Tied to the banks, the wharves, the bridge, to each other rail-to-rail. They stretch out from the shore like stacked cordwood."

"Any gunboats? And how many soldiers?" asked Major Owens.

"Mostly civilian transports. I didn't see any gunboats or infantry," said Jacob.

"We scout from south bank; soldiers on north bank across bridge," said David. "Maybe this many." He held up his fingers and flexed them several times.

"A company perhaps," said the Major. "And they're on the north bank?"

Ruins of White House Plantation burned by Federal forces.
Courtesy, Library of Congress

"They camp in field, arrow shot away," nodded David. "Behind big lodges you call warehouses, where they keep powder and bullets for rifles and big guns and food for soldiers. They not much care about other things."

Captain Parker and Major Owens exchanged glances, as if each had been struck with the same thought.

"So, conceivably," ventured the Captain, "a force could slip cross the bridge, set fire to the warehouses and retreat before the guards reacted."

"Chief Parker think like Indian," smiled David.

"Why not destroy the bridge behind us so they can't interfere at all?" asked Jacob. "Then use that time to destroy the ships and warehouses on the south side?"

"Post my marines along the south bank, and we'll buy you all the time you want," said Major Owens. "My boys are crack shots; they'd enjoy the target practice."

"We could make that base unusable for months!" said Roger, his newly re-grown moustache once again twitching with excitement.

"Now we're getting somewhere," said Captain Parker. "How about timing? Do we go in at night like we did with the *Underwriter?*"

"It depends," said Major Owens. "Tell me, Mr. Two-Feathers, if we attack at night, could you and your men go in first and silence any night guards?"

David broke into a cold grin. "They not hear anything, not see anything, just drop dead. Better we go just before first light, when all sleep. Greycoats come when sky brighten so they able to see in strange place."

"Very good, gentlemen," said Captain Parker. "This gives us a plan. We'll fill in details and assign each of you specific duties. And let's remember the importance of this mission. Its success will depend on *close coordination and absolute secrecy.* That's all for now. Thank you."

* * *

The sunny, spring afternoon reminded Jacob of the day a week before when he had last visited Lydia. Unlike that day, today he wanted to be alone, as he often did when he felt stressed.

He descended the *Patrick Henry's* gangplank, climbed the narrow steps to the top of Drewry's Bluff and walked to the edge of the cliff on the upriver end. From there he could gaze down on the *Teaser,* the *Beaufort* and the other ships of the James River Squadron anchored below. He took a seat on a log.

The opinions of his commanders aside, this mission sounded easier than the *Underwriter* raid, he thought. They would have plenty of men and the base wasn't heavily defended. The Mattaponi braves would precede them. They would go in at night, do what damage they could, and exit. On paper it seemed simple enough.

That was what bothered him. Their mission to pick up the new torpedoes had seemed simple. The raid on the *Underwriter* was risky but not especially complicated. This mission had the potential to inflict more damage on the enemy than both of those missions combined. If a spy existed and was worth his salt, the enemy would surely know in advance and be ready for them.

On top of that, he was to command twenty chosen cadets and a company of sailors. They were to secure the bridge, set fire to the warehouses and ships on the far side and blow up the bridge as they retreated, all before the Federal garrison could react.

He gazed down at the old *Beaufort*, his first ship, now riding peacefully at anchor with her 32-pounder gun still mounted in the bow. He had been the rammer on that gun at Roanoke Island when his nerves caused him to nearly blow his own head off. Then came Cobb Point, Hampton Roads, the *Underwriter...*

How vividly he recalled that night on the *Underwriter*, climbing to her deck in plain view of armed enemy sailors, the screaming and shooting, hand-to-hand fighting, men dying on all sides. Now it seemed he was to court death again, but this time with one big difference. He would be responsible not just for his own life but the lives of the men under him as well.

He wasn't sure he could do it, or if he wanted to. So far he had survived and excelled - even saved lives, he liked to think - by acting instinctively with little thought for his own safety. Now he *must* think of his own safety, for if he went down, it would increase the danger to his men.

Even if God *had* chosen to spare him, it couldn't last. No man was immortal. Or perhaps he had just been lucky so far. Either way, his number was overdue to come up. Didn't that mean he was gambling with the lives of his men?

Then he recalled an old Amish saying from his childhood - *don't try to think for God*. The thoughts he was having were just that. Commanding his fellow cadets could be part of God's plan.

Jacob heard a noise and turned to look. A young marine was approaching, his brass buckle and buttons polished bright, his white cross belts gleaming in the sun.

"Sir, kin I sit fer a spell? Saw you an' thought you might want some comp'ny."

Jacob nodded and motioned the boy to a seat on the log. Company was the last thing he wanted, but the young man looked no more than seventeen, probably not long removed from home, and Jacob suspected it was *he* who wanted company.

"Hope I'm not disturbin' ya, sir. Name's Zachariah Harrison. Folks call me Zack. I come here now an' agin 'cause o'the view. 'Preciate you lettin' me join ya."

"I'm Jacob Buckner, Jake for short. Pleased to meet you. That accent - where you from, Zack?"

"Tennessee. Jist signed up 'bout a month ago."

"Tennessee? How'd you end up in the marines?"

"Said they needed fellas what kin shoot, an' they tell me I kin shoot. 'Course, back home that ain't nothin'. Where I come from, them what can't shoot don't eat. Say, ain't you the fella I hear tell about? Fella who use'ta, you know, be agin killin' an' all, an' then turned out a hero in that big fight awhile back?"

Jacob nodded. "I'm not a hero. I just did what needed to be done."

"Well, jist the same, I'm proud t'meet'cha'. You goin' on this here mission we got a'comin' up?"

Jacob nodded again. "You one o'the marines going along?"

"Yessir, an' don't mind tellin' ya, I'm nervous." He removed his shako hat and put it in his lap. "I done killed a lot o'deer, even bears, but never shot a man before. They didn't tell us much, though. Are we...you know...gonna come up agin Yankees?"

"Good chance of it. How old are you, Zack?"

"Well, told 'em I was seventeen, but truth is, I jist turned sixteen."

"Why'd you do that? You that eager to fight?"

"Don't have nothin' agin Yankees, 'cept they got no biz'ness a'comin' down here botherin' us. Truth is, I wanted t'git away from home. After Ma died, I was jist in Pa's way. Thought maybe I could be some help here."

Jacob glanced at him. "I'm real sorry about your mother, but...aren't you, uhh, on good terms with your father?"

Zack shook his head. "Ma won't hardly in the ground 'fore this woman moved in with us. She an' Pa stay drunk most o'the time. Only time they want me 'round is when the still needs tendin'. But say listen, what's it like, you know, in a fight?"

And he thought he had problems with *his* father, thought Jacob. Combat will probably be a relief to this boy. He hardly knew where to begin.

"Well, I'm glad you're nervous," he said. "Anybody who doesn't get nervous just isn't normal. All you can do is keep your head down, follow orders and pray."

"Ain't been t'church in awhile, but I been thinkin' 'bout it. You know of one 'round here?"

"Yeah, and I think it's important that you go. There's one in town that helped me a lot. I'll give you directions."

Chapter Eleven

Jacob stumbled and fell forward in the darkness, scraping his shin on the stump that had just tripped him. Quickly he righted himself. It wouldn't do for the other cadets to see their leader sprawled on the ground like a careless schoolboy.

"You all right, Jake?" asked Roger, marching beside him.

The twenty cadets brought up the rear of the column. Ahead of them in the faint starlight were two marine companies, one of sailors, and three wagons loaded with kegs of gunpowder and tin containers of coal oil. The column stretched along the narrow forest trail for a quarter-mile. Somewhere out in the darkness, David Two-Feathers and his braves scouted the way.

"I'm fine," said Jacob. "Just wish we had a better road, or a little more light."

"Want me to carry you, darlin'?" came a soft voice.

"Shut up, Henry!" snapped Jacob.

They had left Richmond the previous morning, stopped for a few hours' sleep near New Kent Courthouse, then awakened at 2:00 a.m. to continue the march.

A shadowy figure glided out of the woods toward the head of the column.

"Chief Parker, enemy mile away," said David quietly. "No talk, no noise now."

David moved down the column until he located Jacob.

"Jacob, enemy near. Soon we fight. Remember, wait by end of bridge. I tell you when to cross. May Great Spirit be with you."

"And you, brother. Good hunting." Jacob watched his stealthy Indian friend steal into the forest and disappear before his very eyes.

Fifteen minutes later the column halted. Ahead through the trees, nightlights of ships flickered, their reflections leaving broken trails across rippling water. The smell of

Ships at White House Landing. Courtesy, Library of Congress

Bridge Across the Pamunkey at White House Landing. Courtesy, Library of Congress

coal smoke, bacon grease and latrines grew strong in the night air. Word passed to deploy for the attack.

Following prearranged plans, one marine company filed to the left and the other to the right and marched silently into the darkness. The hundred marines, armed with breech-loading rifles, would take up positions along the river bank and provide covering fire as needed.

At Jacob's signal, the twenty cadets and forty sailors, under Captain Parker but field commanded by Jacob for this mission, started forward. Armed with pistols and carbines, they had been divided into pairs. Each team of sailors took a twenty-five pound keg of gunpowder from the wagons while the cadet teams carried five-gallon tins of coal oil. The cadets would douse the warehouses with the flammable oil while the sailors rigged the bridge and vessels with explosives.

Moving silently, they approached the edge of the forest. On the other side of a clearing, a row of warehouses sat along the river bank.

Jacob signaled everyone to stay low. He gazed around in the dim light to get his bearings. Faint streaks of orange and pink were beginning to show in the eastern sky.

"I don't see the bridge," he whispered.

"David said it crosses where the water gets shallow," said Roger. "So it must be upstream, to the left."

"There, where the ships' lights stop," said Jacob. "That must be the bridge."

"Jake, movement over there!" whispered Henry, tapping Jacob's shoulder.

"I see it. Don't move."

Shadows, moving swiftly and silently like black ghosts, emerged from the bridge. Jacob lost sight of them in the dim light. He readied his pistol.

"Wha...?" A hand appeared on his arm. "David! How'd you do that?"

"No time now. Must move quickly. Light soon and bluecoat soldiers wake up. You come. We show the way."

Jacob turned to the men behind him. "We're going across," he said. "Stay low, and remember, once the powder and oil are in place, the carriers get back across the bridge while their partners light them. But *don't light anything until I signal!"*

The glow in the east was slowly brightening as David and his braves silently led the way across the bridge, a simple open structure similar to a long pier. At the far end, everyone fanned out like ants escaping a disturbed nest. The Indians slipped away in the shadows while the sailors and cadets, moving in pairs, headed for the warehouses and the vessels tied up along the shore. Other teams of sailors had stopped on the bridge to rig fuse-tipped kegs of explosives at key points.

Time was of the essence. Jacob ran along the dock from building to building, speaking in loud whispers to his teams of cadets. "Spread the oil inside if you can! We want the fires to get a quick start!" He turned toward his sailors rushing to board the ships. "If any of their crew resist, kill them – quietly if possible, but kill them!"

A blue-uniformed figure suddenly appeared from around a corner up ahead. He spotted Jacob and quickly took aim with his musket.

An arm slipped around the man's neck, followed by the flash of a knife. Blood shot from his throat and he dropped to the ground. A buckskinned Mattaponi brave, his face black with war paint, grabbed the man's hair. Again the knife flashed and the brave straightened up. In his hand, dripping blood, was the man's scalp.

Jacob and the Indian glanced at each other, nodded, and the warrior slipped away. Jacob turned back to the matters at hand.

The warehouses quickly received a dousing of coal oil and men stood by to light them. Rigging powder kegs aboard the various vessels took longer. The civilian crews of the merchant vessels, awakened and warned that their ships were about to be blown up, seemed to be stalling despite the imminent danger they faced.

David rounded a corner on the run, followed by his braves. "Many soldiers in forest! They come this way! We must cross bridge *now!"*

"Fire the warehouses and head for the bridge!" Jacob yelled at the top of his voice. Silence was not an issue now.

One by one the warehouses burst into flames and the cadets ran for the bridge. Jacob waited for the last to leave – it seemed an eternity - and then yelled to his sailors waiting aboard the ships. "Light the powder kegs and get across the bridge!"

As each team finished their job, Jacob rushed them toward the bridge. The enemy was close and the fuses short, but he had resolved to be the last to leave.

A man ran towards Jacob from one of the big merchant steamers. Jacob noticed something shiny to one side of the man's head. It was an ear ring and the man was Henry. Jacob also noticed a suspicious bulge under his friend's jacket.

"Henry, what in blazes do you have there?"

"Oh, nothin'. Just a flask o'that captain's brandy that I rescued. Wouldn't want it goin' t'waste."

"Just make certain that flask is still full when this mission is over...and take off that ear ring! The thing flashes like a beac..."

A deafening explosion knocked both men off their feet. A powder keg aboard one of the ships had ignited. Timbers rained down around them. They picked themselves up and raced for the bridge as more explosions followed in domino fashion.

The Mattaponi warriors and a dozen sailors and cadets, among them Roger and James, had formed a defense line at the end of the bridge. In a field opposite them, beyond the burning warehouses, a battle line of 400 Union infantry had emerged from the woods and was advancing at route step, two ranks deep, drums beating, mounted officers waving swords.

"That's a regiment or more!" exclaimed James as Jacob and Henry ran up. "Pennsylvania boys I think!"

"Everybody across the bridge! We must blow it up quickly!" yelled Jacob.

Betrayed again, he thought, gazing at the enemy line. That force was many times the normal garrison. Now he knew why the ships' crews had been stalling.

The men on the defense line fired a volley, rose from their kneeling positions and quickly back-pedaled onto the bridge.

Jacob heard orders being shouted. The enemy line halted and the front rank dropped to one knee. Both ranks cocked and raised their muskets.

"Get down!" Jacob yelled, dropping face down on the ground as 400 enemy muskets roared, sending long fingers of fire and smoke cutting through the faint dawn.

A Mattaponi brave, still standing because he had not understood what was happening, grabbed his thigh, writhed in pain and fell to the ground. It was the young Indian whom Jacob had seen taking a scalp. Jacob started for him.

"I've got him, Jake!" yelled Henry, holding Jacob back. "We don't need you gettin' shot! Get across that bridge!"

Jacob glared at Henry. The latter glared back. Jacob blinked. "All right, everyone get across the bridge!" he yelled. "Light the fuses!"

Sailors bent over the fuses while everyone else hurried for the far end of the bridge. Henry put the brave's arm around his shoulder and carried him. The ships and warehouses were all burning now. Secondary explosions began going off as the fires reached stored munitions, sending flames and debris shooting into the sky.

The wounded brave passed out from loss of blood and slipped from Henry's grasp. As Henry struggled to pick him up, David Two-Feathers arrived to help. They carried the man between them and ran for the south end of the bridge.

A powder keg exploded and a thirty-foot section of bridge collapsed into the river behind them. More explosions followed close on their heels as they ran across the bridge narrowly ahead of an advancing storm of flames and flying timbers. They dove to safety just as the last section collapsed behind them.

The men took cover behind a crude breastwork constructed by the marines of cotton bales, cargo boxes and timbers. The wounded Mattaponi brave was carried to the rear where a doctor waited.

David came up to Jacob. "Henry help Running Beaver. My people not forget."

"He's a good man," nodded Jacob. "So is Running Beaver. I saw him dispatch a guard without a sound. But... I didn't know the Mattaponi still take scalps..."

David shrugged. "Some braves young, hear stories. Wish to follow old ways."

With Jacob and his men safely over the bridge, Major Owens barked orders to his marines. The cross-belted men crouched behind their makeshift breastworks and opened fire with their breech-loading rifles. The cadets and Indians, the former with short-barreled carbines and the latter mostly muzzle-loading hunting rifles, joined in but with less effect. Men began to drop on both sides.

Roger tapped Jacob on the shoulder. "Jake, Henry's wounded!"

Jacob spun toward Henry. The latter was lying against the breastworks, not moving, the front of his shirt soaked with blood. Jacob and Roger rushed to him.

"Henry...Henry!" Jacob smacked his friend's cheek. "Henry, talk to me!"

Henry's eyes opened halfway and he stared up at the sky, as if in shock. "My chest...I think I took a bullet..."

Jacob frantically tore away Henry's shirt. The tail end of a bullet protruded from his chest directly over the heart.

"*Henry, dad gum your hide!*" exclaimed Jacob. "The bullet barely broke the skin! That pewter flask stopped it! You bled just enough to turn the leaking brandy red! I think you saw it and *fainted*."

"The flask saved his life?" said Roger. "And folks say whiskey's bad for you!"

"He didn't faint from the blood, it was because the *brandy* spilled," said James.

"Well, at least he smells good for a change," added Roger.

Jacob was torn between laughing and crying. "Henry, I ordered you to keep that flask *full* until this mission was over! Technically, you disobeyed orders. I ought to have you court-martialed just as a matter of principle!"

The fight settled into a standoff with the Federals' numerical advantage offset by the marines' marksmanship. Though surprised by the large enemy force, Captain Parker knew the mission would still be a success if he could destroy the warehouses and ships along the south side of the river, but he debated whether it was worth exposing his men to the heavy enemy fire. A change in the situation made a decision unnecessary.

"Captain Parker, a ship!" exclaimed Major Owens, pointing downriver. "A big one! Could be bad news!"

The Captain followed the Major's pointing finger. A column of heavy black smoke rose above the treetops a half-mile downstream. The ship was moving up the narrow Pamunkey and bearing down on them at flank speed.

Captain Parker grimaced. "Look at that row of gun ports," he said, using his spyglass. "She must mount ten guns per side." He snapped the glass shut.

"Pro'bly 32-pounder rifled guns," said Major Owens. "And us with not even a six-pounder field piece. We may have to withdraw."

Jacob joined his superiors and shielded his eyes against the rising sun for a better view of the approaching ship. He blinked and looked again. His face flushed.

"That's the *Arapahoe*," he said, trying to sound composed.

"How do you know, Mr. Buckner?" asked Major Owens.

"I just know," said Jacob, his voice calm but his fists clenching and releasing repeatedly.

He had a feeling. He had endured three years of unconsummated hatred of Alonzo Peck, three years of seeing Peck's sneering face in his nightmares, his gun sights, the sky, even his washbasin. Now he somehow knew. Peck was on that ship.

"Moving at such speed in this narrow channel, she knows she's late for the party," said Captain Parker. "Her appearance is no coincidence. She was sent to support their infantry. They knew ahead of time we were coming."

"A withdrawal is in order, Captain," said Major Owens grimly. "We can't stand up to those heavy guns."

"Sir, that may not be necessary," interrupted Jacob. He wasn't in the mood to cut and run, not against the *Arapahoe*. "We can take shelter behind the warehouses. If they open fire, they'll be doing our work for us."

Captain Parker rubbed his thick moustache and gazed at the big ship churning the river into foam. "Mr. Buckner's right, Major, no need to run just yet. We'll take shelter, burn the warehouses and everything else we can and *then* withdraw."

The orders were given. The marines abandoned their breastworks and joined the others behind the warehouses along the south shore. David sent six braves to scout the forest, for the Captain feared the enemy might try to encircle them.

The *Arapahoe* slowed its forward advance and halted several hundred yards downstream. The enemy ship, her smokestack and three schooner-rigged masts towering above her massive hull, looked even larger in the narrow, 300-yard wide river.

"Whadaya think she's doing?" asked Major Owens as he and Jacob stood with Captain Parker, watching the enemy ship.

"She pro'bly stopped to avoid those rifles your boys carry," said the Captain.

The Major couldn't hide a smug grin. "My boys can still reach her," he said.

"And she us," said the Captain. "This is pointblank range for those big guns."

As if in answer, white smoke erupted from the *Arapahoe's* bow followed by a loud clap. A shell whistled low over their heads and exploded in the woods behind them.

"That was a deck gun! She's getting our range!" exclaimed the Captain.

"She's running out her main guns!" yelled Jacob. "Everybody take cover!"

A few seconds later the *Arapahoe's* port side exploded in a sheet of smoke and the thunderous roar of ten guns. The whistle of incoming shells quickly gave way to earth-rattling explosions as the deadly projectiles detonated in rapid succession on the now-abandoned breastworks constructed by the marines. Another broadside minutes later and the breastworks were reduced to scattered piles of rubble.

The Confederates crouched behind shelter. Designated marine sharpshooters took occasional shots at enemy officers. Jacob noticed that one of the sharpshooters was Zack Harrison, the Tennessean he had met on Drewry's

Bluff. The young boy seemed to be adjusting well to hunting human game.

"Federal Marines on the *Arapahoe's* deck!" shouted Major Owens, rushing to the others. "I'd know them anywhere! I used to *be* one!"

Captain Parker quickly jerked open his spyglass and braced the tube against a piling. "Looks like...maybe two companies," he said. "They're forming up on deck and disembarking into a...a boat, a big cutter I think, on the far side.

"Whatdaya think they plan to do?" asked Jacob.

"They'll pro'bly land those troops and begin shelling us in earnest to force us into the open," said Major Owens. "Could be time to set the fires and call it a day."

Captain Parker kept gazing through his spyglass. Suddenly his eyes widened. "That cutter is rounding the *Arapahoe's* stern in *this* direction! They plan to land those troops all right, but on *this* shore!"

A fifty-foot steam cutter had emerged from behind the *Arapahoe's* stern and was approaching the south bank some 300 yards downriver. She was loaded to the gunwales with a hundred cross-belted Federal Marines, the brass insignia on their tall shako hats flickering in the morning sun.

"They'll shell us first and then attack with those marines, maybe try to cut off our escape!" exclaimed Roger, failing in his attempt to sound calm.

"Mr. Buckner, have your men fire the warehouses and anything else they can, and *quickly!*" yelled Captain Parker. "Major Owens, form a defense line. Mr. Two-Feathers, move your braves to the woods along our retreat route. Let us know of any attempt to block it."

The cutter's bow slid into the mud along the riverbank and the well-trained Federal Marines disembarked and deployed in a battle line facing upriver toward their Confederate counterparts. The latter did the same facing downriver toward the Federals. The two lines of marines, 300 yards apart, opened fire on each other.

The Confederates suffered five men killed and nine wounded in the first two exchanges. The Federals suffered similar casualties, but the Southerners knew the enemy had a trump card they had only begun to play – the *Arapahoe's* big guns.

Jacob and his men set to work setting fire to the warehouses and vessels along the south bank. Fire was their only weapon, for they had used all their powder kegs. Already smoke rose from several warehouses and flames flicked upward from open hatches on the transports and barges.

Jacob knew that Captain Parker was waiting for them to finish their work before ordering a retreat. He also knew that the *Arapahoe* would soon turn her guns on the Confederate position. The results would not be pleasant.

He gazed across at the enemy ship, cleared for action. The white trim and insignia of her blue-uniformed crew were visible even at this distance.

His attention was drawn to one figure in particular, a big man giving orders to a group of sailors, sharply pointing and gesturing as if short of patience. Jacob flushed, his temples throbbing as if someone was filling his veins with boiling blood. He was certain the figure was Alonzo Peck.

A powerful explosion at his back spun Jacob around. Fire had reached stored gunpowder in one of the warehouses. More explosions followed in quick succession, throwing up plumes of burning debris. All structures on both sides of the river were on fire now as were most of the vessels. He ran to Captain Parker.

"Sir, our work is done! What are your orders?"

Captain Parker was looking across the river with a glazed expression closer to panic than any Jacob had seen on him since Fort Cobb. "Look!" he said, pointing. "They're ferrying infantry across from the other shore to reinforce their marines! Bring your boys here quickly. We must stop them long enough to slip away!"

"We're already here!" came Henry's voice. The other cadets and sailors were with him. "Where you want us, sir?"

Jacob looked sharply at Henry and wanted to ask how he felt, but knew it would be a waste of time. He waved them to the defense line.

Out on the river, being towed by a small steamer, was a large quartermaster's barge carrying 150 men from the Pennsylvania infantry unit that had first opposed the Confederates. The latter would soon be outnumbered two to one.

Jacob redirected his gaze to the *Arapahoe* just as the latter's gun ports erupted with billowing smoke and the thundering report of ten thirty-two pounders. The fierce shriek of incoming shells culminated in ten simultaneous explosions. Nine of the shells overshot their mark. The tenth landed among the marines.

Jacob sprinted the twenty feet to the point of impact. Six marines lay dead, including several who had been gruesomely dismembered. Ten more were dazed and bloody. The doctor arrived quickly and began attending the wounded.

Jacob grimaced. One of the dead was without a midsection, but his young, clean-shaven face left no doubt that it was Zack Harrison, the boy from Tennessee. Jacob prayed silently for this young man who had been so coldly forsaken by his father. He hoped the boy had visited St. John's Church. Something told him that he had, and that he was now at peace in the arms of his mother.

The *Arapahoe* fired another broadside. Again they overshot the Confederates but this time the shells landed closer. Downriver, the Pennsylvania infantrymen, joined by some of the *Arapahoe's* crew, were ashore and taking their place with the Federal Marines. Over 300 Federals now faced 150 Confederates.

"We must withdraw!" said Captain Parker grimly. "They have our range now and the next broadside will be on target. Then those boys down yonder will charge us and I don't think we can stop 'em. "

Jacob and Major Owens both nodded. They knew the Captain was right.

"Major, upon my order, have your men pull back as if retreating. Carry the wounded to the wagons but then form up at the edge of these woods," said Captain Parker. "Mr. Buckner, you and your men do the same, and then slip downriver about a hundred yards and form up in the woods just to the other side of that bend yonder. If the

Federals pursue us, we'll catch them in a crossfire. With luck they'll fall back and lick their wounds long enough for us to slip away."

The plan was brilliant by virtue of its simplicity, thought Jacob. The Federals would assume the rebels, outmanned and outgunned, had lost their nerve and were calling it a day. They would not expect an attack from two directions.

Fifteen minutes later found Jacob and his sixty cadets and sailors crouching in the edge of heavy woods and lush spring undergrowth, weapons at the ready. Five yards in front stretched a broom straw field fifty yards wide that ran along the river. Upriver to their left, around a slight bend, were Captain Parker and the marines. Downriver was the enemy line. Heavy gunfire continued from both directions.

Suddenly the gunfire stopped. Major Owens must have pulled his marines back into the woods, figured Jake. Sure enough, a shouted order to advance rang out from the Federal line. They were taking the bait and moving upriver in pursuit.

"Pass the word," whispered Jacob. "We'll fire in two volleys, sailors first, then cadets. Wait for my order."

Roger and James moved along the line to deliver Jacob's instructions. Henry stayed close to Jacob.

"Can we charge 'em?" Henry asked eagerly.

"Henry, we're outnumbered five to one!"

Within minutes the Federals appeared from the right, advancing through the broom straw at a quick route step in five ranks, each spaced five yards from the next. The marines occupied the first two ranks and the infantrymen the last three. In front, a marine major led the advance with sword drawn. The enemy's precision and large numbers caused many a heart to skip a beat among the waiting men.

Jacob extended his hand with palm down, signaling silence and patience as the enemy approached. One by one, the ranks drew even with them. Henry shot an anxious glance at Jacob, but the latter's palm remained down. The last Federal rank passed by. Now the Confederates were looking at the backs of their enemy.

Then came what Jacob had been waiting for. A blistering volley echoed down the river from Major Owens' marines. The first Federal rank disappeared into the broom straw. The others recoiled in shock and confusion.

"Sailors fire!" screamed Jacob.

Forty carbines blazed and half the rear rank fell. Panic broke out.

"Cadets fire!" Jacob yelled. Twenty more carbines erupted.

A second volley from upriver delivered the final blow. Those Federals still able to walk broke for the rear. They had not fired a shot.

A few cadets and sailors ran out onto the field to fire at the fleeing enemy.

"Let them go!" Jacob yelled. "Let's get out of here before they reorganize!"

As if to confirm his point, the *Arapahoe* fired a broadside that cut down trees and limbs just behind the Southerners. Her gunners had aimed high to avoid their own wounded lying on the field.

Jacob led the way deeper into the forest. Twenty yards into the thick woods, they angled upriver toward Captain Parker and the others. With no visible target, the *Arapahoe*'s guns ceased firing.

Jacob glanced over his shoulder at the big ship riding at anchor out in the river, becoming less visible now as they retreated deeper into the woods. He felt certain Alonzo Peck was out there. He was willing to bet he had even *seen* this demon that had haunted him for two years. Now he was walking away. With a shake of his head, he turned back to the trail ahead. He must think only of his men now.

The sharp crack of a gunshot echoed through the forest. Bark fragments stung Jacob's face. The bullet had splintered the tree next to his head.

"Take cover!" he yelled. His men were way ahead of him.

More gunshots sent bullets thudding into trees and whining past the men. Fifty yards in front, through the foliage, puffs of white smoke curled upward.

"About a dozen men," said Henry, peering around a tree with one eye. "Dark blue uniforms with white trim – they're Yankee sailors, sir!"

"*Arapahoe* crewmen who came ashore with that Pennsylvania infantry," said Jacob. "Pro'bly sent out as skirmishers when their line advanced." He gazed behind him. His men were crouched behind cover anxiously awaiting orders.

"Skirmishers? *That's* workin' out well!" said Henry sarcastically, ducking as a bullet whistled past. "They couldn't spot us when we were waitin' to ambush 'em, now they stumble headlong into us!"

"That's why we learn infantry tactics at the academy," said Jacob. He cupped his hands and spoke in a loud whisper. "James, take ten men and circle left! Roger, do the same to the right! The rest of you, let's make it hot for those fellas!"

James and Roger signaled to the men they wanted and stole off in opposite directions. The other forty men opened a blistering fire that prevented the enemy sailors from getting off more than an occasional shot.

The Southerners fired nonstop for ten minutes, picking off two of the enemy and suffering no casualties. Jacob eagerly joined in. The fact that they were facing *Arapahoe* crewmen was not lost on him.

Shooting erupted on the left. James and his men had flanked the enemy and begun an enfilading fire. An instant later, Roger's men opened on the right. Up ahead, a blue-clad sailor darted away through the forest, then another and another.

Jacob fired his carbine at a running figure but missed. He dropped the empty gun, drew his pistol and sprinted forward.

"Jake! Where you goin'?" called Henry, but to no avail.

Jacob had seen something, an officer trying to rally his men, a big man with a sour temper and insignia on his sleeve, the same man he had seen on the *Arapahoe*.

Peck, he thought to himself. But he must find out for sure.

He stopped behind a tree twenty yards from where he last saw the figure. Pistol poised, he sneaked a glance around the tree but saw nothing. Apparently the man had fled. He leaned forward for a better look.

A hand and face popped out from behind a tree. The hand held a pistol. The face sneered. The pistol fired.

Jacob felt pain but ignored it. He had seen the face. It was Alonzo Peck.

Peck was busily fumbling with his pistol. Apparently he had fired his last round, and was racing to replace the empty cylinder with a loaded one from his pocket.

Jacob could feel blood trickling down the side of his head. He ignored it, pulled back the hammer of his pistol and took aim. At the sound of the hammer clicking into position, Peck looked up and their glaring eyes met.

There he was, thought Jacob, in all his ugly, hated detail, the man who killed Joshua. How many times had he fanaticized about having this man in his sights? It seemed surreal. He wondered if Peck even remembered.

"You killed my little brother in cold blood, you son-of-a-dog!" He spit out the words as if they were poison.

"Killed a lot'a young whelps. Can't remember 'em all. You got the guts t'do anything about it?" Peck continued to reload, seemingly mocking Jacob with no attempt to seek cover.

Jacob's nostrils flared and he sucked in hard. "This is for Joshua!"

He pulled the trigger. The hammer fell with a thud. The pistol had misfired.

Peck snapped the new cylinder into place, grinned sadistically and leveled his pistol at Jacob.

Jacob braced for whatever was about to come. He mouthed a prayer for his mother and father, for Amy, Lydia, his comrades...

Peck cocked the pistol and his finger went to the trigger.

A gun roared. Smoke engulfed Jacob's head and the concussion left his ears ringing. The bullet buried itself in a tree. Peck bolted away through the woods.

"Sorry, Jake. Reckon I need lessons on how to shoot a pistol."

Jacob spun around to find Henry standing there, the pistol in his hand still smoking. He had never been more than two steps behind Jacob the whole time.

Jacob swiped a hand across the side of his head and gazed at his blood-tipped fingers. Peck's earlier bullet had creased him just above the ear.

"That makes two of us, Henry, and how to *avoid misfires* as well," he said. "We must see to those things before we next meet that man."

Chapter Twelve

The marine sergeant buttoned his coat, strapped on his accoutrements and moved among the sleeping men. He kicked the leg of one, shook the shoulder of another, and whacked the rears of several more with the back of his hand.

"Everyone up! We march in twenty minutes!"

The men arose rubbing their faces, buttoning coats, shaking slow-to-awake comrades. Jacob and Roger were among the former, James and Henry among the latter. Soon all were up and preparing for departure. There would be no breakfast today, for they had no food nor time for fires.

They had slipped away from White House Landing in mid-afternoon and marched until dusk. That put them less than a safe distance from Federal troops, but the physically and mentally exhausted men could go no further. They hadn't slept in twenty-four hours, eight of which were spent in deadly combat that cost the lives of seventeen of their number. When Captain Parker ordered a halt for the night, they stretched out on the ground still in column, fully clothed, without fires or blankets or food. The horses were left hitched to the wagons.

"How far to Richmond?" asked a groggy James, back from relieving himself.

"Too far to suit me," said Jacob. "Maybe noon, if there's no hitches."

"How's that head o'yourn?" asked Henry.

"Sore," said Jacob, gingerly touching the wound. The doctor had cleaned it and left it without a bandage. "It didn't keep me awake though. I was too exhausted."

"Fall in! Prepare to march!" shouted the marine sergeant.

The men gathered weapons and accoutrements and stood in rank awaiting the order to move out, still tired but eager to get back to their permanent quarters. The badly wounded rode aboard a wagon, others depended on hastily-made crutches or, for some, the help of a comrade.

Captain Parker climbed up on a wagon and shouted for attention.

"Men, before we get to Richmond and disburse, I wish to commend you on a job well done. We were obviously betrayed by an informant and faced twice our number, plus a twenty-gun Federal warship, yet our mission succeeded beyond all expectations. The White House supply depot will be shut down for weeks, perhaps months. If General Grant comes this way, he'll have to bring his supplies with him!"

A cheer erupted but fell away as the Captain raised his arms for silence.

"I share your enthusiasm, but remember, the enemy is still near," he said. "My report to the navy will detail the valor you all displayed. However, there is one whom I wish to recognize now. Cadet Buckner, step this way, please."

Startled, Jacob hesitantly moved to the wagon on which the Captain stood.

"Mr. Buckner, you were given an important command - your first command - and you responded with leadership and valor that far exceeded the standards used to judge normal men. You played no small role in our success. It gives me pleasure to promote you to the rank of brevet lieutenant. The paperwork making it official will be submitted with my report. Congratulations, Lieutenant!"

The groundswell of another cheer rumbled among the men, but quickly died away as they remembered the Captain's request for silence.

Jacob stood without sound or expression, as if he had suddenly become a deaf mute. Indeed, he wondered if he had heard right. He didn't deserve this, he thought. He had simply done what was expected of him.

"Column forward!" shouted Major Owens.

Jacob waited silently for the last-place cadets as the rest of the column marched past. The marines and sailors, told not to cheer, instead raised their hats in silent tribute as they passed him. Then came the cadets, every man snapping a salute. Jacob returned each and then fell in, glad to no longer be the focus of attention.

* * *

Lydia attacked her rosebushes as if they were somehow responsible for the fact that she hadn't heard from Jacob in two weeks. She applied her garden knife like a machete, cutting here, pulling there, eliminating dead wood, selecting the most suitable stalks. It was a ritual of spring that she usually enjoyed, but this year it was far more therapeutic than pleasurable.

Lydia was worried. She had gotten word that some of the cadets were away on a dangerous mission, said to be an attack on a major enemy post with heavy fighting expected. That would explain why she hadn't heard from Jacob, but it did nothing to calm her concerns for his safety.

She pulled a dead stalk from one of her prized rosebushes, a fiery red Gallica, and swore under her breath as a thorn penetrated her glove through to her thumb. With a growl of pain and anger mixed with frustration, she slammed the stalk into a tub with the rest of the day's clippings.

"Sure glad I'm not that rosebush!"

Lydia flinched and spun toward the voice. "Jacob!" She ejected her gloves into space and rushed for the gate, flinging herself into his arms as he opened it.

"Whoa!" he said, dropping a bag. "You gonna throw me in that tub too?"

"I just might if you don't stop running off trying to get yourself killed! I've been worried *sick* about you."

They gazed into each other's eyes, her arms around his neck, his hands caressing her hair, giving no thought to who might be watching. She pulled him down to her lips and kissed him, holding him against her body. A moment later they strolled arm in arm toward the front door.

"Uhh, your roses will...soon be beautiful, Lydia. You did a good job," said Jacob as they went inside. He was still shook up by the heat of Lydia's welcome and found it impossible to say anything more constructive.

"You know about roses?" She led him to their usual seat on the parlor sofa.

"My mother raises them; roses are her favorite flower."

"You miss your mother, don't you?" She caressed his cheek.

"Yeah, I guess I do," he nodded. Lydia was working her magic, he thought. Already the tensions of battle were melting away.

"I understand," she said. "I miss mine too. I'd like to see her again, but I'm not sure what kind of reception I'd get."

"I expect she'd welcome you. Mothers are like that..."

"Perhaps. But tell me, what's this bag you brought? Is it dinner? Don't you like my cooking? Maybe *that's* why you miss your mother!"

Jacob smiled. "No, it's my uniform jacket." He pulled out the jacket and two small insignia. "I need to have these shoulder bars sewn on, and I was hoping you'd do it..."

"Jacob, those are *lieutenant's* bars! Are you...did you...?"

"The Captain called it a brevet promotion. He says it isn't official until the navy gives its approval. I don't feel I deserve it."

"I know all about brevet promotions. They aren't given loosely. If you got one it's because you *deserved* it! And it usually means you risked your life more than you needed to. Is that what you did? Is that how you got that cut on your head?"

Jacob sidestepped her questions. "It was a hard mission. I was in command of sixty men, and we were given a difficult job. *Everyone* had to be aggressive or we wouldn't have succeeded. Never commanded men before and I must tell you, Lydia, I don't like it. I don't like being responsible for other men's lives."

"Well, it's ironic, but my fiancé was a brevet lieutenant in command of a company of sixty men when he was killed, and he felt just as you do. But in war a commander's duty is to get the job done with minimum deaths. If you can do that, then you've actually *saved* lives. You must simply do your best, Jacob, and always ask God for help. The burden of responsibility grows lighter with the help of wings."

"I lost six men – good men."

"I'm...sure the other commanders had similar or perhaps greater losses..."

Jacob frowned and nodded. "The marines lost heavily. There was a boy of sixteen, from Tennessee. He had fallen out with his father and left home, kind'a like me. We had talked at Drewry's Bluff and he told me this would be his first action. He was scared, so I suggested he go to St. John's Church. Then he ended up being hit by a shell and killed. So young, his whole life ahead of him...I can't get him out of my mind..."

"Jacob, you couldn't save his life, but you may well have saved his soul." She gazed up at the cut on his head. "Now are you gonna tell me about that cut or not?"

Jacob smiled. He thought he had avoided the subject. "It...was a close call, and not pleasant. We were retreating through the woods...and I came face to face with the man who killed my brother, a man named Alonzo Peck. I'd been watching for him since I first enlisted and suddenly there he was, right in front of me."

"Oh, Jacob! That must have been horrible! How? What happened?"

"Peck was leading a patrol and we ran into them. After we flanked them, they fled. I ran after Peck and suddenly he jumped from behind a tree and shot at me. That's when I got this." He touched the side of his head.

"I *thought* so! I *thought* that was from a bullet! Another inch and you'd be *dead*, Jacob Buckner! And over a two-year-old grudge! Don't you know any better?"

"It's no ordinary grudge, Lydia! He killed my brother in cold blood! I tried to kill him right there but my pistol misfired. He was about to shoot at me again, but Henry Stiles fired first and Peck took off through the woods."

"I don't know this Henry Stiles, but he must be one of those guardian angels you seem to have," said Lydia. "Perhaps one day I can thank him."

Jacob smiled. He couldn't stay angry at Lydia for long. And she was right. He had escaped so many close calls that he *did* seem to have guardian angels.

"It's hard for me to imagine *Henry* as a guardian angel," he said.

"God's instruments come in all shapes and sizes," said Lydia.

"Perhaps," Jacob said. "The enemy knew we were coming and yet we managed to get the job done, so we must have had God's help. But all in all, it was a day in hell, one I'd like to forget if I ever can."

"Well, I'll be glad to sew your lieutenant's bars on - but never again tell me you don't deserve them!"

"I survived, Lydia. That was my greatest achievement."

* * *

"You sent for me, sir?"

"Yes. Good morning, Lieutenant, please have a seat," said Captain Parker.

Jacob glanced about to see if someone else was present, then remembered that 'lieutenant' was *his* rank now, though still not official. He slipped into an easy chair across from the Captain.

"You no doubt remember our previous talks about a possible spy," continued Captain Parker. "Well, the White House mission removed all doubt from my mind. Clearly we're dealing with a spy, perhaps more than one. Do you agree?"

"I do, sir," said Jacob. "That regiment of infantry might have been a coincidence, but to have the *Arapahoe* arrive ready for battle an hour after we got there, with two companies of marines on board, was no coincidence."

"Exactly," said the Captain. "But how do we catch him? Any ideas?"

"Well, I don't see an easy way unless he makes a mistake. I suppose we could come up with a list of possible suspects and then watch for suspicious behavior. But the list would have to cover both the academy *and* the Navy Department..."

"That would be a long list," said the Captain.

Jacob nodded. "Perhaps we should examine our own house first. If we don't find anything, we'll ask the navy to examine theirs."

The Captain thumped his desk, pondering something. "What about the duty logs? When someone leaves the ship they must sign out and give their reason. When they return, they must sign back in. We could examine the logs for patterns - you know, like someone signing out every time there's a mission in the works..."

Jacob sat forward. "That's an excellent place to start, sir. Then we could eliminate those with legitimate reasons and look closely at the rest. I enjoy solving problems, sir. I'd like to conduct this study."

* * *

May 1, 1864

My dearest mother,
I hope everyone is well. My health has been excellent except for a scratch I received on my head, but for once in my life being a hardhead served me well, so you have no need to worry.

I have only time for a few lines before I must return to my studies. We have missed a great deal of time on navy business. In the last month, we have conducted two missions against the enemy. Both were hard. On the first we fell short of our goal but the second was a great success.

On the second one, I was placed in command of sixty men, my most important job so far, and everything went well. My captain promoted me to lieutenant. In my opinion others deserve the credit, chief among them our old friend David Two-Feathers.

I have written you about how the first mission failed despite David's help. Well, he played an even greater role in the second one, along with some of his Mattaponi tribesmen. We could not have succeeded without them. David has returned home to his family. If you see him, please convey my thanks.

I must tell you, dear mama, that my duties have placed me at risk on many occasions and I have experienced several close calls. On each occasion, I have suffered nothing more serious than the aforementioned scratch on my head. A girl with whom I am friends accuses me of having guardian angels. Though she may be right, I think the more likely cause is the prayers you have been offering on my behalf. I ask you to please continue those efforts.

Speaking of close calls, I had one recently with my old enemy, Alonzo Peck, the man who killed

Joshua. We tried to kill each other but apparently God did not intend it to he, at least not on that day. My lady friend says the grudge is foolish, and I agree that most grudges are, but this one is too personal to be easily settled.

I have become very close with this girl. Her name is Lydia Schenk. She was born and raised as Amish, in Pennsylvania, but decided not to return following her rumspringa. However, she remains very religious and together with my close friends in the navy, has been a godsend to me. I pray that one day you may meet her.

Well, dear mama, sadly I must now return to the finer points of navigation and seamanship, plus a special study that Captain Parker has assigned to me. I remain your loving son who misses you very much and who hopes one day soon to see you again.

Jacob

A tired Isaac Buckner washed up at the well and entered the house. He and the other men had spent the day working in the fields, putting in the spring planting. They had planted ten acres of corn and planned to start on the wheat tomorrow.

He entered the study to have a smoke and wait for supper. As he filled his pipe and applied a match to it, he noticed a letter lying on the table next to him. He read the letter quickly, flipped it back to the table with a frown, and relit his pipe. After two hard puffs, he sat back and gazed out the window toward the barn.

"Is that it? Don't you have anything to say?" asked Sara Buckner as she entered the study. She took a seat in the chair next to her husband.

Mr. Buckner frowned and lowered his pipe to his hand. "This...individual...has sinned against God, and it's a sin for us to have contact with him! Yet you opened this letter and read it, and I suspect there have been others. Then you put it where I would see it, and I succumbed to the devil's temptation and read it also. We have sinned, Sara, and we must ask God to forgive us."

Sara glanced toward the kitchen and the wooden figurine sitting atop the cook stove. "If that's the price for loving my son, then I accept it."

"That's not the point! He's my son too, but so was Joshua! Jacob violated the most basic Amish principal, and it cost Joshua his life! He *had* to be punished! If we allow exceptions, our whole society will disintegrate!"

"Isaac, he lives with the memory of what happened every day, and will for the rest of his life! Don't you think that punishes him enough?"

"You read that letter, Sara! Violence is all he knows now! He has abandoned us altogether!"

"No, the letter shows that he still has his faith, and this girl Lydia seems to be influencing him in that direction. If he can get past what those men did to Joshua, I think his life will turn around."

"He'll likely be killed first. His only salvation is to forgive Mr. Peck, renounce violence and confess his sins, but his thirst for revenge has poisoned his mind and blinded him to that fact. Sara, we must face the truth. We no longer have a son."

* * *

True to predictions, in the spring of 1864 General Ulysses S. Grant moved his massive army south, 'bringing his supplies with him' as Captain Parker had said he must. He first confronted Lee on May 5th in the Wilderness near Chancellorsville, the same ground on which the armies had fought a year earlier, and where Lee had lost Stonewall Jackson. Without Jackson, and weakened by losses in the previous year's campaigns - losses that were as irreplaceable as Jackson - Lee nonetheless repulsed the northern invaders in heavy fighting.

But the Union Army was no longer led by the likes of McClellan or Hooker. Ignoring the defeat, Grant circled Lee's right flank and on May 9th attacked him at Spotsylvania Court House. Again he was beaten in desperate fighting. Still refusing to retreat, he put his men in motion around Lee's right for yet a third time.

It was the beginning of the Overland Campaign, a series of 'meat grinder' moves, always to the east and south, closer to Richmond. Grant was using his superior numbers as the ultimate weapon, capitalizing on the North's far larger pool of manpower.

While Grant was grinding his way toward Richmond, a second Union army, under Benjamin Butler, was transported up the James River to Bermuda Hundred, ten miles below Drewry's Bluff. Butler's orders were to cut the rail lines bringing supplies to Lee, take Petersburg and advance on Richmond from the south while Grant converged from the north and east. The men at Drewry's Bluff found themselves in the crosshairs of an approaching Federal pincer movement.

* * *

Summoned by Captain Parker, Jacob took a seat in the Captain's office aboard the *Patrick Henry*. With him were Roger, James and Henry.

"Mr. Buckner, let me start with you," said the Captain. "I have received word from the Navy Department that your promotion to lieutenant is official. That rank is unheard of for someone who hasn't even graduated from the Academy yet, but given details, Secretary Mallory readily agreed. Congratulations!"

"Thank you, sir," said Jacob. "Most of the credit goes to these fellas."

"Take the basket off your candle, Jake, and let it shine a little," said Henry.

"I have news for the three of you as well," said the Captain. "It was clear from Lieutenant Buckner's report that you each played a key role in the recent mission, so I requested, and the Secretary has approved, a promotion for each of you to the rank of 'passed midshipman', effective immediately. Based on length of service, you will be senior, Mr. Stiles, followed by Mr. Morgan and Mr. Phillips in that order. I wish to congratulate all of you!"

The three stared at Captain Parker and then rose to shake his outreached hand.

"Congratulations," said Jacob, offering his own handshake. "You deserve it."

"You know, I've been in a navy uniform – first blue, then grey - for eight years," said Henry. "I was beginning to wonder if I'd *ever* command anything, and now I get to command *these* two scoundrels! I hope that doesn't mean I hav'ta be nice to 'em!"

"There's no justice," said James, shaking his head.

"Well, look at it this way," said Roger. "This makes us eligible for the lieutenant's exam, and now we have a clear incentive to pass it."

Captain Parker listened to the banter of his new officers with satisfaction and pride, and a touch of sadness. All but James had served with him aboard the old *Beaufort*. They were proven veterans who would be a tribute to any navy, but he knew they would soon be tested to their fullest, for he had alarming news to share with them.

"One other thing, gentlemen, and I'm afraid this isn't good news," he said. "As you know, Grant was beaten twice in a week with heavy losses, yet continues to advance. You also are aware that General Butler and about forty thousand men have landed at Bermuda Hundred, south of here."

The Captain got up and went to a map on the wall behind him.

"We're here," he said, pointing to Drewry's Bluff. Then his finger drifted to a spot further down the James River. "Here's Bermuda Hundred. From there, Butler moved west toward the Richmond Turnpike and the rail lines bringing supplies from the south, but then halted his advance. Now there are reports that Grant is nearing Richmond's outskirts and that Butler is shifting his divisions north toward us. It would seem they're planning a coordinated assault on Richmond."

"And we're right in their path," said Henry, swallowing hard.

"Richmond will be practically surrounded," said Roger grimly.

"Why should they bother to attack?" asked James. "They could just wait us out."

"Because they have a hundred fifty thousand men and Lee has less than half that many," said Jacob. "Captain, are there any reinforcements available to Lee?"

"General Pickett's division is in Petersburg," said Captain Parker. "General Hoke has been recalled from North Carolina, and General Beauregard is said to be coming. That will add another thirty thousand at best."

"That isn't enough," frowned Jacob. "So I guess we can expect an attack."

"I think we can count on it," said the Captain. "Drewry's Bluff is on alert as of now. Classes are canceled until further notice. Things look bleak, gentlemen, but they've looked bleak before. We must prepare ourselves for anything."

* * *

Dear Lydia,

As much as I want to see you again, it appears the Federal Army has other plans. As you may know from the papers, the enemy is moving on Richmond in great numbers from both north and south, and poses the most serious threat the city has ever faced. Drewry's Bluff is on high alert and I cannot leave as long as the alert persists.

We cannot tell when the attack will come, but I fear it will not be long. You must leave the city if possible, otherwise you must buy what food you can, and should the city fall, shutter your windows and remain inside.

Lydia, I long to be with you, but cannot. You must remember Psalm 23: "Ye though I walk through the valley of the shadow of death, I will fear no evil." We can only trust in God's words and pray for His deliverance.

Until we meet again, I remain your loyal and loving friend,

Jacob

* * *

Jacob leaned against the breastworks atop Drewry's Bluff and trained his field glasses, not toward the river as usual, but toward the fields and forests to the land side. His gun crew lounged about their eight-inch rifled Columbiad, listening to the rumble of distant artillery and musket fire, watching smoke rising in lazy clouds over the area and straining to follow the blurred movement of flags and men.

A major battle had begun at daybreak along the Bluff's outer defenses a mile distant. The sound of guns had sent sailors, marines and cadets alike scurrying to their posts. Now they anxiously watched the fighting, following its ebb and flow like a partisan crowd at an athletic contest, but with far more riding on the outcome.

The battle raged back and forth, but as the day wore on, Federal commanders warned Butler repeatedly about the size and strong position of the rebel forces. The administratively talented but combat-weak Butler grew increasingly tentative. In early afternoon he ordered his men to withdraw back inside their defenses at Bermuda Hundred. By nightfall they were again in their original positions. The men atop Drewry's Bluff watched them go and breathed a sigh of relief.

On June 2nd, Grant drew close to Richmond and attacked Lee again, this time at Cold Harbor just east of the city. Impatient for victory, he ordered his brigades to frontally assault heavily fortified and stoutly manned rebel breastworks. The attack failed and cost Grant 6,000 men in twenty minutes. Years later, he would state in his memoirs that it was the only attack of his career that he regretted making.

Thus thwarted in his plans to take the Confederate Capital by storm, Grant crossed the river, linked with Butler's men, encircled Petersburg (an important rail center), and cut the rail lines bringing supplies to Lee. With Lee thus bottled up on three sides, his supplies reduced to a trickle and his army being reduced daily by sickness, casualties and desertion, Grant settled down to outwait his opponent.

Chapter Thirteen

Jacob descended the *Patrick Henry's* gangplank and walked across the dock to the path leading around the base of Drewry's Bluff. There he stopped and gazed in both directions. To his right, a man sat alone on a bench next to the path. Jacob paused, took a deep breath, and proceeded toward the man.

"Sorry to disturb you, sir. They told me you wouldn't mind," said Jacob. "It's about my study of the duty logs. If you'd rather discuss it another time..."

Captain Parker looked up. "Well, I come here to be alone and think," he said, "but since this discussion requires privacy, I'll forgive you this time."

"Thank you, sir. I come here sometimes myself. Something about a flowing river that seems to cleanse my mind and make it work better."

"Exactly. So tell me, have you identified our spy?"

"No, but I've come up with a few possibilities." Jacob sat down beside the Captain and opened a notebook. "The logs show that eleven men left the ship shortly before the *Underwriter* and White House missions and returned within two hours. Three were members of the ship's crew on official business. Another three are from the area and went to see their families. Of the remaining five, two visited sweethearts in town."

"I'm sure they told a sad tale of needing affection before going out to risk their lives," said the Captain. "Men have been using that ploy for centuries."

"Yessir," said Jacob, grinning. "Of course, we can't be sure they went where they said they went, but it's well known that both men have sweethearts in town."

"What about the other three?"

"Well, that's where it becomes interesting, sir." He pointed to three names in the notebook. "All are cadets who listed their reason as 'personal business'."

"Surely it couldn't be any of *them!*" exclaimed Captain Parker, scanning the names. "Those men are among our best cadets!"

"Yessir. I tend to think it's one of the two Romeos, or maybe one of the three with family in town. But I feel certain we'll find our spy among those eight names."

"Well, whoever the spy is, he'll likely not have much to do as long as Grant plays his waiting game. Of course, with us on high alert no one can sign out anyhow, so we may have to play our own waiting game before we can flush him out."

* * *

As 1864 progressed, Grant's siege of the rebel capital grew tighter. Digging replaced fighting as the main occupation. Vast earth-and-log fortifications sprang up in a double semi-circle that enclosed Richmond and Petersburg on three sides, with just the west side remaining open. Only a few hundred yards – in some cases less than a hundred yards - separated the Confederate inner circle from the Federal outer circle.

The fortifications grew into a maze of trenches with strategically-placed forts, gun emplacements, bomb-proofs and storage tunnels. A man could walk miles and never show himself to the enemy. Fighting diminished to a game of potshots at careless opponents and periodic skirmishing among smaller groups. Large-scale assaults grew rare. More insults than bullets flew between the trenches.

Conditions in Richmond grew steadily worse. Propelled by shortages and the deteriorating value of Confederate currency, prices of food and other essentials rose to ridiculous levels. By the end of 1864, a pound of bacon cost $20.00, flour and corn meal $100.00 a bushel and cotton cloth $15.00 per square yard.

* * *

Jacob hunkered down under his blanket. Bitter cold and a half-foot of snow had greeted the new year of 1865, but to conserve scarce fuel, heating stoves aboard the *Patrick Henry* were kept low or not lit at all.

He pulled the blanket tight about him and dozed off again. Reveille would not be for another half hour.

"Bring boilers to full pressure! Secure guns! Stand by to raise the gangplank!" The voices came from the deck. Jacob bounced up, got dressed and hustled up the companionway. On deck he found the crew busily preparing the ship for departure. James Morgan stood by the rail.

"James! What's going on? Are we going downriver?"

"No, I'm afraid we're headed in the other direction."

"Toward Richmond? Why? And why wasn't I told?"

"Orders just arrived for the squadron to pull back."

"That doesn't make sense! What good are navy ships in Richmond?"

James frowned and shook his head. "We weren't given a choice. They say the enemy's too strong downriver, so we won't be going there anyhow."

Jacob turned away in disbelief. Without the squadron, Drewry's Bluff would be strictly a defensive outpost! The enemy would know that they need not fear attack and that with a little patience they could win without firing another shot.

A force strong enough to get past Drewry's Bluff couldn't possibly be stopped in the narrow confines of the James River nearer Richmond. The squadron would be no better than toy boats in a bathtub, and the cadets no more than a highly-trained caretaker crew, waiting to hand over the city to the enemy.

Later that day, after guiding the *Patrick Henry* up the James to a birth near Rockett's, Captain Parker assembled the cadets and crew. With a grim face, he gazed out over the 150 men standing at attention on the ship's main deck.

"At ease, men," he said in his deep voice. "This meeting is informational. I'll make a brief statement, and then you may ask questions."

The cadets and sailors looked around in surprise. They had never before been allowed to question a captain in open assembly. A few cautiously relaxed while others remained at attention simply out of habit.

"An attack on Drewry's Bluff appears imminent and may include ironclads and a strong infantry force," began the Captain. "As a precaution, the navy has pulled us back here to Richmond so that we can better defend the Capital and assist our Government if needed. Now, are there any questions?"

Surprised by Captain Parker's brevity, the men stood silently as if not sure he had finished. Finally Roger raised his hand.

"Sir, wouldn't Richmond be best defended by stopping the enemy at Drewry's Bluff? If they can't be stopped there, surely they can't be stopped here."

"Other troops will be moved to the bluff. It will remain fully manned."

"But...wouldn't it be better to use those troops elsewhere while *we* man the big guns?" asked another cadet. "After all, we have experience with those guns."

"The navy's bringing in a heavy artillery unit from the coast to man the guns. We will join a well-trained reserve unit that the navy wishes to establish here in Richmond."

Jacob listened to the banter. The Captain was not being his usual open, soft-spoken self. A possible attack on Drewry's Bluff? Nothing new about that. Assist the government? That was the function of *any* military. A well-trained reserve in the city? A poor use of men, he thought. The cadets and sailors of the squadron were well-trained, but not for fighting the enemy in the streets of Richmond.

Then the pieces fell into place. They weren't here to defend the city at all. The War Department was concerned that Lee's lines might be broken. They were laying contingency plans for the evacuation of the Confederate Government.

* * *

The Officer of the Deck tapped on the door of the small cabin assigned to Jacob. "Lieutenant Buckner, a visitor here to see you, sir."

"Oh? Did he give his name?" Jacob asked. He was just getting dressed.

"He's a she, sir...and no sir," said the nervous young cadet. "But she's a very attractive she, uhh, lady, if I may say so, sir."

Jacob scanned his memory banks and found only one possibility - Lydia. He buttoned his shell jacket, grabbed his hat and hurried up on deck. Even before he reached the gangplank, he heard Henry's voice on the dock below.

"Yeah, he's done well, but he owes it all to me. Why, I remember when he was nothin' but a farm boy with seed in his hair and manure on his shoes, but I brought him along slow and...oh! Good morning Lieutenant! This lady's here to...to see you."

Lydia looked up and smiled. "Hello, Jacob, I heard your ship was here." Her smile turned to a playful grin. "Mr. Stiles has been telling me about your adventures together. Such a sweet 'guardian angel'! I didn't realize you *owed* him so much!"

Guardian angel indeed, thought Jacob. "Thank you, Mr. Stiles, and I'll try to find an appropriate way to *repay* you."

He led Lydia across the dock away from the ship. "Lydia, what are you doing here? We're still on high alert. We could be attacked at any time..."

"Poo on the navy's high alert! I don't see any danger! They wouldn't let you come to me, so I came to you! I couldn't stand not seeing you, Jacob."

"Many's the time I've thought about you being just up that hill yonder, Lydia. Let's find a place more private, but I must stay within earshot of the ship."

They walked along the dock, heading downriver away from Rockett's. The dock gave way to a path that led through scattered trees and brush along the river bank. They were in an area Jacob had used for fishing when he served aboard the old *Beaufort* two years earlier. It was close enough to the *Patrick Henry* that he could hear an alarm should one be sounded.

The day was sunny and comfortable, typical of days that frequently occur in Virginia in late winter. They stopped at a spot visible only to vessels passing by.

"I've missed you, Lydia."

They kissed and he held her close. A deep sigh eased from Lydia's chest.

"Oh, Jacob, I've missed you so much. Will this war *ever* be over...?"

"I'm afraid it will," uttered Jacob in a near whisper. "And soon now, I think."

They sat on the river bank. Lydia leaned against his shoulder as they quietly watched the current flowing gently past.

"I had a feeling things weren't going well," she said softly.

Jacob nodded. "The army's starving. Replacements are nonexistent. They're releasing the walking wounded from hospitals and sending them back to their units. There's even talk of putting slaves in uniform in return for their freedom..."

"The army isn't the *only* ones starving," said Lydia. "Yesterday, I visited three shops before I found a loaf of bread and a pound of bacon, and then had to pay fifty dollars. It takes *three months* for me to earn that much in my flower shop."

Jacob thought of his parents. How fortunate, at times like this, to be part of a self-sufficient, close-knit community with little need for money. He prayed that God would keep them and their farm safe from enemy raids.

"Is there any way I can help? I've got a little money..."

"No, Jacob! You risk your *life* for the pittance they pay you. I love you for offering, but I could *never* accept money from you." She reached up and kissed him on the cheek. "I'm glad they moved you here to Richmond, but I hope it doesn't mean you're about to go off on another dangerous mission somewhere..."

He shook his head. "I have a feeling our next mission will be right here."

Lydia glanced at him. "To do what, help defend the city?"

"Well, maybe, but if the city is about to fall, the government will evacuate. I suspect we're here to help with the evacuation."

"You mean to escort officials? Maybe help keep order?"

"More likely to escort government officials."

"And we'll be left to the mercy of the Yankees, just like the people in Atlanta. I've been trying not to think about that."

"As have I. Do you have somewhere outside the city you could go?"

"I'd rather stay here. An empty house is more likely to be looted or burned."

"Then at least pack your valuables and hide them, maybe up the chimney, or buried in a flower bed. Do you have a gun?"

Lydia shook her head. "A gun would just get me killed. But don't forget, I'm from Pennsylvania. Maybe that will help."

"I doubt it. But if you mention it, just be sure you're talking to *Union* troops."

They chuckled and grew pensive, momentarily captured by the hypnotic effect of the flowing river. The time was near when she must leave and he must return to his ship, but neither wanted to spoil the moment by bringing it up.

At least the river had a known destination, Jacob thought, whereas he and Lydia had no idea where they were headed or when they might next see each other. She was beautiful, the most beautiful girl he had ever seen and he treasured her, yet he felt helpless to protect her against the chaotic events he suspected were barreling toward them. He helped her up and they embraced, quietly and somberly, hesitant to let go.

"We may not see each other for awhile, Lydia, but I... want you to promise me you'll take care of yourself..."

She laid her hand softly on his cheek. "Jacob, *you're* the one in danger, not me. Just promise me you'll be back as soon as you can. You're my...whole world."

They kissed with the clinging passion of two people in love who were about to be thrown into an abyss, one with no discernable bottom. Reluctantly, hand in hand, they walked slowly back up the path toward the ship.

* * *

Sunday morning, April 2, 1865, dawned warm and clear in Richmond. Bright sunlight greeted the peel of church bells summoning worshipers to services. A light green blanket, just beginning to emerge on the maples and elms lining the streets, heralded the imminent arrival of spring.

At the intersection of Ninth & Grace Streets, across from Capital Square, the sanctuary of St. Paul's Episcopal Church quickly filled with worshipers - women in black mourning dresses, convalescing soldiers in uniform, old men in suits and a scattering of government officials.

In his usual pew halfway down the center aisle, President Jefferson Davis sat alone as the late morning sun streamed through the tall windows on his left side, facing the capital. He followed along in his Bible as Dr. Minnigerode, rector of St. Paul's, read from Psalm 46, verses 7-9:

"The Lord of hosts is with us; the God of Jacob is our refuge. Come, behold the works of the Lord, what desolations he hath made in the earth. He maketh wars to cease...he breaketh the bow, and cutteth the spear asunder; he burneth the chariot..."

How appropriate under the present circumstances, thought the President. Indeed God *is* the only true refuge. Everyone would do well to pray to Him for an end to this war and its horrible desolation.

He glanced through the window at the capital. It reminded him that he must go by his office after the service and check the latest dispatches from General Lee. The news yesterday had been encouraging and he prayed that nothing had changed.

As the congregation prepared to take communion, a messenger entered the church and quietly handed a folded note to the sexton. The latter, an elderly gentleman, walked down the aisle, touched President Davis's shoulder and handed him the note.

Suddenly all color drained from the President's face. Lee's lines were broken. The army was in retreat. Richmond must be evacuated tonight.

The President quietly got up and strode out of the church.

* * *

Captain Parker spent Saturday night in town and arrived aboard the *Patrick Henry* just in time to conduct the Sunday morning muster, prayer, and inspection of cadets. As the inspection ended, Jacob came up to him.

"Any news about the fighting, Captain?"

"Why yes. I ran into Secretary Mallory last night and he said the news from Lee is good. He seemed very much encouraged."

"Glad to hear that, because I've heard some worrisome stories lately," said Jacob. "Seems there were wagons at the railroad depot, putting boxes aboard the trains."

"Pro'bly just some nervous citizens taking...taking precautions," said the Captain. His attention was distracted by a company of men marching past. "Look there," he said. "That's part of the Home Guard. Wonder where they're headed."

Most of the men were above or below normal military age. Some walked with limps or bore other signs of old wounds. Others wore the heavy clothing of factory workers. One man in particular looked familiar to Jacob, and he realized it was the husky iron worker from Tredegar who had killed Calico Sam McClung.

"I don't know, sir," said Jacob. "But my guess is the outer defenses."

Both men fell silent, preferring not to speculate. The Captain retired to his cabin to finish a report. With no classes on Sunday, Jacob joined his friends on the aft deck for a day of checkers and chatting. He anticipated heavy ribbing, notably from Henry, about his recent beautiful visitor. The constant rumble of big guns drifted across the hills and fields from the direction of Petersburg.

Shortly before noon, an officer rode up to the ship, saying he had an urgent message for the Captain. He was piped aboard and directed to the Captain's cabin.

Five minutes later the messenger left the ship, and five minutes after that, those time-worn words known to every sailor rang out:

"All hands on deck! Fall in!"

The ship's drummer beat out the urgent cadence of the long roll. The off-duty watches tumbled up the companionways and fell into formation, along with the cadets. Captain Parker, looking shaken and ashen-faced, emerged from a gangway and walked to the front. His demeanor told them that something was up and that it was serious.

"Gentlemen, Secretary Mallory has sent devastating news. General Lee's lines are broken and he is in retreat. Our government will flee the city by nightfall."

The news fell upon the men like a bombshell. The unthinkable was happening. The Captain took a deep breath and gazed around the drawn-up ranks, engaging as many eyes as possible as he tried to convey a sense of assurance and orderliness to the stunned men. He knew that what he was about to say would be equally shocking.

"The *Patrick Henry* must be burned. We are to abandon her within the hour. All sailors are to join General Lee's army as infantry. Midshipman Stiles, you are to lead the cadets to the railroad depot and await orders. Lieutenant Buckner, you will stay behind with a detail of cadets, burn the ship and then go to the depot. I must go by the War Department and then will join you at the depot. Before leaving the ship, every man will be issued a carbine, forty rounds of ammunition and three days' rations."

He inhaled and let it go, trying to get control of himself.

"This is a sad day, gentlemen. Our country needs us as never before, and I call on every man to do his duty to the fullest, knowing that the peace of God will ultimately return to us. Now, we have much to do, so let's get started. Dismissed."

Jacob was shocked, not so much by the news as by the speed with which it had come about. His assignment to burn the *Patrick Henry* hit him equally hard. It had been his home for the past two years. It had transformed his life and given him many happy memories. Burning it would not be pleasant.

The cadets and sailors broke ranks and rushed to carry out dozens of details. Over the next hour, haversacks and suitcases were packed, blankets rolled into bundles and tightly tied, provisions prepared and arms issued.

Jacob finished packing and toyed with the idea of a quick visit to Lydia. But a group of cadets - Roger, James, Henry and six others - gathered outside his cabin door. They carried a collection of haversacks, suitcases and blanket rolls.

"Well, guess we don't get to graduate after all," said Roger.

"Guess not," said Jacob. "But we have more important things to do now than to cry over spilt milk." He had no idea why the group had gathered outside his door, but he was anxious to get on with his assignment.

"That's why we're here, Lieutenant," said James. "We've been through just about everything together on this ship, from classes to combat, good times and bad, and it shouldn't be any different now. We wish to volunteer for your detail."

"That's right, sir," said a senior cadet whom Jacob did not know well. "We'd consider it an honor to join you." The others echoed his sentiment.

"I appreciate that," nodded Jacob. "I wasn't looking forward to burning our ship, but you fellas just made it easier." He looked over the group. "Henry...why are you here? You're supposed to lead the other cadets to the railroad depot..."

"I simply came to ask you a question. Didn't know anythin' about these fellas volunteerin'...not that I wouldn't if I couldn't...I mean, not that I wouldn't if..."

"I understand, Henry. What's your question?"

"I just wondered why we're goin' to the railroad depot. Seems a little strange, us bein' in the navy and all."

"Well, I'd say they have something in mind for us," said Jacob. "Like perhaps escorting the government officials, maybe even President Davis himself."

Faces that had been serious quickly blossomed into smiles at the prospect of such a high honor. It was a sad day, but instead of being mere pawns, they might well play a role important enough that it could get them in the history books.

"Guess I'd better get the cadets moving," said Henry. "Wouldn't want t'keep old Jeff waiting."

"The rest of you take your luggage to the wagons so it can be sent ahead, and please take mine also, if you will," said Jacob. "I'll gather the materials we'll need and meet you on the dock in ten minutes."

Jacob went to find coal oil, but found that the bosun's mate had half-a-dozen containers of it waiting on the foredeck, along with stick matches. Jacob did a quick survey of the ship, mentally noted what should be done, and then went to the dock to meet the others. Most of the fifty-odd cadets were already in line, weapons in hand, their luggage piled high on two wagons.

"We're missing Carter, Fleming and Harris!" hollered Henry impatiently. He had just finished calling the roll. "We march in five minutes, with or without them!"

"Carter and Harris are in my detail! Haven't seen Fleming!" hollered Jacob.

"I'm here!" yelled a voice. Fleming appeared, struggling to drag an oversized suitcase down the gangplank. "Forgot something and had to go back!"

"Was it your brain you forgot, or something equally useless?" yelled Henry in the man's ear. He enjoyed being in command. "Next time we'll leave you behind!"

The mood grew noticeably more somber and reflective as the column stepped off toward the railroad depot, a quarter-mile away. Henry knew the cadets were distressed that their ship would soon be destroyed. He took up position at the rear of the column.

"Eyes straight ahead, gentlemen!" he bellowed. "We're moving forward and can't take the past with us! We must focus on the future!"

Jacob watched the cadets depart and then led his detail, comprised of Roger, James and six other cadets, to the foredeck where the coal oil waited.

"We'll form teams of two like we did at White House Landing. Each team take coal oil and matches and go below, two teams forward and two aft. Set the fires deep in the hold; I'll tell you where. Open the hatches and portholes to create a draft. Use furniture and anything else handy to make sure the fires get a good start."

Jacob outlined where each fire should be set and assigned a location to each of the four teams, noting the best escape routes. Then he invited questions.

"What about the ship's magazine?" asked Roger.

"The magazine and the Captain's cabin are mine. No more questions? All right, we'll meet back here in ten minutes. Let's go."

Jacob watched the others depart for their assignments, then grabbed a can of coal oil and headed below deck. The magazine was deep in the hole amidships and housed a ton of gunpowder in five-pound bags. He poured coal oil on a few of the bags, opened another bag and laid a trail of powder out into the passageway. The fires would ignite the powder trail, which would ignite the oil-soaked bags and the magazine would explode. The fire and subsequent explosion would leave little of the ship.

That completed, Jacob ran for the last can of coal oil and headed for Captain Parker's cabin. Already he could smell smoke wafting up through the ship.

"Five minutes to be off the ship!" he yelled, mindful of the exposed powder.

He entered the Captain's cabin and looked for confidential papers left behind in the rush to leave the ship. He had no doubt the Captain had taken care of that detail himself, but still, it was his duty to make sure nothing survived.

He thoroughly doused the desk, the cabinets and the rest of the room with coal oil, stopping only long enough to take an item from atop a bookcase and stick it in his jacket. Once out the door, he threw a lighted match in behind him and ran for the deck.

Smoke was rising in hot, swirling columns from the passageways and hatches. Three of the teams had returned to the deck, but Roger and his partner were not back, nor had the others seen them.

Jacob knew they had entered the bow of the ship. He ran forward and peered down through a hatch, and promptly jumped back as thick smoke bellowed up in his face. He recalled a barn fire back home where a man died, not from burns, but from being trapped in the smoke. A cold chill ran up his spine.

"Roger, are you down there? Roger? Roger?"

Now his scheme to blow up the magazine didn't seem like such a good idea. The smoke had grown too thick to breathe and the fire was spreading rapidly.

He didn't know the other cadet well, but Roger was his best friend. They had fished together, shared personal secrets together. On the *Underwriter*, Roger had saved him from a bullet. He had sent his friend into this hole. Now he must get him out - and quickly, for the powder could explode at any moment.

He covered his nose and mouth, skidded down the ladder and felt his way through the acrid, suffocating smoke. There was no sign of the two men.

"Roger? Roger?" He could barely see his hand in front of his face.

A weak sound up ahead, then nothing. Carefully Jacob felt along the walls.

"Roger, where are you?"

He stumbled over something. Eyes closed, holding his breath, he felt around his feet - two bodies, both unresponsive. His lungs screamed for air but he knew that two lives, perhaps three, hung in the balance. Somehow he managed to lift one man and head back toward the steps.

"James! Quick! Help!"

Smoke was streaming up the steps as if through a chimney. To his relief, the faint, ghost-like forms of James and another cadet appeared at the top. They grabbed the man's arms and pulled him up.

With his lungs ready to burst now, Jacob gasped a quick breath of fresh air, again descended the ladder and crawled back to where he had left the second man. His heart pounding like a sledgehammer, he dragged him back to within reach of helping hands.

A moment later the three men lay sprawled on the deck. All were dizzy, coughing and gasping. Jacob recovered quickly but the others took longer. It had been a close call. A few more minutes would have been fatal.

Flames curling up through the hatchways and the deck growing hot under him reminded Jacob that the danger wasn't over. Later he would recall thinking what a good job his men had done for the fire to spread so fast - and how stupid his idea involving the magazine had been. He rose up on his elbows.

"The magazine is about to blow! Get off the ship!"

Jacob staggered to his feet and joined the others running for the gangplank, the cadets helping the two smoke victims. Jacob stopped and counted each man as he passed. When the count reached eight, he joined them on the dock.

They quickly headed upriver along the same path that Henry and the other cadets had taken. A hundred yards from the gangplank, a thundering roar sounded behind them that shook the ground and sent a shockwave crashing painfully against their ears that nearly knocked them down. The magazine had exploded.

Timbers rained down from a debris-filled plume of smoke overhead. The ship settled quickly into the river. Large sections of her deck and hull were gone. Jacob realized, with mixed feelings, that his plan to assure destruction of the ship was working to perfection.

They proceeded toward the depot. Richmond bustled with activity - soldiers running, citizens scurrying about. Clearly news of the evacuation had spread.

"Look there!" exclaimed Roger, feeling stronger now. "Smoke rising!"

They looked up the hill. Smoke drifted upward from buildings in a mostly industrial area between the river and the capitol building.

"The army has set fires!" said James. "They're burning warehouses holding anything that might be useful to the enemy!"

Jacob thought of Lydia. "You'd think they'd let the citizens have it."

"If there ain't enough security, things are gonna get bad," said a young cadet. "My folks were in Atlanta when it fell – fire, drunkenness, looting. It weren't pretty."

"Some of those people *are* drunk! Look at them!" said James. "And have you noticed the wind? Fire, wind, alcohol - they don't mix well."

Jacob felt sick to his stomach. Every bone in his body ached to go to Church Hill and protect Lydia. But he must honor his loyalty to the academy, to Captain Parker, the navy, his friends...

The Richmond & Danville Railroad Depot sat along the north bank of the river at the foot of 14th Street. From there the trains crossed a bridge and headed for Danville and points west. Captain Parker and the cadet corps were waiting.

"Congratulations, gentlemen," said the Captain. "It was a thankless job but you seem to have achieved it in fine fashion. The explosion shook the whole city."

"Thank you, sir," said Jacob. "It was a job we hated, but everyone did well. Will we, uhh, be departing soon?" He was still having thoughts of visiting Lydia.

"Very soon. The President and most of his cabinet are already on board. Each car is marked as a department – Executive, Treasury, War and so forth. We'll be the only escort for what will truly be a constantly moving government."

"How shall we deploy the cadets, sir?" asked Jacob. He knew now that he must put thoughts of visiting Lydia out of his mind.

"Divide them into two watches and assign six to the first and last cars. Spread the rest over the other cars. We should reach Danville tomorrow morning, then we'll see."

"Yes sir. By the way, sir, I have something here I thought you might want," said Jacob. He reached in his jacket and took out an object wrapped in paper. "I removed it from your cabin just as we were setting the fires..."

"My picture! Of Maggie and me! It was made ten years ago, soon after we were married! We've had to be apart so much...I've always kept it with me wherever I went." His eyes left the picture and went to Jacob. "I thought...I'd lost it forever. I can't...tell you how much..."

Choking with emotion, Captain Parker grabbed Jacob's hand in both of his. His voice had failed him, but his feelings spoke loud and strong.

Chapter Fourteen

Jacob and his friends watched curiously as Captain
Parker approached across the depot platform. Head down,
hands behind his back, he seemed preoccupied with
something. Jacob had noticed it earlier, and passed it off
as shock from seeing his ship destroyed, or perhaps
homesickness caused by recovering the photo he had
thought lost.

"Gentlemen, I have something to tell you," said the
Captain, pursing his lips. "I've received a rather startling
message from Secretary Mallory. Only a handful of cadets
are to be aboard the President's train."

A change of plans perhaps, but certainly not all that
startling, thought Jacob.

Roger asked the obvious question. "What about the rest
of us, sir?"

"We'll escort a second train, likely to be the last one out
of Richmond."

"But why, sir?" asked James.

"Because, gentlemen, that train will be carrying the
Confederate Treasury."

The boys didn't react; they didn't know how. Finally
Jacob ventured a guess.

"Sir, you mean...Treasury Secretary Trenholm...his
staff...all the records..."

"No, I mean the *treasury itself*. Half a million in gold,
silver and minted coin. It's already packed aboard that
train sitting yonder."

"And *we* are to guard it?" exclaimed Henry.

The Captain nodded. "Lower your voice. This isn't
public information."

"So they picked *us* over the army or marines?" said
James in a loud whisper. "What an honor - and what faith
and trust in us!"

"Indeed!" said Roger. "This could be the academy's
finest hour."

A wispy smile played on Jacob's face. He felt the same rush of pride as the others, but also read something less positive into the situation, something that could explain the Captain's unusual mood.

Trust and honor carry responsibility, in this case *major* responsibility. If the South hoped to continue its struggle, it must be able to pay its bills in hard currency, for its paper money was fast losing its value. Yet the bullion that would make that possible was being entrusted to forty young naval cadets. Yes, it could be their finest hour, but anything less than an honorable result could make it their worst hour.

Jacob knew the Captain had full faith in the cadets. That wasn't the issue. The issue was that a veteran regiment of 300 men would have been chosen if one had been available. But none was - sad proof of how far things had deteriorated. What practical chance, then, did the cadets have of an honorable result?

"I'll join you on the treasury train shortly," said the Captain as he walked away to speak to someone. Jacob caught up to him.

"Sir, if you have a moment, I have an idea," he said, speaking in a low voice. "Do you remember the eight cadets on my, uhh, list?"

"Hard to forget 'em, Buckner. Why?"

"Well, when you divide the cadets between the two trains, make sure those eight are among the ones aboard the treasury train..."

"Isn't that like putting the fox in the chicken coop?"

"It might seem so, but if handled right, a chicken coop can become a trap."

"How do you plan to do that?"

"I don't know yet."

* * *

The treasury train finally left the depot shortly after midnight, several hours behind the President's train. By then crowds of citizens, aware that it was the last train, had mobbed the platform and squeezed into every available space on board, even the car roofs. Captain Parker was forced to arm the cadets with two pistols each and order them to let no one else aboard.

They pulled away and headed west across Mayo's Bridge, stopping in the town of Manchester on the south bank to take on fuel. While this was being done, Jacob stood on the tailgate of the rearmost car, his anxiety mounting as he watched a horrible scene of panic and destruction unfolding behind him in Richmond.

Fires set to warehouses near the river by the army were spreading out of control and threatening government offices, the financial district and residential areas to the north and west. Whipped by high winds, flames leaped like ravenous monsters from windows and rooftops. Entire blocks were aglow. Huge landmarks like the Warwick Flour Mill and Gallego Mills were balls of fire from foundation to roof.

There was no sign of fire wagons, only shadowy figures running through the streets. Barrels of whiskey had been rolled out of warehouses by the authorities and smashed with axes, sending the contents gushing into the gutters. Thieves, deserters, vagrants and other types that always seem to appear at such times were scooping up the pungent liquid in any available container, including their hats, and drinking it. Drunken, demonic yells mingled with frenzied shouts as looters fought over stolen goods. Shots rang out, fired by law-abiding citizens trying to protect their property. Law and order had disintegrated. A state of anarchy existed.

Near Rockett's, the *Patrick Henry* and other vessels still burned violently, the flames reflecting off the water as if that too were on fire. From further downriver came the rumble of artillery as the rearguard of Lee's army defended a pontoon bridge so that the last of Lee's retreating troops could cross the river and head west.

Jacob gazed toward Church Hill but found his view impeded by smoke and flames. His heart came to his throat as he realized the fires were licking at the very base of the hill. As usually happens in moments of panic, his imagination took over and the images came faster than he could expel them – looters, drunks, marauding soldiers, houses burning, Lydia screaming for help...

No, he told himself. Lydia was strong and resourceful. She would be all right. He must steel himself and think of his duties, which right now must supersede any personal concerns. He prayed to God to protect her and keep her safe.

A massive explosion shook the ground as if from an earthquake. The train's windows rattled like tambourines. The eastern night sky came alive with exploding missiles resembling a huge fireworks display.

"The *Virginia II* just exploded," said the Captain. He had joined Jacob on the train's tailgate. "The explosion threw her shells in the air and lit their fuses. Now they're exploding. She's putting on quite a final show, isn't she?"

"Yeah," nodded Jacob. "Sad how anything so tragic could be so beautiful."

"And look there behind us. The army engineers are about to fire the bridges. You can see now why people were so anxious to get aboard this train."

A whistle sounded and the train lurched forward. The Captain left to check on other matters and Jacob stayed on the tailgate, watching the burning city retreat behind him. The engineers had set fire to turpentine-drenched logs piled along the bridges and trestles. Flames flicked upward, adding to the growing conflagration.

"Goodbye, Lydia," mumbled Jacob. *"Please be with her, God, until I return."*

* * *

The Presidential Train reached Danville, a tobacco and textile town to the west of Richmond near the North Carolina border, early on April 3rd. The citizens on board disbursed. Confederate officials hastened to set up a temporary government.

The treasury train with its cargo of $500,000 in gold, silver and minted coins, and escort of forty cadets, pulled in later that day. Jacob had walked the length of the train several times, inspecting the cars, the cargo, the cadet guards and their weapons. He found that only six of the eight cadets on his 'suspect' list were on board. Two from Richmond had decided to remain there with their families.

Neither Secretary Trenholm nor any high-ranking treasury official had made the trip from Richmond. A lowly teller was the ranking official present. Much to his chagrin, Captain Parker was forced to take charge of the treasure.

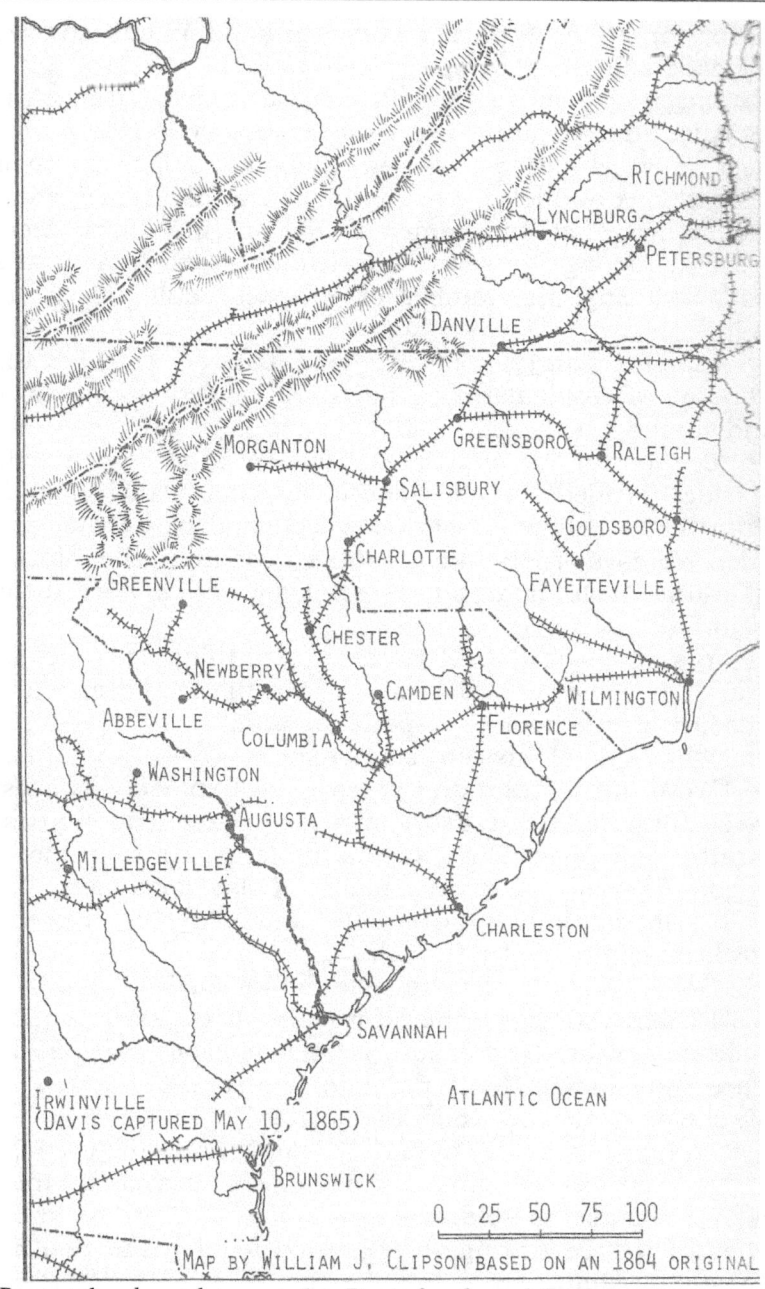

Route taken by cadets escorting Davis family and Confederate treasure.
Parker: Recollections of a Naval Officer

He promptly had the train pulled to a siding and ordered the cadets to set up camp adjacent to it.

They remained in Danville several days, guarding the treasure and awaiting Lee's army, said to be retreating west toward them. Seven cadets tendered their resignations and left for home. Since two had remained in Richmond, only thirty-one of the original forty were present. Among the seven who left were two from Jake's 'list', reducing the number of 'suspects' still present to four.

Apprehension grew by the hour. Late on April 6th, the Captain received alarming news. He pulled Jacob aside and shared it with him.

"Lee lost at Saylor's Creek. Half his army is gone. He appears headed for the mountains, not Danville, with Grant close behind. Enemy cavalry could be here at any time. We have orders to convey the treasure to the mint in Charlotte. Have the cadets break camp and go aboard the train."

"Yes sir," said Jacob. He hesitated, thinking. "Sir," he said after a moment. "I have an idea that could save the treasure, but it involves a special mission."

"What kind of mission, Lieutenant?"

"Word of this train and its cargo will spread. I suggest we secretly load the treasure on a wagon and send it cross-country to Raleigh. The Federals will look for a train, not a wagon. Raleigh's the state capital and also has a mint. The train can continue to Charlotte, but with the treasure boxes on board filled with rocks."

"Good. Will you take charge of the wagon?"

"I think you and I should remain on the train, sir, to make it appear the treasure is still on board. I'd like to place Midshipman Henry Stiles in command of the wagon. We can work out the other details later."

"All right. Who do you suggest should know the truth?"

"As few as possible unless we're attacked, then everyone must be told. The men have a right to know whether they're risking their lives defending the South's treasury or simply boxes full of rocks."

That afternoon, the cadets broke camp and moved aboard the treasury train. The Captain went to President

Davis and got approval to use 'any means necessary' to keep the treasure safe. Departure for Charlotte was set for the next morning.

Late that night, a freight wagon pulled up to the railroad siding and stopped beside the boxcar holding the treasure. The wagon carried a dozen sealed boxes filled with rocks. Henry was at the reins of the four-horse team, and with him on the wagon were four cadets hand-picked by Jacob.

Jacob stood in the door of the boxcar. Waiting beside the boxcar were Roger, James and four cadets also hand-picked by Jacob. They would switch the rock-filled boxes on the wagon with the treasure-filled ones in the boxcar.

"Bring those boxes from the wagon over here and set them in the doorway," Jacob whispered. "Quietly now, we mustn't attract attention."

The cadets in the wagon handed the boxes, one by one, to the cadets waiting on the ground. The latter carried them to the boxcar and sat them on the floor just inside the door. Jacob dragged them further inside from there.

Once the wagon was emptied, the reverse process began. Jacob slid the boxes in the boxcar to the door, where cadets hoisted them off and carried them to the cadets waiting in the wagon.

Ten minutes later the switch was complete. No one had noticed nor been disturbed, not even the sleeping cadets aboard the train. Henry flicked the reins, spoke softly to the horses and the wagon rolled off into the night. The four cadets aboard the wagon cradled their carbines and settled in for the long ride to Raleigh.

* * *

The treasury train left Danville for Charlotte on April 7th. Enemy cavalry was reported nearby. The train stopped in Greensboro where Captain Parker attempted to telegraph President Davis to confirm a message he had received from Charlotte. He had no success. He called Jacob, James and Roger together.

"It appears enemy cavalry has cut the telegraph between here and Danville, probably the railroad line too," said the Captain. "We must have left just in time. It's possible that President Davis has been captured."

"Should we go back, sir?" asked Roger.

"No, I'm praying the President left just after us, but there's nothing we could do anyhow. Besides, I've received a message that we have urgent business waiting in Charlotte. Supposedly the President's wife, Varina, and their children are there and need an escort to somewhere in Georgia."

"But sir...with all due respect to Mrs. Davis...is she aware that this is the treasury train?" asked James. "Protecting the treasure must be our first priority. I know it's no longer on board, but we must keep up appearances as if it were..."

"She's probably not aware that it's the treasury train," said the Captain. "But don't worry. We'll do nothing to jeopardize our mission. Varina will understand."

Jacob hoped the Captain was right, but he had serious doubts. Mrs. Davis might be the First Lady, but she was also a mother. It would be natural for her to place the well-being of her children ahead of the treasure. With her on board, the train would draw far more attention. His scheme, simple in concept, was fast becoming more complicated.

* * *

When the treasury train pulled into Greensboro on April 9th, President Davis was in Danville learning that General Lee had surrendered to Grant at Appomattox Court House. The President left Danville six hours later, one step ahead of Federal Cavalry, and headed south toward Greensboro.

On April 10th, the treasury train reached Salisbury, a town halfway between Greensboro and Charlotte, and parked on a siding for the night. A report of enemy cavalry just ahead had sparked fears that the train's engine noise would alert them.

Jacob had a hunch. The enemy close by, the train halted and about to reach Charlotte – if the spy was looking for a chance to tip off his friends in blue that the treasury was no longer on board the train but aboard a wagon bound for Raleigh, this would be the logical time and place.

Already the trap had been baited. The four cadets Jacob had picked to help Roger, James and him switch the boxes were, in fact, the four on his suspect list.

Jacob picked out a hidden spot on a knoll overlooking the tracks. From there he could see any activity around the train. He settled down for the night.

He relaxed and gazed down at the sleeping train, bathed in faint moonlight and quiet but for the soft hissing of the boiler's safety valve. He was struck by the serenity of the scene, far more serene than it had a right to be. Richmond in flames, Lee's army crumbling, the government in flight, Grant and Sherman closing in – it was clear that this war would end soon and not well for the South.

The war had changed the life of many people, but few more than him. The Amish boy who left home four years ago was gone now, replaced by a man. He had tasted every emotion from triumph to defeat, from fear to fulfillment. He had learned to fight, to love, to hate, to kill...and it wasn't over yet. Here he sat, hungry, tired, cold, trying to catch a fellow cadet in the act of spying while at the same time witnessing the last dying vestiges of the Confederacy. He couldn't imagine two more distasteful acts.

To top it off, catching the spy could be meaningless. If the Confederacy fell, with it would go all authority to prosecute the guilty party. Three years of treachery, of putting men in greater danger and likely costing lives, would go unpunished.

Then there were the decisions he would face. The Confederate Navy would be gone and with it his plans for a navy career. (He had no desire to be in the same ranks as Alonzo Peck.) His future would become a blank page. He knew only that he would begin by asking Lydia to marry him, then perhaps a brief visit to his mother...

Movement below! A figure emerged from a boxcar and strode silently through the shadows alongside the train. It appeared to be a cadet, but beyond that Jacob couldn't tell. The man stepped out of the shadows and broke into a trot.

Jacob descended the knoll and cautiously trotted after the man, just close enough to keep him in sight. He ran the descriptions of his four suspects through his mind but found the light too poor to come up with a match.

A dirt road ran near the tracks, then veered into the woods and led away from town. A citizen had informed them that the road was occupied by Federal Cavalry. The mystery cadet took the road. Now Jacob knew for sure. He was following the spy.

Twenty minutes had passed when suddenly up ahead the sharp challenge of a sentry broke the night silence. Jacob saw his quarry halt. Words were exchanged, and the sentry led the man toward a cluster of campfires. Jacob withdrew a safe distance back toward the train and sat down beside the road to wait.

He felt sick to his stomach. Light from the campfires had revealed the identity of the man.

* * *

"Where's Lieutenant Buckner?" asked Captain Parker.

"Don't know, sir. Haven't seen him this morning," said the cadet, snapping to attention. He was standing guard on the rear platform outside the Captain's car.

"Strange. We must get underway soon. Please find him and say that I wish to see him." The Captain went back inside his quarters.

Another day was unfolding. The sun had not yet appeared, but already the cadets had eaten breakfast and were at their posts. The Captain thought about going outside to enjoy a bit of fresh air before getting underway...

The door opened and the cadet to whom he had just spoken, beside himself now with excitement, awkwardly stumbled in, righted himself and quickly saluted.

"Sir, we've located Lieutenant Buckner, sir! He's in the lead car, just behind the locomotive. He...he asks that you come to him, sir!"

Captain Parker's eyebrows lifted. "Come to *him*?" he said gruffly. "I assume he has a good reason for that..."

"He's, uhh, holding a prisoner, sir."

The Captain's expression filled with a question, then an answer that led to more questions. But he decided those questions were best saved for Lieutenant Buckner.

He rushed from his car and charged headlong through two cars used as cadet sleeping quarters, the car holding the treasury boxes, then another car used as quarters. Cadets lined his way, all with questions on their faces that none dared ask right now. He reached the lead car, used for baggage, and barged in.

Jacob sat on a trunk holding a pistol. Standing nearby was James Morgan, also holding a pistol. In a corner across from them, sitting on the floor, was Roger Phillips.

Captain Parker stared at Roger, then Jacob, then James, then Roger again. His jaw fell further with each shift of direction.

"Don't tell me! Mr. Phillips? There *has* to be a mistake!"

"I followed him straight to a Yankee cavalry camp, sir," said Jacob grimly. "I saw him go in and grabbed him on the way out. I'm afraid there's no mistake, sir." He turned his back in disgust rather than look at his former friend.

Captain Parker stepped closer to Roger and bent over him. "Is it true? On second thought, save your breath! I can see it's true from the look on your face!"

The Captain looked away. When he turned back, his fists had clenched and his face was blood red. "You've been with me longer than anyone! I trusted you as I would my own son! How could you do this?"

Roger had his eyes lowered, clearly shaken and embarrassed. "I'm...sorry, sir, but I'd rather not talk about it."

"As you wish, Mr. Phillips. I'm placing you under arrest for treason. You will be tried by court-martial. If found guilty, you will face a firing squad."

Captain Parker turned to leave but changed his mind. "Mr. Buckner, I'm told the enemy cavalry has gone. No doubt this traitor told them of the wagon and its supposed cargo, and they've gone to search for it. Your double-switch worked to perfection. Congratulations."

"Double-switch?" asked James. In the corner, Roger's ears perked up.

"The treasure never left the train," said Jacob. "The boxes we put on the wagon were the same ones that came off the wagon in the first place. Henry and the Captain were the only ones besides me who knew."

Chapter Fifteen

Captain Parker opened his old, well-traveled sea chest and held up a bottle. "This is the last of my brandy, Mr. Buckner, but I expect we could both use a little right now. Will you join me?"

They sat in the Captain's quarters as the train rumbled and creaked toward Charlotte. With Roger arrested the previous day, neither had slept well.

"Thank you sir, but no," said Jacob. "My brother and I got into some bad wine once. Made us sick for days. Never had any real desire for alcohol since."

"Well, if you don't need it now you never will. Hope you don't mind if I have a little." He filled a pewter tumbler with the amber liquid.

Jacob nodded his understanding. "You know, Roger was my best friend," he said, shaking his head. "I never *once* suspected him. He wasn't even on my *list!*"

"If he'd been on your list, I'd have thought you were out of your mind," said the Captain. He timidly tasted the brandy, followed the taste with a healthy sip, and soon the tumbler that had been lifted full was set down empty.

"The hardest thing for me is trying to understand why he did it," said Jacob.

"For me also," nodded Captain Parker, refilling his tumbler. "He betrayed us and now he'll most likely face execution."

"How soon do you think a court martial can be convened?"

"Hopefully in Charlotte. We must move quickly or the war will end and he'll go free. Friend or not, we can't allow that. He likely cost some men their lives."

* * *

The treasury train pulled into Charlotte on April 11th, nine days after leaving Richmond. Everyone was fatigued and shaken by the chain of hectic events, not the least of which was the arrest of one of their own. Captain Parker deposited the treasure in the mint and breathed a sigh of relief at being rid of it.

But when the Captain went to the navy office to request that a court martial be convened, he found that all naval personnel had fled the city. Federal Cavalry was reported advancing through Salisbury, the town they had left just the day before.

Captain Parker also learned that Varina Davis and her children were indeed in Charlotte. He visited her and offered his command as an escort. Not knowing her husband's whereabouts, Mrs. Davis at first declined in favor of staying in Charlotte to await word from him, but when told of the advancing enemy, she accepted.

Henry Stiles and his four-cadet squad thundered into Charlotte later that night aboard their wagon, empty now, for the rock-filled boxes had been jettisoned. The Captain summoned Henry, James and Jacob to a meeting in his quarters.

"Well, instead of ridding ourselves of the treasure, it appears we now have responsibility for both the treasure *and* the President's family," he said.

"The *enemy's* on our trail!" exclaimed Henry. "Wouldn't she be in less danger traveling alone? I mean, I hear she was enough of a looker to attract men's attention when she was younger, but now..."

"It would still be risky for her," said the Captain. "There are those who blame her husband for recent events and might direct their frustration at her."

"What the First Lady *looks* like isn't the issue, Henry. Our first priority is the treasure," said Jacob. "But since you have such a sharp eye for the ladies, how about if you be her personal escort? Perhaps she can improve your taste in ear rings."

"Uhh, anything to...to be helpful," said Henry. "How... far is she going?"

"She only wishes to avoid capture and rejoin her husband," said the Captain. "I told her that to keep moving was more important than the destination right now, but that we'd pro'bly head for Macon, Georgia and then let events dictate our route."

"Any word from the President or General Lee?" asked James.

"No, but the signs aren't good," said the Captain. "Both the telegraph and railroad lines coming from Virginia are cut. We'll be leaving here shortly. Have the cadets pull the treasure from the mint and put it back aboard the train."

* * *

For the next two weeks, the cadets and Captain Parker escorted the treasure and the President's family on a twisting, roundabout route through South Carolina and Georgia. From Charlotte the train traveled to Chester, S.C., where the absence of a rail line running south forced them to go aboard wagons for a forty-five mile overland trip to Newberry, S.C. There they went back aboard a train for the short ride to Abbeville, S.C., then again switched to wagons for a second overland trip, this one forty miles to Washington, Georgia, crossing the Savannah River by ferry.

Not relishing a second trip aboard a wagon, Mrs. Davis chose to remain in Abbeville to await word of her husband. Henry's duty as her escort ended there. Despite initial doubts, he had enjoyed his brief time with the First Lady.

In Washington, Captain Parker learned that Macon, their destination, had fallen to Federal Cavalry. The enemy was now ahead *and* behind them. Disaster appeared imminent. Dire reports circulated, including one that General Lee had surrendered to General Grant a week earlier at Appomattox.

The Captain had the treasure again put aboard a train and decided to change course, heading for Augusta, Georgia. He knew there were Confederate forces in Augusta, including a naval officer senior to him. He hoped also to find a treasury official to whom he could turn over the treasure.

"Sir, if Lee has indeed surrendered, isn't the war over?" asked James. He and several others sat with Captain Parker as the train headed for Augusta.

"Not at all, Mr. Morgan," said the Captain gruffly. "The war isn't over as long as there are Confederate forces in the field, and as far as I know, Generals Johnston and Beauregard are still fighting Sherman."

"And remember, we've been charged with guarding the treasure no matter what," added Jacob. "That will remain our duty until we're properly relieved."

"That's correct," nodded the Captain. "I don't intend to relinquish the coin and bullion to anyone except the President himself or a top treasury official."

The group scattered. Jacob walked toward the head of the train to see if the engineer planned to stop for fuel before reaching Augusta. He found himself passing through the car in which Roger was being held, guarded by two armed cadets.

"Hello, Jake."

Jacob ignored the voice. He had not talked with Roger nor even laid eyes on him since the night he brought him in. Despite his better judgment, he relented and glanced sullenly at his former friend.

"Hello, Roger."

"Is that the Savannah River? Guess I won't be fishing much for awhile..."

Jacob gritted his teeth at the lame attempt to gain sympathy. "You can stow that, Roger! You betrayed us! We plan to see that you *never* fish again."

"Well, we had some good times. What...does the Captain plan to do?"

Jacob knew he shouldn't share information with a prisoner, but either Roger was feigning, or he didn't fully appreciate the seriousness of what he had done.

"He plans to have you executed," said Jacob with a sneer. He was deliberately trying to sound cold-blooded. A traitor deserved nothing less in his opinion.

Roger, momentarily taken aback, composed himself and nodded. "I expected as much. My only regret is that I disappointed you and the fellas."

Jacob felt a twinge of compassion but quickly funneled it into anger. "You're a traitor, Roger! You cost men their lives! Why? Why'd you do that?"

"I'm not sure you'd understand..."

"The *Underwriter* raid, White House Landing – you betrayed us time after time! You're right, I'll prob'ly not understand, but try me anyhow."

Roger sighed. "Well, you remember I told you how my foster father beat us, kept us locked up, gave us hog slop for food and even, you know, raped my sisters?"

"Yeah, I remember. So you decided to get even by 'raping' your friends?"

"No, but it reminded me of how slaves are treated. Every time he beat me or took one of my sisters, I'd think 'this is the way slaves live'. It got so I identified with slaves. I developed a...a sympathy, a kind of...bond with them."

"Don't know much about slaves. The Amish do their own work," said Jacob.

"Yes, but suppose you were made to do another man's work while he sat and watched and reaped the benefits? And on top of that, suppose he whipped you or raped your family members? Those are things slaves live with, part of their world."

"I've known folks who owned slaves. It's not like that, at least not often."

"Well, once is too often," said Roger. "I know this war is about more than just slavery, but there's one fact you can't deny. If the South wins, slavery goes on. If the North wins, it doesn't. That's all that matters to me."

"If you're against the Confederacy, why didn't you just volunteer to fight for the Union? At least that would have been honorable! After my brother died, I didn't join the side that *killed* him, I joined the other side so I could *fight against* his killers!"

Roger nodded. "Perhaps I should have, but I wanted to be near my sisters. If I'd joined the Union, I'd have been stuck miles away without a chance to even visit."

Jacob could understand Roger's strong feelings about how his sisters were treated. He could even understand how that might turn him against slavery. But to go from there to treason was a big jump, one he didn't understand at all, and clearly one not justified by simply wanting to be near his sisters.

Roger's childhood obviously messed up his thinking, figured Jacob. He had seen cases like that before. It was hard enough for a person with a *good* upbringing to turn out as expected. In his case, for example, he had undergone endless hours of teachings against violence, yet he joined the military.

"Jake, I'm ready to face a firing squad if I have to," said Roger. "I deserve it, and besides, I didn't expect to survive this war anyhow. But what if the war ends?"

"The war is over when the Captain says it's over. He plans to declare Martial Law if need be, and have the trial and execution quickly, probably in Augusta. He says we can't let you go unpunished after what you did. I happen to agree with him."

Roger nodded. "I see. So...the firing squad will consist of cadets. That's fitting. I like that. Perhaps you'll let me choose the members."

Jacob was trying to scare Roger, to punish him in his own way, but instead Roger seemed to be enjoying this talk with his ex-best friend. Jacob decided to change course.

"Who was your contact?"

"My what?"

"Your contact, your middleman, the person who received your information and passed it on."

"I didn't have one."

"That's a lie, Roger. We know you weren't alone." Jacob was bluffing again. "Now, if you give us his identity, things might go easier for you."

"Did Captain Parker send you here?"

"No, but I could talk to him."

"Well, you side-stepped my question about the war, but I hear General Lee has surrendered," said Roger, "and your little 'double-switch' may have extended the life of the Confederate treasure, but sooner or later it'll be captured. The Confederacy's time is short, Jake, a matter of days. Call it Martial Law if you like, but if you execute me after the war ends it'll be murder."

"I wouldn't rule that out," said Jacob, caressing the pistol on his belt. "There's confusion in the last days of a war. Feelings run high and things happen."

"I know you better than that, Jake. But I *will* admit I had a contact. Tell you what, if this war ends and I'm still alive, I'll give you the name."

* * *

The Savannah River forms the boundary between South Carolina to the north and Georgia to the south. Augusta sits on the south bank. The train arrived there at noon on April 21st. Captain Parker reported to Brigadier General Fry and Commodore Hunter, the senior army and navy officers present.

"Federal Cavalry will be here by morning," said General Fry, "and our forces are far too meager to mount an effective defense."

"A Union ship is on its way upriver from Savannah," added Commodore Hunter. "Her heavy guns can destroy the town. Our only choice is to surrender, but first we plan to destroy records, burn military supplies, and scuttle a small gunboat that's in our harbor. We have much to do. You may want to head for a safer place."

"Scuttle a small gunboat? My cadets can handle that," said Captain Parker. "Then we'll board the train and be on our way."

"Surely you plan to pay out the treasure to our soldiers first, don't you?" said the General. "There's no point in surrendering it to the enemy..."

"Are those by chance the same soldiers who aren't available to defend your city? No, I have no authority to do that," snapped the Captain, irked at the attitude of the two men and half sorry he had volunteered his men to help them.

The Captain returned to the train and issued orders for the cadets – and the treasure - to remain on board ready for quick departure. Then he dispatched Jacob, Henry and James to the waterfront to scuttle the gunboat.

* * *

"Reminds me of the old *Beaufort!*" said Henry as the three boys came into view of the docked gunboat. "This should be easy work."

"Looks like some of her crew are still on board," said James.

"Good. We haven't much time and they can help," said Jacob.

"Uh-oh, hold on!" said Henry. "I don't think those men are part of her crew."

Henry nodded toward a much larger warship, bristling with guns, anchored out in the harbor among smaller ships. The three cadets quickly ducked behind cover, for the big ship flew the Union flag.

"My God, how'd we miss that?" exclaimed James.

"Failure to study our surroundings – a basic rule of tactics," said Jacob with a frown. "We nearly walked into a detail of Yankee jack-tars."

"That ain't all," said Henry, gazing at the big ship. "I hate to tell you, Jake, but those are your old friends. That's the *Arapahoe* out there."

"What?" Jacob spun toward his friend. "You're wrong! I'd know the *Arapahoe* anywhere! That ship is different..."

"She's been refitted," said Henry. "Different rigging, the hull painted. But look at the superstructure, the gun deck, the shape of the bow - it's the *Arapahoe*."

Jacob looked again. Henry was right. It was the ship that had haunted him, that had terrorized his waking hours and tormented his sleep, and that set his blood to boiling at first sight.

He had struggled to relegate the ship and Alonzo Peck to the back of his mind in the belief that he would never see them again, but here was the *Arapahoe*, a year later and 400 miles from where he had last seen her. It ignited a flood of bad memories - of Joshua's death, the hatred, the obsession for revenge...

Also flooding back came the same feeling that had proven correct at White House Landing, the ominous feeling that Peck was close at this very moment. He had given up all hope of avenging Joshua's death, but now he felt certain he was about to get another chance.

"What do we do now, Lieutenant?" James asked. "Lieutenant...?"

Jacob's mind was in limbo, caught between leaving to warn the train and staying to look for Peck. He shook his head, trying to clear the emotional fog.

"Uhh, you and Henry go and warn Captain Parker. The train must leave soon or we'll lose the treasure. If I'm not back, leave without me."

"But what are you...?"

"I said go! That's an order!"

The two midshipmen slipped away and Jacob turned his attention back to the waterfront. Four Union sailors on board the Confederate gunboat were busily bringing up items from below and packing them in crates – papers, log books, a sextant, a pistol. One sailor worked to free the ship's brass bell from its mount. They were looting the ship of anything important as well as souvenirs for themselves.

A few moments later, an officer emerged from below deck, gestured toward the crates and pointed to the *Arapahoe* out in the harbor. The sailors picked up the crates and headed down the gangplank and along the dock to a waiting launch. The officer went back below deck.

Jacob's eyes followed the officer closely, glaring at him as if he were the devil himself. Indeed, to Jacob he was. The man was Alonzo Peck.

If he had boarded the ship and unwittingly walked up on Peck, it would have been like putting his hand on a copperhead snake, thought Jacob. But now with the snake's presence known, things were different. He stood up and strode toward the ship with his hand resting on his revolver.

Peck reappeared on deck carrying a box and sat it near the rail. As he paused to catch his breath, he spotted Jacob and quickly drew his pistol.

"Get'cha hands off that gun, rebel, or I'll shoot you dead!" yelled Peck.

"Not a chance, Peck!" yelled Jacob. He slipped his revolver from its holster and continued walking toward his enemy.

"Do I know you, rebel?"

"You killed my little brother, Peck, and a year ago you almost killed me. This time it's my turn."

"Yeah, I remember you, and I remember that little whelp you called a brother! Just keep comin', reb! The closer you get the easier you make this!"

Jacob bristled and kept walking, pistol at his side, his grip tightening around the handle. He ascended the gangplank onto the deck. He was twenty feet from his adversary, the closest he had been since the day Peck killed Joshua. Shaking with anger and tension, he said a silent prayer, for he knew one of them would likely die in the next few minutes.

Peck gritted his teeth. "I warned you, rebel!" In one quick motion he cocked his pistol and fired, the gun's sharp report echoing across the harbor.

The impact staggered Jacob. Searing pain shot through his right arm and blood poured down his sleeve from just below his shoulder. But he wasn't about to back down. He would rather die than back down. He switched the pistol to his left hand, leveled it at Peck and continued forward, trailing a stream of blood across the deck.

Peck's eyes grew wide and froze. He had fired too quickly. Jacob's intentions were clear to him now, and he knew that he was courting death and if he cocked his pistol again, it would come quickly.

Jacob placed the muzzle inches from Peck's forehead and cocked the hammer. Peck dropped his pistol, all of his courage gone and replaced now by fear. He stared at Jacob, shaking, the blank look on his face turning to panic.

"This...war's over! Lee surrendered...!"

Jacob showed no repentance. He moved the pistol closer, until the muzzle rested squarely against Peck's forehead.

"Not quite over," he said calmly. "This is for Joshua." He pulled the trigger. The gun roared. Peck's head disappeared in a burst of smoke.

Peck fell backward onto the deck. As the smoke cleared, he righted himself and frantically searched for blood, but found none. Jacob had moved the muzzle just enough to send the ball whistling past Peck's head.

Jacob turned and walked away, in a daze, weak from loss of blood, not at all sure why he had moved the gun.

He had walked ten feet when he sensed movement behind him and spun around, so lightheaded from loss of blood that he nearly lost his balance. Peck had picked up the pistol and was leveling it at him. Jacob blinked hard and fired.

The ball entered Peck's forehead and exited the back, taking a section of skull with it. Peck was dead before he hit the deck.

Weak, barely able to stay erect, Jacob dropped the pistol and peered down at his lifeless enemy. He felt no emotion. The last five minutes seemed like a dream, a theater play in which he was but a spectator. He wasn't even sure he understood everything that had happened. Maybe tomorrow he would feel...

The sound of thunder rumbled from out in the harbor, followed by the high-pitched whistle of an incoming shell. A second later the shell screamed through the ship's rigging and exploded in an embankment on shore. The *Arapahoe's* captain had witnessed what had happened and was trying to defend his officer.

His blood-soaked shirt and spinning head told Jacob that he must get back to the train quickly or die from loss of blood - or a shell. He pressed his left hand against the wound and tried to clear his head enough to get his bearings, then staggered away in the direction he thought he had come.

Chapter Sixteen

"You were fortunate, Lieutenant. The bullet just missed the bone," said the medical officer. "A half inch to the right and we'd be amputating your arm. Just keep it clean and bandaged for a couple weeks and you should be fine."

Jacob had staggered up the steps of the train's rearmost car, pushed through the door into Captain Parker's quarters and collapsed on the floor. The Captain quickly summoned a medical officer who stemmed the bleeding and bandaged the arm. Jacob lay on a bunk now, gradually recovering his strength.

'Thank you, doctor," he said. He turned his head toward the Captain. "Sir, we must...get underway immediately! It's the *Arapahoe*...they'll be looking for us!"

"Mr. Stiles and Mr. Morgan told me," said the Captain. "Steam pressure is up and we'll be leaving shortly. I understand you went to look for your old enemy. You shouldn't have done that alone. Is he the one who shot you?"

Jacob nodded. "Something I had to do, sir, but...it's over now."

"I assume you killed him and that it was self defense. Were there witnesses?"

Jacob shook his head. "I don't...think so, sir, and yes, it was self defense."

The Captain nodded. "I had to know in case there are questions. The war is very nearly over. Lee's surrender is confirmed and General Johnston has arranged a truce with General Sherman. If the truce turns into surrender, that's the end of it."

"A sad day," said Jacob. "What...will we do now, Captain?"

"Mrs. Davis' presence in Abbeville will likely draw the President there," said the Captain. "So we'll head back to Abbeville and if he appears, we'll turn the treasure over to him. It's nothing but an anchor around our neck, and frankly, I'm tired of dealing with it. If it were up to me, I'd as soon dump it in the river!"

The train shuddered into motion and gained speed as it headed back toward Abbeville by way of Washington, Georgia, the town the cadets had left two days before. Jacob, his bandaged arm in a sling, lay on his bunk gazing out the train window.

He had suffered a wound that nearly cost him an arm, and he had witnessed two monumental events that would leave even deeper scars – the death of Alonzo Peck and the probable end of the war – all in the same day. It seemed surreal, as blurred as the Georgia pines slipping past the window.

He remembered facing Peck on the deck with guns drawn. He remembered the pain and blood as the bullet tore through his arm. Then a haze closed around him and grew thicker as he continued to lose blood. He could not recall returning to the train.

He had no doubt that he had fired in self defense. His vision might have been impaired but there was no mistaking Peck leveling his pistol at him. That image would remain chiseled in his mind forever. Nor did he have any doubt that he had given Peck every chance to live. The burning question, the thing most unclear and most haunting, was why had he done that?

He had confronted Peck for the sole purpose of killing him. Most legal and religious laws - Amish law being an exception - condoned killing in time of war. But the war was ending and so was his window of opportunity. When he put the gun to Peck's head, every fiber of his heart and soul screamed at him to kill this man who had killed his brother, and to do it while he had the chance. There would be no guilt, no regrets, and no consequences.

Why, then, had he pulled the muzzle to one side at the last second? His focus had been clear enough. His hand did not slip. Yet almost subconsciously, he had swung the gun to one side, and he didn't know why.

* * *

After leaving Augusta on April 23rd and experiencing several delays due to roaming Federal cavalry, the train reached Washington, Georgia on the 26th. There they again went aboard wagons for the overland trip to Abbeville and arrived in that town two days later. Captain Parker had the treasure stored in a building on the town square and ordered the cadets to take up quarters in the same building.

They found the town full of paroled soldiers from Lee's army making their way back home. These men had not been paid in months and word of the treasury's presence quickly spread among them. Hearing a rumor of a possible night attack, the Captain doubled the guard and went to bed for a few hours of uneasy sleep.

He was awakened early and told that a troop of cavalry had been spotted on a hill outside town. He dispatched two scouts, who returned with word that the horsemen were in fact President Davis' advance guard. The scholarly gentleman himself rode into town at ten o'clock that morning. The Captain had guessed the President's route exactly.

Eager to rid himself of the treasure and receive new orders, Captain Parker promptly arranged a meeting with President Davis. An hour later, he returned and gave the cadets an update.

"Secretary Mallory and acting Treasury Secretary Reagan are with the President," said the Captain. "We are to turn the treasure over to Secretary Reagan."

"What will happen to it then?" hollered a cadet in back.

"Yeah, there are plenty of scallywags about, not to mention those traveling with the President!" yelled another cadet. Scattered snickers rippled through the ranks.

"Why not distribute part of it to these paroled fellas passing through town?" asked Jacob. "They stayed with Lee to the very end, they haven't been paid, and they'll surely need it for their families when they reach home." Others nodded.

"I suggested that very thing to the President, and he said he'd consider it," said the Captain. "Clearly it'll not be needed by the government anymore."

"Whadaya mean, Captain?" asked another voice in back.

"The war's over, gentlemen. The President and his cabinet are wanted men now. They're fleeing to avoid arrest."

One of the strangest of human phenomena always seemed to occur when something of a sad or dreaded nature, even though widely expected, actually happened. It evoked the same shock and dismay as if it were a total surprise. That was what happened now.

The cadets stood as lost for words as a group of mutes. Henry dropped to his knees and stared at the ground. James gazed skyward as if the world were ending. Jacob subconsciously rubbed his injured arm. Others openly wept. It was as if they had lost their parents and home in one fell swoop. In a sense, they had.

"What...will happen to us, Captain?" ventured Henry. As one of the most senior cadets, he felt more lost than most.

"Our duty is done. You'll each receive a letter from me shortly giving you freedom to follow your own pursuits. I must say that I am richer for having known each of you. Commanding you has been a pleasure greater than any I could have wished for. I thank you for your loyal service and ask God to look over you in your new endeavors. I'm afraid we'll all need His help. Cadets – attention! Dismissed!"

* * *

A few days later, the cadets received the letter promised by Captain Parker. Hoping for a reunion at some point, he directed them to stay in touch with Secretary Mallory, but the reunion never occurred. The letter appears below, verbatim:

Abbeville, S.C., May 2, 1865
SIR: You are hereby detached from the naval
school, and leave is granted you to visit your home.
You will report by letter to the Hon. Secretary of the
Navy as soon as practicable. Paymaster Wheless will
issue you ten days rations, and all quartermasters
are requested to furnish you transportation.
Respectfully your obedient servant,
Wm. H. Parker, commanding

* * *

The downhearted cadets slowly dragged themselves to the empty building that had served as their quarters and began packing what little of their belongings remained. They had brought little with them from Richmond and a month of constant movement, guarding the treasure night and day, had left them with worn-out bodies and equally worn-out clothing.

Everyone wandered around the big room as if lost, speaking with this person or that, wishing each other well, all the time dreading the final goodbye. They had been through much together - the classroom, manning the big guns, raids, back to the classroom, a blend of academia and action that molded them into first-rate naval officers. Camaraderie had grown to high levels. They would miss it.

Jacob glumly made the rounds and said his goodbyes, speaking with most of the thirty cadets still present. Saving the hardest for last, he approached Henry and James as they collected their personal items and tied them inside their blanket rolls.

"Well Jake, I guess it's over," said James. "Makes me sad, because I have a feeling this could be the highlight of our lives."

"You might be right," nodded Jacob. "We've seen and taken part in a lot of history being made. Just be grateful we lived through it."

"Had some close calls, didn't we?" said Henry, tossing his blanket roll over his shoulder. "Roanoke Island, the *Underwriter*, the York River...but you know what? I'll miss it, and I'll miss you fellas too."

"We'll *all* miss each other," nodded Jacob. "What'll you do now, Henry?"

"Oh, I'll go home to New Bern, be the mate on my pa's fishing trawler."

"Once a sailor, always a sailor, huh?" said Jacob."What about you, James?"

"Well, with most of the slaves gone, my father will need help with the land. Might have to sell most of it, maybe keep the best thousand acres. Even with me and my two brothers, and a few loyal hands, there'll be plenty to do."

"A thousand acres?" exclaimed Henry, his eyebrows going up. "How much land ya'll own down there in Loosy'anna anyhow?"

"We're small for a rice plantation. Maybe twenty-five hundred acres."

"Heckofva time to find out we've got such a rich friend, huh Jake?" exclaimed Henry. "Think of all the beer he could've bought us!"

"That's why I never told you," smiled James. "But I'll tell you this. Ya'll come down to Cajun country, and I'll treat you to the best shrimp and catfish supper you ever ate. Cornbread, okra, fresh tomatoes and butterbeans..."

"Sounds mighty good. We might just do that. I know Jake here likes fish," nodded Henry. "What *about* you, Jake. What are your plans?"

"I'm heading back to Richmond to ask a certain beautiful lady to marry me. We'll get hitched, and then decide what we want to do."

Later that day, at the request of Captain Parker, a Federal officer arrived from nearby Washington, Georgia. The officer accepted the surrender of the Captain and cadets, administered the oath of allegiance and issued them the proper papers.

Captain Parker had a supply of bacon, coffee and sugar distributed to each man along with two $20 gold pieces he had withheld from the treasure as back pay. Thus supplied, the cadets departed in all directions. The Confederate Naval Academy had passed into history.

* * *

Eager to see Lydia, Jacob lost no time heading for Richmond. Traveling by train and wagon, he went from Abbeville to Newberry, then Chester and Charlotte and on up the line, reversing the path the cadets had taken with the treasure heading south.

Ironically, traveling the same route was Roger Phillips, free now and on his way home to Amelia County, just west of Richmond. Jacob noticed his former friend setting alone in one of the cars as they passed through Greensboro. They had not spoken since their talk ten days earlier aboard the train heading for Augusta.

"Jake, would you join me for a minute?" called Roger as Jacob passed by.

Jacob paused. "Well, for a minute." He slid into the seat next to Roger.

"I hear you finally settled the score with Alonzo Peck," said Roger. "He give you that wound to your arm?"

"Yeah," Jacob said, frowning. He preferred not to talk about that day.

Roger misinterpreted Jacob's frown. "I guess you're disappointed about me cheating the firing squad..."

Jacob shrugged. "That's the way the chips fall. War's over now."

"Well, it seems silly to apologize for not being dead, so I'll just say I did what I had to do. My only real regret is ruining our friendship."

"Actually, I've been thinking about what you did. We both had grudges, but of a different kind. You wanted to abolish slavery and I wanted to settle a score. My grudge was with an individual and yours with an institution. Looking at it that way, I get a better idea of why you did what you did."

"You don't know how much it means to hear you say that, Jake."

"Yeah, well, that may be, but I still say you should've just joined the Union. If you intended to kill me, I'd have preferred you do it to my face, not my back."

Roger cringed. The remark cut deep, but he couldn't deny the truth in it.

"I understand," he nodded, his chest heaving. "So, with the war over, what're your plans now?"

"I intend to ask Lydia Schenk to marry me. We'll make our plans after that."

"I...didn't know ya'll were that serious. Do you think she'll have you?"

"Without a doubt," Jacob nodded. "We've grown very close."

The look on Roger's face turned deadly serious. He grew quiet for the first time since Jacob sat down.

"I just remembered something I promised you awhile back," he said. "It isn't going to help our friendship, but that's wrecked anyhow and it's something you need to know. I told you that if I survived the war, I'd tell you the name of my contact."

"Yeah, I remember, but what good will that do now?"

"Given your plans, it could do a lot of good. My contact was Lydia."

"You lying sonofa...! That's impossible! Why are you telling me that?"

Jacob arose and clenched his hands into fists. He was sorry he had sat down and wanted to get away from Roger. His only decision was whether to hit him first.

"Because it's true, Jake, and if you plan to marry her, you needed to know."

"You're lying, Roger! You're lucky I don't kill you!"

"She's a Northerner! Didn't you wonder how she could make a living selling a few flowers? In winter? Did you ever see any customers? She was a *paid spy!*"

Jacob stormed out of his seat and started up the aisle. Three strides later he spun around, returned to Roger and bent low over his face.

"I'll be going to see Lydia the minute I get off this train," he said, gritting his teeth. "If you're lying, you'll need somewhere a lot bigger than Amelia County to hide, you understand?"

"I did you a favor, Jake! Why would I lie?"

* * *

Trains going south from Virginia in the spring of 1865 were full, while those heading north to Virginia tended to be less crowded. It was a normal consequence of the war's end as ex-Confederate soldiers and officials headed back home.

Given his choice of seats, Jacob chose one several cars removed from Roger, where he could sit in solitude for the rest of the trip. He gazed out the window but saw little scenery of any note, or at least he wasn't aware of seeing any.

It made no sense to him. Yes, Lydia was from Pennsylvania, and yes, she had insisted on staying in Richmond after the evacuation. And it was true that her flower shop seemed to generate little activity.

But she came from an Amish background. She hated war, crime, violence of any kind. She had lost her fiancé at

Gettysburg. Her fiancé's parents still helped her with food and no doubt money too. Any suggestion that Lydia was a spy was laughable.

Of course, he would never have suspected Roger either, thought Jacob. And to quote Roger, why would he lie?

Then it all clicked. Roger was a *spy*, and spies were habitual *liars*. He had *lived* a lie for four years. To him it was a way of life, a habit probably formed to cope with his rough childhood, and that habit had come out as he tried to get even for being caught. He intended no physical harm to Lydia, only mental anguish to the man who had caught him. He would go and see Lydia first, thought Jacob, just to make sure of his ground. Then he would pay a visit to Amelia County.

He sat back and gazed out the window, feeling better, enjoying the scenery for the first time since they left Greensboro. Funny, he thought, but before he left home he had never ridden a train. They were a symbol of that way of life the Amish renounced and viewed as sinful. Now, as if branded for rejecting Amish ways, his bottom was calloused from hours of riding trains.

He looked out the window, his anticipation growing. They appeared to be nearing Richmond. Soon he would be in Lydia's arms.

* * *

Even before the train crossed the newly-repaired bridge over the river into Richmond, Jacob could see that the latter wasn't the same city he had left.

The center section, from the capital to the canal boat turning basin and from 9th Street down to Rocketts, looked as devastated as a gutted body, a wasteland of roofless brick walls, tottering chimneys, and scattered stacks of salvaged bricks. Primary streets had been cleared but most others remained clogged with debris.

Seeming strangely out of place, sentries in bright blue uniforms guarded the intersections. The capitol building still gleamed atop its hill like the Parthenon, except now the Union stars and stripes flew from the tallest flagpole on its roof. In the waters of the James near Rockett's, a salvage vessel worked to remove the burned and sunken

Richmond after evacuation fire - Capital building on hill. Courtesy, Library of Congress

hulks of the school ship *Patrick Henry*, the *Virginia II* and the *Jamestown*.

The train pulled into the station at the foot of 14th Street and came to a stop. As Jacob disembarked, it occurred to him that this was the same station from which the cadets had departed Richmond a month earlier, their spirits high at the prospect of escorting their government and its treasury to safety. The outcome was not what they envisioned, but everyone knew that no one could have done more.

Jacob swung his blanket roll over his shoulder and strolled toward the dock area, stretching his legs. Downriver, he could see the wreckage of the *Patrick Henry* and the work going on to clear it from the river. He knelt down, rested his wounded arm on one knee and watched for a moment, his mind drifting back.

Virginia II, Patrick Henry and Jamestown scuttled in James River by their crews. Courtesy, Library of Congress

The navy had given him the home and family he had sorely needed, and most of it was spent aboard that ship. Experiences there had changed him and created memories he would never forget. Now, like so many other things, the last earthly vestige of those experiences, those memories, was being summarily discarded as if no one cared. He sighed, brushed a tear from his cheek and turned away.

Following the route he had traversed many times, Jacob walked up 17th Street to Broad Street, turned right onto Broad and headed up Church Hill. As he neared St. John's Church, a Federal sentry stepped in front of him.

"Halt, mister," said the sentry, a boy of about eighteen. "You a rebel soldier? I need t'see your parole papers!"

221

"I was a sailor, not a soldier," said Jacob, irritated at this delay in reaching Lydia. "When you get old enough t'shave, be careful o'those razors. They're sharp ya'know." He yanked a slip of paper from his pocket.

The young sentry snatched the paper and glanced over it. "All right, you may proceed about your biz'ness, rebel, but *watch your mouth!*" He handed the paper back.

Jacob knew he shouldn't have ribbed the sentry; the boy could have arrested him - but it sure made him feel better. He hurried along towards Lydia's house.

At the top of the hill Jacob passed St. John's Church. He glanced at the heavy wooden entrance and his mind flashed back to the day he went inside. Even now, he was certain he had been in the presence of God that day.

The familiar fence and rose garden in Lydia's yard were still in place. He was concerned, though, that the roses had not received their usual spring pruning, and their roots weren't covered with pine needles. But the war had just ended. Many things were in need of attention. They'd have time later to care for the roses.

The brass knocker was gone, its former spot outlined by the faded paint on the door. No doubt confiscated and melted down for its metal, Jacob figured. He rapped on the door with his knuckles.

No answer. He knocked again.

The door cracked open enough to reveal two peeking eyes. The eyes quickly grew into saucers.

"Jacob! What...where'd you come from?" Lydia threw the door wide. "Come in! Let me..."

Before Lydia could finish, Jacob entered and eagerly pulled her to him. He smothered her with a kiss and held her as if afraid to let go.

"You're as beautiful as ever, Lydia. I've missed you."

"And...I you!" she answered, taken back by his impulsiveness. She pulled away and gazed at him. "Are you all right, Jacob? I heard the cadets aided the treasury and...and the President's family to escape! Are they...after you?"

Jacob shook his head. "No, I'm paroled. We left the treasure with the proper officials, and I last saw the President and his family in Georgia. How are things here?"

"They're good. Federal troops came as soon as you left and put out the fires, restored order, brought in food..."

Lydia didn't seem quite herself, thought Jacob. She seemed a bit nervous or something. "But what about *you*?" he asked. "Is there anything wrong?"

"Well, I heard you caught a cadet committing treason, and I wondered if he was perhaps a...a friend..."

Jacob was amazed at how fast news traveled. Going south, folks ahead of the train knew of the treasure even though the lines were cut and no one passed them.

"He was actually my *best* friend," nodded Jacob. "Roger Phillips."

"I'm so sorry. Where...is he now? Have you...uhh, talked to him?"

"We wanted to court-martial and execute him but the war ended, so now he's free. He was actually on the train with me and we talked, but I'll never forgive him."

Lydia began fiddling with a linen cover on the hall table below a mirror. She glanced up and her eyes met Jacob's in the mirror. She quickly looked away.

Jacob knew something was up. "Lydia, we both have something on our mind and there's no point in dancing around it. We must simply tell each other."

Lydia nodded and took him by the hand. "Come," she said.

A moment later they were sitting on the parlor sofa, where they had often spent time during his visits.

"Jacob, there are things you need to know about me," she said, clasping her hands in her lap. "I'm not who you think I am."

Jacob's face reddened. His temples pulsated. He sensed what was coming.

"Are you..." The words stuck in his throat. "Are you telling me that...what Roger told me...was true?"

"If he told you I was his, his contact, then yes. I'm sorry."

Jacob's stomach jumped to his throat. He stared at Lydia as if she had just grown a second head. He tried to speak but found his shock-filled thoughts so jumbled that he couldn't translate them into words.

"Jacob...are you all right? Say something."

Jacob slowly shook his head. "Lydia...you're Amish. Your...fiancé...gave his life at Gettysburg. How could you..."

"Well, I'm from Lancaster, but I was never Amish. That was just a cover-up. My fiancé – actually my husband - was killed on Cemetery Ridge, but he wasn't in Lee's army. He was a member of the 69th Pennsylvania Infantry. I'm returning to Lancaster in a few days to live with his family. We have a son there."

Jacob sat dumbfounded. "But his family was *here*, helping you, bringing you food. And you led me to believe we had...you know...special feelings. Was it a lie?"

"All a cover-up." Relaxing now that she had broken the news, Lydia smiled as if proud of what she had achieved. "But I'll tell you, I could never get anything out of you, except a little information that day on the river bank just before the evacuation, and that proved useless. I had to depend on Roger. Now, what'd you want to tell me?"

A cynical grin crossed Jacob's face. Lydia's guise was gone, stripped down to the naked, ugly truth now. She was a cold-blooded, calculating spy who had used him. The revelations cut deep, but the casual, matter-of-fact manner in which she told him cut even deeper.

"I intended to propose, Lydia, but now I'll tell you something quite different." Jacob spoke with a bitter, throaty growl. "I just killed the man who killed my brother, but you deserve to die more than he did! At least he wore a uniform! You and Roger may go free now, but you must live with yourself, and one day you'll answer to God!"

Jacob could say no more. He arose and stormed out of the house.

Chapter Seventeen

Jacob bolted from Lydia's house and down the walk. He stopped for a moment and leaned on the front gate, shaking with anger, most of it directed toward her but no small portion toward himself.

Lydia might be an accomplished professional, but he was supposed to be a professional too, and yet he allowed himself to be taken in like a lovesick schoolboy. He racked his brain trying to remember if he had let anything of value slip during his visits, but could only recall the day on the river bank that Lydia had mentioned, when he spoke of conditions in the army and the role the cadets might play in an evacuation. Though the former was well known and the latter only speculation, just the fact that he had made such a slip aggravated him.

He slammed the gate behind him and started down the street, trying to let his anger cool but not having much luck. He had suffered yet another humbling blow to his pride and self esteem, again delivered by a woman.

But at least Amy Unger had been up front with him. She had broken off their relationship because of honest differences between them, with no attempt to lie or deceive him. The simple truth was that he had been taken in and played for a fool by an older and more deceptive woman. How could he be so stupid? He picked up a stick and hurled it against a tree.

"Whoa! Hold your fire, I'm not a Yankee!"

The man stepped from behind the tree. He was about forty, hatless, and wore a dark vest over a brown shirt. Far more telling was the white collar around his neck.

"Sorry, sir. Didn't know you were back there," said Jacob. "You look like...are you a minister?" He realized now that the tree stood in the St. John's churchyard.

"Guilty as charged! Actually I'm Father McGill, the priest here at St. John's," said the man. "Also the gardener, it would seem. I've seen you pass by here before, but you've never *thrown* anything at me. If you're troubled about something, perhaps I could, you know, be of service..."

Jacob fondly recalled the inner peace he had found when he visited the church before, and he sorely needed that now. "Well, if you have time, I could use someone to, to talk to right now..."

"Of course, sir. These weeds can wait. I only wish my parishioners were this plentiful. Let's go inside, but leave all *missiles* outside, please." He led Jacob into the sanctuary, to a pew near the front.

Nothing had changed - the cross hanging behind the pulpit, the Bible on the table, Christ gazing down from the stained glass window. It seemed like magic how inanimate things could instill such a sense of peace and tranquility, Jacob thought.

"Now," began Father McGill. "What would you like to talk about?"

"Well, it's like this. In the past ten days I've killed the man who killed my brother, found out my best friend was a spy, learned that my girl friend was the spy's accomplice, and seen my side lose the war."

"No wonder you need to talk! I only hope I can help."

"I should mention that I'm Amish by birth. Don't know much about, you know, other religions."

"Not important. God speaks Amish. But you know, you're a young man, you survived the war and you're smart enough to come to God for help, so things can't be all that bad. Now, what concerns you the most?"

"Well, I turned my back on my family and went to war. I've sought revenge rather than forgive. I've hated, killed, dishonored my parents...I wonder if the things that have happened to me recently are punishment for all that."

"I doubt it. We're all sinners. God specializes in forgiveness, not revenge."

"There's also a reverse side to this," said Jacob. "There've been times when I should have died, but I escaped by a close miss, or a misfire, or some other miracle that luck just can't explain. It's happened to me perhaps a dozen times."

"God doesn't deal in luck. He does know a little about miracles, though. He just wasn't ready for you, son. Now, about this man you killed who killed your brother..."

"It was self defense. I could've killed him after he shot me, but I walked away and let him live. Then I looked and be dogged if he wasn't about to shoot me again!"

"I noticed your arm," said Father McGill. His brow furrowed. "Now, this man killed your brother and tried to kill you, yet you gave him a chance to live? Why?"

"I don't know. I had every intention of killing him."

"Uh-huh," nodded the priest. "So let me be clear on this. You rejected your family and your religion and went to war. Are you on good terms with your parents now?"

"My mother, yes. My father wants nothing to do with me. I miss them both."

"How do you view Amish life now?"

"It isn't perfect, but what bothers me is all the evil in the rest of the world."

"Good and evil are my stock in trade, and believe me, my trade is *well* stocked with the latter," said the priest. "With the war and spies for friends, I'm sure you've seen plenty of it as well. As for the 'miracles', I think God wants you around for awhile. He may have plans for you, possibly involving your family. But to me the most important thing is how you tried to spare your enemy."

"Why? What're you getting at?"

"Well, aside from doing a poor job of picking friends, you don't seem an evil sort at all. In fact, you reject evil. You also consider your family important, and you show compassion sometimes whether you want to or not. Let's see, what does that describe – an *Amish* man perhaps?"

"If you're advising me to return home, I can give you reasons why that isn't a good idea – my father, an old girl friend, a thing called the *Ordnung*..."

"No, I'm advising you to *think* about it. Any man who has a home and family he cares about can never go wrong by returning to them. More importantly, son, I think God is pointing you in that direction."

* * *

Jacob descended Church Hill and headed up Broad Street toward 9th Street. Lydia had discarded him as callously as the unwanted remains of a deer carcass, and then Father McGill had rescued him from the depths of despair, all within thirty minutes. It was almost too much for him. He needed time to think.

Instinctively he was drawn toward the river. He turned south on 9th Street and headed downhill past the Capitol, St. Paul's Church and the canal turning basin. A block nearer the river stood Tredegar Iron Works, its tall smokestacks standing like silent sentinels guarding the damaged complex, its once humming machinery no longer turning out guns and munitions for Lee. The scene, so cruelly symbolic of defeat, wasn't what Jacob needed to see right now.

He crossed the canal on a footbridge and walked a little further downstream to an area that allowed access to the riverbank. He was at the fall line of the James where the river, swollen by spring rains, tumbled over rocks and around tiny islands in swirling, rushing currents as it moved from the shallow waters above the city to the navigable waters below. He walked toward the bank and found a spot on a rock, near enough to the turbulent water to feel the cool, blowing mist in his face.

He sat listening to the powerful roar of the three hundred yard wide river. It was mesmerizing, a sound not heard on his placid Mattaponi. But like the Mattaponi, the James was beautiful in its own way.

The same couldn't be said for Richmond. Behind him, a wasteland of burned buildings and debris stretched up the hill. How ironic, he thought, that the South had seceded because of differences with the central government, and the result was nothing but death, destruction and lack of a meaningful voice in that government that could last for decades. Better to have stayed in the system and worked to improve it, even if it meant abolishing slavery.

The hypnotic effect of the rushing water wasn't enough to deter thoughts of what his two "friends" had done. Roger was bad enough, but Lydia's actions cut even deeper because he had been about to propose to her. Nothing cut deeper than injured pride and being made to feel like a fool.

Father McGill had described him as an "Amish man". Deep down, maybe he was, Jacob thought. Certainly he was sick of the violence, the destruction, the death. Indeed, something within him – or perhaps a divine hand – had guided him to give Alonzo Peck a second chance. Even when he killed Peck, he felt no pleasure.

And what if Father McGill was right about the close calls? What if God *did* want him alive? Did that constitute divine approval of the path he had chosen to follow? Or was God pointing him home because his family needed him?

His event-filled venture among the 'English' had laid bare the worst evils of the outside world – cruelty, rape, violent death, not to mention betrayal by his closest friends. On the other hand, it had also yielded a successful navy career in which he displayed leadership and excelled in responsible positions.

Perhaps his criticism of the South applied to himself as well. He had 'seceded' from the Amish. Perhaps he should have stayed and helped bring about changes.

He heard a rumble and looked up as a huge section of brick wall three blocks away, part of the old Warwick Flour Mill, collapsed in a cloud of smoke and debris.

He no longer could call the navy home. Henry, James, Captain Parker and his other friends had left. Lydia and Roger had taken themselves out of the picture. He was alone with no plans or place to go. Father McGill had given him good advice. A visit home might prove contentious but wasn't likely to do permanent harm.

* * *

Jacob headed east through New Kent County, his blanket roll tied across his shoulder. The hot, dry, May weather had converted the usually packed soil on the West Point Road into a grey powder that coated his shoes and trouser bottoms. He had walked all the way from Richmond except for a five mile stretch in Hanover County where a farmer gave him a lift.

He was approaching New Kent Courthouse when a four-horse freight wagon came thundering down the road behind him. It was the first traffic he had seen in ten miles. He stepped aside to let the big wagon pass.

"Whoa! Whoa now!" roared the driver, leaning backward and pulling hard on the reins. The wagon rumbled to a stop in a thick cloud of dust. "Need a ride, reb?"

As the dust cleared, Jacob noticed 'U.S. Army' stenciled on the wagon's side.

"Sure could use one, yessir," he said. "You goin' anywhere near West Point?"

"Goin' to White House Landing t'pick up supplies. I'd enjoy the comp'ny."

The irony wasn't lost on Jacob, but he thought it best not to mention his last visit to White House Landing.

The ride went well but for the driver's constant chatter. A veteran with fifteen years service, all as a teamster, he was starved for company. They shared mutual complaints about army food and then began to trade war stories. Jacob kept his fingers crossed that the subject of the raid wouldn't come up. To his relief, it didn't.

Ten miles past New Kent, the road to White House Landing forked off to the left. The right fork continued to West Point. Here Jacob took his leave, thanking the driver and waving as the latter cajoled his horses into a canter. Jacob shouldered his bed roll and set out walking. It was three miles to West Point.

Each step closer to home gave the butterflies in his stomach new energy. He didn't know what to expect. Likely his reception would be cold, but what worried him more was Father McGill's hunch that his parents could have a problem of some kind.

The last letter from his mother had been in February, and she had stated that Isaac seemed lethargic and complained about his 'cold weather miseries'. Jacob had assumed it was just his father's advancing age. He wondered now if the elder Buckner had been ill, perhaps unable to join the other men in the fields when time came to plant the spring crops.

A stream of dust came over a rise up ahead and moved rapidly closer. It was a rider galloping toward him, pushing his mount harder than he should in the heat. Jacob eyed the rider as he drew near. He was a small man with dark skin, dressed in buckskins with black hair braided into a long pigtail. It was David Two-Feathers. The Indian reined in his stallion in a cloud of dust, and dismounted.

"Good to see you, brother!" said Jacob. "It's been a long time!" They locked forearms and Jacob winced. His sling was gone but the arm remained tender.

David nodded. "Two winters now, my brother. Hope you well. Arm sore?"

"A little souvenir from Alonzo Peck, but it's the last one he'll ever hand out."

"Good. Score settled," nodded David. "Also good we meet. I ride to Richmond to find you. Much fever along Mattaponi. People die."

A knot formed in Jacob's stomach. "Why...why are you coming for *me?*"

"Your mother much sick. High fever. White medicine man say not good. You must come."

The knot in Jacob's stomach grew to the size of a cannon ball. "What...kind of fever? Malaria, Scarlet Fever, Swamp Fever...?"

"Medicine man say it yellow death. We hurry. You ride with me!"

Yellow Fever! Jacob mounted behind David and they thundered toward West Point. They crossed the Pamunkey and the Mattaponi on ferries just upriver from the town, reversing the route Jacob had followed four years earlier when he left.

His heart pounding, Jacob prayed that it wasn't Yellow Fever. There had been past outbreaks along the Mattaponi that always brought bad results. Many thought the dreaded disease was caused by the marshes and swamps in the area. A score of people had died the last time, including one of Jacob's grandparents.

After what seemed an eternity but in fact was less than an hour, they arrived in front of the Buckner farmhouse. Though Jacob's mind was on his mother, it was hard to overlook the missing roof shingles, broken fence rails and other signs of neglect. Even his mother's roses needed tending.

They circled to the backyard and stopped next to a horse and buggy tethered to the well pump. Jacob recognized the rig as that of old Doctor Grainger from town. His heart sank. The Amish called in outside help only as a last resort.

Jacob left David with the stallion and rushed in through the back door. His father stood in the kitchen. Isaac registered only mild surprise at seeing his son.

"I wasn't looking for you this soon," he said in a tone cold and reserved. "David made good time..."

"We met on the road." Jacob was surprised his father had sent for him.

"You were already on your way? You knew of your mother's illness?"

"Kind of. I see Doctor Grainger's here. How is she?"

"Not well. It's Yellow Fever." Mr. Buckner's stony countenance softened a touch. "The doctor says her chances are...fifty-fifty..." He turned away.

Jacob had never seen his father cry, and he knew Isaac was struggling to prevent it now. It was a clear indication that things were serious. Jacob swallowed hard.

Joshua, Amy, Lydia, Roger, his mother – was life simply a procession of bitter pills to be swallowed? If this wasn't punishment, he would hate to see the real thing. He must have faith and remember Father McGill's words. God is forgiving, not vengeful.

"Our community's being...hit hard," said Isaac. "The Horst girl, Mrs. Hostetler, old Mr. Schlabach, Rudy Detweiler - the Detweiler boy's funeral is in the morning. Many others are sick..."

"I...want to see her, Father."

"All right, but let me tell you, Jacob, you're being allowed here only because your mother is sick. Other than that, nothing has changed. Now, she *must not* see us arguing, is that clear? It will upset her."

Jacob frowned and nodded. Arguing in front of his sick mother was the *last* thing he wanted. But his father was right; nothing had changed in four years.

Isaac led him toward the back bedroom. The former went in, but Jacob hesitated outside the door, apprehensive about the scene he was about to see. Doctor Grainger's low whisper drifted out of the room.

"Take your time, Mrs. Buckner. This'll make you feel better. A little bit more, that's it. Don't want to overdo it."

Jacob entered the room. Doctor Grainger, holding a spoon and bottle, looked up and greeted him with a nod.

The scene took away Jacob's breath. His mother's complexion was mustard-yellow. She was perspiring heavily and had a wet cloth on her forehead. A chamber pot sat on the floor within easy reach and smelled of sour vomit.

"Mrs. Buckner, look who's here," said the doctor. "Mrs. Buckner...? I'm afraid she's drifted off, Jacob. I've sedated her and...oh...Mrs. Buckner, look who's here!"

Her eyes had opened, but just a sliver. "Who is it? Who's...here?" She spotted her son and lifted a feeble hand. "Oh, Jacob! I've prayed so hard...for you to...to...!"

Jacob took her hand and found it hot with fever. "I'm here now, Mother, just rest easy. You must save your strength."

"I've...missed you so, but...the beard...will you return to that...awful war?"

"The war's over, Mother. I'll not leave you."

"Praise God! So much killing...I've been...so worried about you!" She glanced at her husband. "Isaac, are you sure it's all right...for him to...to stay a little while?"

Isaac nodded. "The elders have said he may stay until you feel better, Sara."

Jacob felt awkward. He was being treated like a stranger in the home he had grown up in - and with his mother lying deathly ill. He *belonged* here. His father and the elders would just have to...

He caught himself, remembering his father's warning against arguing. He must also remember that his father and the other elders were responsible for the structure that was key to Amish society, the discipline that differentiated it from the English world of betrayal, violence and death that he had come to know all too well.

"You must try to get some sleep, Mrs. Buckner," said Dr. Grainger. "Your family will be right here when you awake."

Isaac Buckner led Jacob and the doctor back to the kitchen and drew each a cup of water. Doctor Grainger took a swallow and began repacking his bag of instruments. He had a busy schedule of patients to visit in the area.

"Doctor, just how...bad is she?" asked Jacob, hesitant to ask the question for fear of the answer.

The doctor shook his head. "I don't like the direction of things, Jacob. Her fever's very high, her jaundice is worsening and she's vomiting blood. I'm afraid all of those are signs that the disease is advancing. We'll know in a day or two." He picked up his bag and hurried out to his next visit.

Jacob followed the doctor outside and brought David Two-Feathers up to date. The sinewy Mattaponi excused himself and said he would return the next morning. Jacob watched him go and rejoined his father inside.

"We must pray, Father," said Jacob. "It's important that we pray."

Mr. Buckner looked surprised. "I hope you're not saying that for my benefit, Jacob. We've been praying for everyone for days now, but it doesn't seem to be helping."

"Father, I can't believe you of all people are losing faith. God will help you if you ask, but you *mustn't* lose faith!" Jacob sensed that he must set an example.

"You're right, of course," nodded Mr. Buckner. "We must never lose faith."

"And by the way, if Mother is stable in the morning, I'd like to attend Rudy Detweiler's funeral," said Jacob. "I knew him well. They're our neighbors and we should support them." For him to leave his mother would also show faith, he figured.

That night, Jacob and Isaac knelt beside Mrs. Buckner's bed and prayed. Sara slept uneasily, her breathing weak and shallow. Sometime after midnight, Isaac retired to bed, but Jacob stayed by his mother's side through the night.

* * *

Isaac Buckner arose just after sunrise the next morning and found Jacob dozing in a chair in his mother's room. His wife appeared to be sleeping well, so he nudged his son and told him the funeral service would begin at 8:00 a.m.

"Jacob, I must tell you that some folks may object to you being there," said his father when they reached the hallway.

"I thought the elders had temporarily suspended all of that..."

"There may be those who object to the suspension, or perhaps to your English clothes or your beard. Everyone is aware of the things you've done."

A little before 8:00 a.m., Jacob crossed the three hundred yards of field to the Detweiler farm. About forty friends and family members were gathered inside the home. The handmade coffin sat in the main room with the viewing lid open. The deceased, a boy Jacob's age, lay inside dressed in his best Sunday clothes.

It was the community's third funeral in two days with another to follow, so the service went quickly. Speakers recalled the respect with which the deceased was held, several hymns were recited - not sung - and several scriptures read. In less than an hour the service was over and would be continued at the cemetery.

For Jacob, it brought back heart-wrenching memories of Joshua's funeral. Visions of undergoing the same thing again in a few days haunted him and gave him resolve to pray that much harder for his mother.

Jacob said his goodbyes. He wished to return home quickly and didn't plan to attend the burial or the meal afterwards. Many had been surprised to see him. Some asked about his mother, some kept their distance, but none openly questioned his being there. He thanked the elders for allowing it and turned to leave.

"Hello, Jacob, how've you been?"

The feminine voice came from behind Jacob. Even before he turned, he knew it was Amy Unger – Amy Webber now. He had spotted her earlier from a distance.

"Hello, Amy. I've been better, but good to see you." Jacob smiled politely.

"I'm sorry to hear about your mother. I pray she will get better."

"Thank you, Amy. I'm afraid it's very serious. The doctor is...concerned."

"Oh no, I've always thought so much of her! I pray God will intervene!"

"As do we," nodded Jacob.

A twinge of old memories stirred in him. Amy was still the deeply thoughtful person she had always been, and even more beautiful, he thought. Clearly her religious faith was still strong and seemed to rest better on her now than four years ago.

"Who's this young man with you?" asked Jacob, bending down.

"This is my son Adam. He's two. Can you shake Mr. Buckner's hand, Adam?"

Jacob took the tiny hand being shyly extended to him. "Hello, Adam, you're a good-looking boy! Amy, how's your husband Crist? I don't see him here…"

Amy's smile turned somber. "He…passed away…a week ago. One of the first."

Jacob wanted to go and hide. He scrambled to find the right words but none seemed appropriate. "Amy, I'm sorry. I didn't know."

"It's all right. Mr. Webber was…subject to illnesses, I'm afraid. Our neighbors have been very supportive. With their help, Adam and I will be fine."

The silence that followed only increased the awkwardness. Amy knelt and busied herself rearranging her son's hair. Jacob rubbed his beard and looked away.

As Amy arose, their eyes met for a brief instant, but in that instant thoughts passed between them, thoughts that were inappropriate for this time and place, thoughts that both knew they must purge from their minds and leave unsaid.

"You look nice, Jacob. The navy has been good to you."

"As do you, Amy. Motherhood becomes you."

* * *

Jacob left the gathering and hurried home. He went straight to his mother's bedside and found Dr. Grainger examining her. His father anxiously looked on.

The doctor took Sara's temperature, checked her heart, her eyes. She had vomited fresh blood a short time before. In a moment, the doctor ushered Jacob and Isaac into the hallway. His grim frown told them more than they wanted to know.

"I'm afraid she's taken a bad turn," he said. "Her temperature's very high and there's a lot of blood. The disease is fast overcoming her internal organs – the liver, the kidneys. The bleeding is increasing and she's lapsed into a coma now that seems to be deepening. She...likely will pass before the day is out."

Isaac's stoic fortitude crumbled and he began emitting a low wail mixed with sobs. Jacob bit hard on his lip. Soon both men were openly crying.

Jacob walked out into the back yard for fresh air, and Isaac followed. The rising sun glimmered off the waters of the Mattaponi, the marsh grasses swayed in the early morning breeze, egrets waded in the shallows hunting breakfast – all was normal but for the heavy weight of dread hanging like a millstone over their heads.

"Thirty years we've been together," said Mr. Buckner, teary-eyed. "It's hard to imagine being...without her."

Jacob nodded, barely able to speak. "I...love that woman," he mumbled, staring straight ahead but visualizing images of happier days with his mother.

"It means a lot to her that...that you're here, Jacob. I still don't...understand why you had decided to come, but I know she's grateful."

"God directed me to come, Father."

"He directed you? Don't lie at a time like this, Jacob."

"I'm not lying, Father. God has made himself known to me many times and in many ways. I've felt His presence beside me more than once. I would not have survived the war without His intervention."

Mr. Buckner stared at Jacob, searching, questioning, still uncertain whether to believe his son. "But you were so full of...of hate, bitterness, lack of faith..."

Jacob nodded. "I've led men in battle, sought revenge, killed...but there were many times when I should have been killed and survived in ways that could only be God's work. On two occasions He kept me from being taken prisoner. He controlled my hand so that I gave a second chance to the man who killed Joshua. He led me to a priest who convinced me that it wasn't just my imagination..."

Mr. Buckner was taken aback. He had to admit that something had caused Jacob to head for home, after four years, without knowing for sure that anything was wrong. That was a lot of coincidence for Providence not to have been involved.

"You gave your enemy a second chance?" Isaac asked. "I wonder if perhaps God is giving *you* a second chance."

Jacob nodded again, his face serious. "I'm certain God brought me here for a reason, and I'm just as certain that He...wishes me to stay."

"Is that what you want? How do you feel about the English world now?"

"My time there altered my perception of things. It's a world so full of evil that it makes the faults of the Amish look trivial. I want no part of it."

Mr. Buckner made no response. As much as he wanted his son back, he wanted it to be through an acceptance of the Amish, not a rejection of the English and not as a result of emotions arising because his mother faced eminent death.

David Two-Feathers rode into the yard and dismounted. Not good timing, thought Jacob, but still he was glad to see his old friend.

"How Mrs. Buckner today?" asked David.

Jacob grimaced and shook his head. "The doctor says she'll not...see today's sunset. But please, come inside with us." He led the way back to his mother's sick room.

"Any change, Doctor Grainger?" asked Jacob as they entered.

The doctor frowned. "Her coma is continuing to deepen. Her fever is higher, her breathing weaker. It...won't be long now..."

"I was hoping she would wake up enough for us to...to tell her about the special bond you seem to have developed with God, Jacob," said Isaac, "and how you want to return home. That would make her very happy. It's weighed heavily on her."

"And on me..." said Jacob.

"Come home, bury hatchet, all good," nodded David.

Suddenly their attention was diverted to Sara. She was emitting gasping sounds, struggling for breath. The doctor waved them out of the room. He had heard the sound many times. It was the death rattle that precedes death. The three men again filed out into the back yard.

Despair descended like a black fog. All knew this was the end. Mr. Buckner sat on the well top, his face in his hands. Jacob stared forlornly toward the distant river. David walked away from the others and went into a low, guttural Mattaponi prayer chant, rocking back and forth and gazing skyward with arms extended.

Several times Jacob glanced toward the back door, praying that it wouldn't open, dreading what it might mean if it did. Mr. Buckner got up and began pacing. Thirty minutes passed – thirty minutes that seemed like half a day. Not a word was spoken, each man ensconced in his own cocoon of thoughts, memories, dreads...

Jacob went to his father's side and the two leaned against the rail fence facing the river, praying. Isaac asked God to take him rather than Sara. Jacob repented his sins, and like his father, offered his life in exchange for his mother's...

Suddenly the door opened and Dr. Grainger emerged. The three waiting men quickly turned to him and anxiously held their collective breath.

The doctor shook his head. Jacob and Isaac slumped. Lumps formed in their throats. It couldn't be, they thought. Please tell them it wasn't so.

"I've never seen anything like it!" said the doctor. "Her fever has broken, her breathing is easier...!"

"What? Whadaya mean?" exclaimed Jacob. He rushed to Doctor Grainger.

"It's too early to tell - but I think she may have turned the corner. She's drinking water, talking, asking for you and her husband. It's...like a miracle!"

Jacob glanced at his father and both choked with emotion. They were sharing the same thought. It wasn't *like* a miracle, it *was* a miracle. They ran for the house.

The doctor grabbed Jacob's arm as he passed. "Jacob, your presence was stronger than any medicine we have," he said. "And when you two were in her room talking about you returning home, she may have heard you. That could have tipped the scale for her – you know, the scale that weighs determination!"

Jacob heard the doctor but in his rush to see his mother it took a minute before it hit him. God had brought him here not to witness his mother's *death*, but to give her his presence, his love, his prayer – things that created a reason for her to *live*.

Jacob went in and found his father leaning over the bed, tearfully embracing his wife. As Isaac straightened up, Sara spotted her son and reached for his hand.

"Oh Jacob," she said. "I feared I would never see you again...but God sent you when I most needed you."

"Yes, Mother, He did," Jacob nodded through tear-filled eyes. Her hand was cooler now and her color had improved. "We must thank Him for that, and for your improvement. Are you feeling better?"

Sara nodded weakly. "I had a...a dream...voices...you and your father..."

Isaac and Jacob stared at each other across the bed. Sara *had* heard them. Now they were convinced beyond a doubt that they had witnessed a miracle and that Jacob's return had been the catalyst.

Mr. Buckner moved around the bed and halted a step from Jacob. He had a searching, questioning look on his face.

"Jacob..."

He moved closer and put his arms around his son. Both broke into tears. They held each other in a way they had not done since Jacob was a small child.

Without warning, Jacob rushed from the room, leaving his parents mystified. Isaac wondered if he had made a mistake.

In a moment, Jacob returned holding something in his hand. It was the carved figure of himself that had sat atop the kitchen stove since that morning four years ago when he left. He carefully placed it on the nightstand beside the bed.

From his pocket came the figure of his mother that he had carried with him and treasured since that morning. He fitted the two interlocking figures together.

The message was loud and clear. Her eyes pouring tears, Sara reached for the two most precious things in he life - her son and her husband. They leaned down and held her. The millstone had lifted from their shoulders. The Buckner family was again united.

"Father, I wish to speak to the elders," said Jacob.

"I will...go and arrange it," nodded Mr. Buckner, happier and more proud of his son at that moment than he had ever been.

Jacob knew then that he would never leave his parents again. He was the only child. He must be here to care for them. It was the Amish way.

Epilogue

On the Sunday following his mother's recovery, a clean-shaven Jacob appeared before the church congregation, confessed his sins and asked forgiveness. It was granted without objection. In the following days, he completed much-needed repairs to the Buckner farm and took his place in the fields beside his father and the other men.

Jacob never missed church services, always sitting with his parents and showing a sincerity and devotion that soon became obvious to all. The following spring, he was baptized into the Amish Church.

Six months later, Jacob and Amy were married. "English" attendees included Henry Stiles (minus the ear ring), James Morgan, David Two-Feathers, Captain William Parker and Father McGill of St. John's Church in Richmond. With a beard now allowed because he was married, Jacob promptly began growing a new one.

Jacob, Amy and Amy's son, Adam, moved in with the Buckner's, who treated the three-year-old Adam as the grandchild they had long wanted. Eleven months after their marriage, Jacob and Amy presented the Buckner's with another grandchild, a baby brother for Adam. They named him Joshua.

Jacob's statue in the community grew steadily until, at age 29, he was elected a church elder, the youngest "elder" anyone could remember. It was also the first time anyone could recall a father and son serving concurrently as elders. Isaac and Sara said nothing (it was against church rules to boast or show pride), but each time Jacob took part in church services, a twinkle came to their eyes and the hint of a smile to their lips.

When speaking before the church, Jacob always emphasized the importance of having high moral standards, avoiding situations that could be misinterpreted, and most of all, being aware of the evils of violence.

Quite often in private he was asked to talk about the war and his experiences. Some even asked to see his "other" scar, the one on his arm caused by Peck's bullet. He always refused, believing that to do so would be to glorify war and himself.

More often than not, such requests came from the young boys of the church. Jacob detected a certain fascination with war, a tendency to think only of the glory and excitement with little attention given to war's true nature. It did not please him, for he had two boys of his own and no desire to see them repeat his mistakes.

But who among the Amish, he asked himself, was better qualified to tell about the ugly side of war and violence than him?

So he became open and vocal about his experiences, holding back nothing. He talked about how his temper resulted in his brother's death. He described the horrors of war - the petrifying fear, the blood, the awful killing, seeing friends mutilated. He told of the waste and destruction, the nightmares and feelings of guilt, the pointlessness of it all. He became recognized as the leading Amish spokesman on the subject.

His message had a lasting impact. A noticeable reaffirmation of anti-violence took place in his community and other nearby Amish communities, helping preserve one of the pillars on which Amish life is built. War and violence became known as the "tools of the devil" and discussions usually included a referral to the lessons of "Mr. Buckner - you know, the man who lived it".

It became clear to Jacob that God's reasons for putting him through such horrible experiences, and bringing him home alive, went beyond just returning to his parents. There had been a bigger plan.

* * *

Jacob remained in touch with his war-time friends, exchanging letters and seeing them at veterans' reunions in Richmond. Henry and his father expanded their fishing business until they owned four trawlers. James Morgan became involved in politics and world affairs, traveling extensively and holding several important diplomatic positions. In 1917, he penned his memoir, <u>Recollections of</u>

a Rebel Reefer. He passed away in 1928 at age 83. No one saw Roger Phillips again. There were rumors that he took his own life.

James Morgan in later years - a diplomat and world traveler.
Morgan: Recollections of a Rebel Reefer

Captain Parker served as a commercial ship captain, diplomat, and president of what later became the University of Maryland. In 1883, he wrote Recollections of a Naval Officer, 1841-65, his memoir in which he detailed his war-time experiences including those as commander of the Confederate Naval Academy. He retired to the Washington, D.C. area and died in 1896 at age 70, still married to his faithful wife Maggie. The couple had no children.

The Confederate Treasure was never captured or found. Its final disposition remains a matter of conjecture to this day. Evidence indicates that a good portion of it was disbursed to Confederate officers and soldiers as it made its way through the Deep South. However, the recorded amounts disbursed fall far short of the total amount that left Richmond. Many believe that at least a part of it still lies hidden in Danville, Virginia or elsewhere along the route, but it seems more likely, based on large expenditures made soon after the war by certain former Confederate officers and officials (none of whom were members of the top echelon), that much of the treasure met with a less than honorable end.

After the war, the U.S. Navy refused to welcome former Confederate Naval officers into its ranks, but many former cadets of the Confederate Naval Academy became local leaders in reconstructing the South. Several in addition to Captain Parker and James Morgan, notably Thomas Scharf and Hubbard Minor (see List of Suggested Reading which follows), wrote books or left diaries detailing their experiences. Many others remained unapologetic champions of the southern cause, reminding one Union Naval officer of the phrase, "The Old Guard dies, but never surrenders".*

*Winston Folk, "The Confederate States Naval Academy", U.S. Naval Institute Proceedings, September 1934, p. 1235.

Note: All people and events mentioned in the last three paragraphs above, beginning with the words 'Captain Parker', were real. Conversely, the Buckner family, Henry Stiles, Roger Phillips, David Two-Feathers, Amy Unger, Father McGill and Lydia Schenk, among others, were fictional and any resemblance to real people living or dead is purely coincidental. White House Landing existed but the raid never occurred, nor did the mission on the York River to obtain torpedoes. Other major events including the battles of Roanoke Island, Elizabeth City and Hampton Roads, the Naval Academy aboard the *CSS Patrick Henry,* the *Underwriter* raid, and escorting the President's family and the Confederate Treasure south, all occurred in broad terms as depicted but differ in detail from the actual. For further edification, see the List of Suggested Reading which follows.

List of Suggested Reading

Campbell, R. Thomas. *Academy on the James: The Confederate Naval School.* Shippensburg, PA, The Burd Street Press, 1998.

Coski, John M. *Capital Navy: The Men, Ships and Operations of the James River Squadron.* Campbell, California, Savas Woodbury Publishers, 1996.

Conrad, James Lee. *Rebel Reefers. The Organization and Midshipmen of the Confederate States Naval Academy.* Cambridge, MA, Da Capo Press, 2003.

Good, Merle, and Good, Phyllis. *20 Most Asked Questions about the Amish and Mennonites.* Intercourse, PA, Good Books, 1995.

La Bree, Ben, Editor. *The Confederate Soldier in the Civil War.* Preface by John S. Blay. Numerous other contributors. Paterson, New Jersey, Pageant Books, Inc. 1959.

Miller, Francis Trevelyan, Editor in Chief. *The Photographic History of the Civil War. Part Six: The Navies.* Castle Books. New York. 1957.

Millett, Wesley, and White, Gerald. *The Rebel and the Rose: James A. Semple, Julia Gardiner Tyler and the Lost Confederate Gold.* Nashville, Tennessee. Cumberland House, 2007.

Minor, Hubbard T. *Confederate Naval Cadet: The Diary and Letters of Midshipman Hubbard T. Minor, with a History of the Confederate Naval Academy.* Edited by R. Thomas Campbell. Jefferson, NC. McFarland & Company, 2007.

Morgan, James Morris. *Recollections of a Rebel Reefer.* Houghton Mifflin Company, The Riverside Press, Cambridge, 1917.

Parker, William Harwar. *Recollections of a Naval Officer, 1841-1865.* New York, NY, Charles Scribners' Sons, 1983. Reprinted in the Classics of Naval Literature series, Annapolis, MD, Naval Institute Press.

Scharf, J. Thomas. *History of the Confederate States Navy.* New York, Gramercy Books, 1996.

About the Author

Photo of author courtesy, Patricia Nuttall

Preston Nuttall is a lifelong resident of Chesterfield County, Virginia, where his family dates to the 17th Century. He holds a Bachelor's degree in Economics from the University of Richmond and a Master's degree in finance from the Wharton School of the University of Pennsylvania. He spent forty-five years as an investment manager but is now retired.

Preston had nine known ancestors who served in the Confederate Army, including two in Pickett's Division who fought at Gettysburg. His lifelong hobbies have been the Civil War and writing, and retirement has provided him time to combine these two activities. *The Amish Rebel* is his fourth historical novel, all focusing on the Civil War.

He and wife Pat have four children, eight grandchildren and one great-grandson.